David R. Gross graduated from Colorado State University's veterinary school in 1960 and was in private practice for ten years. He enrolled in graduate school and earned a M.Sc. degree in 1972 and a PhD degree in 1974 from Ohio State University. He taught and did research at Texas A&M University's College of Veterinary Medicine for sixteen years, then became director of the cardiovascular and thoracic surgery research labs at the University of Kentucky's College of Medicine for five years. He retired in 2006 after twelve years as professor and head of veterinary biosciences at the College of Veterinary Medicine, University of Illinois, Urbana-Champaign.

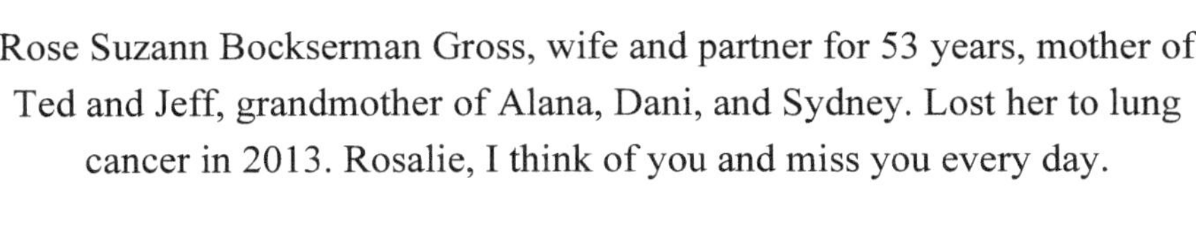

Rose Suzann Bockserman Gross, wife and partner for 53 years, mother of Ted and Jeff, grandmother of Alana, Dani, and Sydney. Lost her to lung cancer in 2013. Rosalie, I think of you and miss you every day.

David R. Gross

INEVITABLE CONSEQUENCES?

AUSTIN MACAULEY PUBLISHERS™

LONDON * CAMBRIDGE * NEW YORK * SHARJAH

Ordering Information
Quantity sales: Special discounts are available on quantity purchases by corporations, associations, and others. For details, contact the publisher at the address below.

Publisher's Cataloging-in-Publication data
Gross, David R.
Inevitable Consequences?

ISBN 9798891557345 (Paperback)
ISBN 9798891557352 (ePub e-book)

Library of Congress Control Number: 2024910734

www.austinmacauley.com/us

First Published 2024
Austin Macauley Publishers LLC
40 Wall Street, 33rd Floor, Suite 3302
New York, NY 10005
USA

mail-usa@austinmacauley.com
+1 (646) 5125767

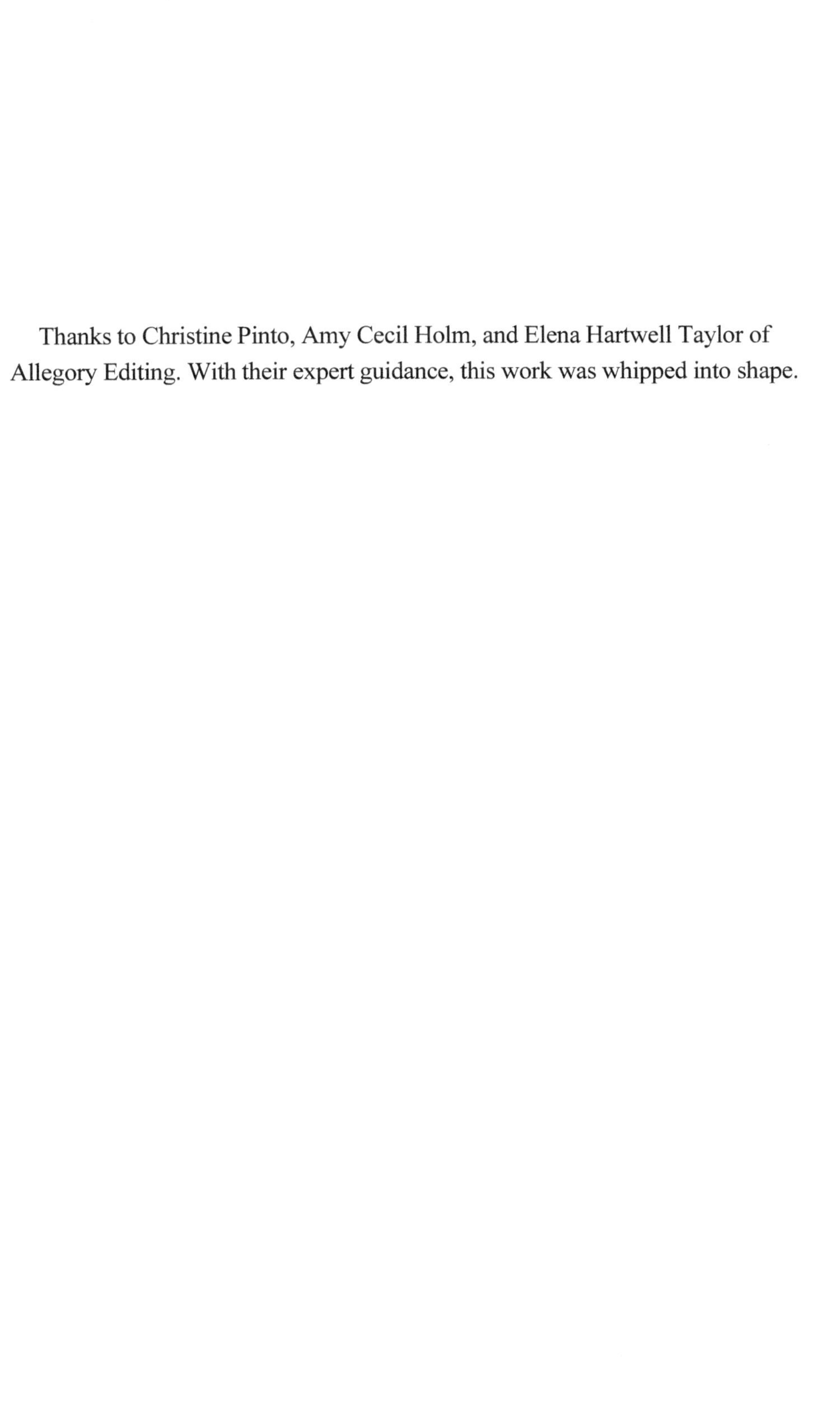

Thanks to Christine Pinto, Amy Cecil Holm, and Elena Hartwell Taylor of Allegory Editing. With their expert guidance, this work was whipped into shape.

Tables of Contents

Chapter 1: Tom Tobin · 13

Chapter 2: Felipe Niero Espinosa · 17

Chapter 3: Tom Tobin · 20

Chapter 4: Felipe Niero Espinosa · 24

Chapter 5: Tom Tobin · 29

Chapter 6: Felipe · 43

Chapter 7: Tom Tobin · 53

Chapter 8: Felipe · 60

Chapter 9: Tom Tobin · 70

Chapter 10: Tom · 83

Chapter 11: Felipe · 93

Chapter 12: Tom · 97

Chapter 13: Tom · 107

Chapter 14: Tom · 112

Chapter 15: Felipe · 115

Chapter 16: Tom · 125

Chapter 17: Felipe · 141

Chapter 18: Tom · 154

Chapter 19: Felipe · 169

Chapter 20: Felipe · 194

Chapter 21: Tom   **200**

Chapter 22: Felipe   **208**

Chapter 23: Tom   **211**

Chapter 24: Tom   **217**

Author's Note   **222**

Bibliography   **223**

Map of the San Luis Valley and Environs

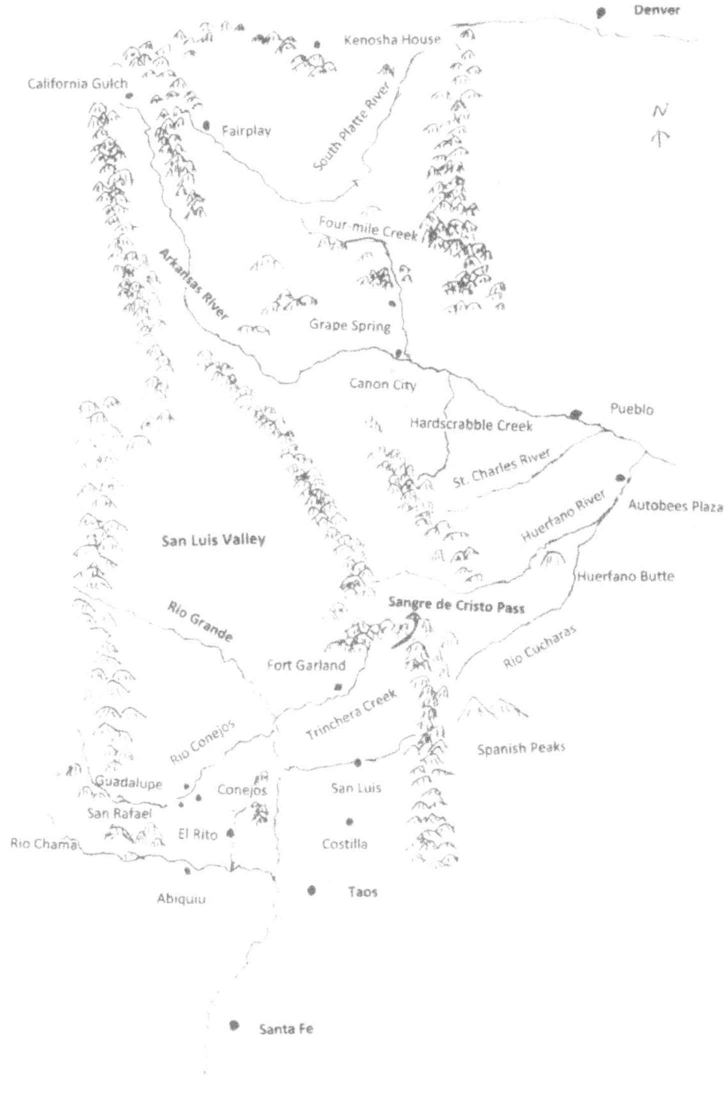

This book is a work of historical fiction. Almost all of the characters lived their lives and did the deeds depicted. The fiction is my words coming from their mouths.

Chapter 1
Tom Tobin

My beginning was different, but I never started out to be a killer. Life happened, I made choices, and here I am.

I was born on 15 March 1823 and christened Thomas Tate Tobin. Eleven years earlier, my mother arrived in St. Louis, wearing a frayed calico dress and carrying the rest of her belongings, including her papers of manumission, in a square of homespun cloth tied into a pouch. She had cared for a sick, stubborn, cranky master during his last years. Despite his apparent bad nature, he rewarded her loyalty by freeing her in his will. She was eighteen years old.

Mama was a mulatto. She told me she was barefoot when she walked down the gangplank of the steamboat from New Orleans. Having heard there was work in St. Louis, she traveled late in the summer on the open deck, hoarding her small amount of cash. Her bare feet were dirty, and the skin on her heels was cracked and rough. Although her fingernails were broken and dirty, she considered her hands elegant, her long, thin fingers aristocratic. She was always proud of her hands.

As soon as she cleared the gangplank, she stepped over to avoid obstructing the path of those following her off the boat. She paused on the dirt road, looking toward the town. It was late in the summer of 1812 and the middle of the morning. The sun warmed her face. The faint scent of flowers blended with that of manure and newly turned earth. Before her stretched two roads, the one she stood upon and another to her right. No streets fronted the river, but on the bluff, she could see glimpses of traffic on a street running parallel. All the houses faced that street with their backs to the picturesque view of the river and the boats on it.

Mama marched up the incline to the street above and saw a second bluff rising in the distance. A dozen or so of the town's twelve hundred inhabitants meandered past. A few stared, but most ignored her. There were two mercantile stores on opposite corners of the intersection. She chose the closest and went through the open doorway.

The man behind the counter turned to face her. "Yes, girl, can I help you?"

"I hope so, I'm looking for work."

"What kind of work do you do?" He asked.

"Most anything. I can cook, clean, do laundry, hoe the garden, whatever work needs doing."

"You're in luck. My missus and I have been looking for a girl with those skills. What's your name?"

"I be Sarah Tissman Tate," she said proudly, "and I kin write my name."

"You stand right there and I'll get the missus. She'll decide if you'll do."

Mama made a good impression on the wife, and they hired her. They provided her with a partly empty storeroom, a thin cotton mattress on the floor, and a chamber pot. She took her meals in their main room after serving the childless couple. She worked from sunup until long after dark, earning two dollars a week plus her room and board.

A year later, Mama married her first husband, Francois Autobees. He was born in Nova Scotia, the son of a French soldier and a native woman of unknown heritage. Mama told me he was a waterman, working the river, doing anything that required a strong back and little imagination. Mama said he was charming, always in good humor. He was short, not more than five and a half feet tall, but broad of shoulder, narrow of hip, and dark-skinned. They communicated in a unique language, part bayou English, part French, both involving much waving of the arms and hands. After a brief courtship, they were married in the Catholic Church, and Francois rented a one-room house for them. Their first child, my brother, was named Charles. When Charles was only three years old, his father drowned while working for a logging contractor floating logs down the St. Lawrence River.

Mama was one of only three freed slaves in town. The population consisted of a few families of means who owned slaves, whites too poor to afford slaves, and slaves. After Autobees' death, she managed to support herself and Charley by doing the heavy house cleaning and laundry for two different families.

During the growing season, she also took care of their gardens. Mama took in laundry from other folks, and Charley told me it seemed to him there was always water boiling for another load and clean clothing hanging from ropes crisscrossing their one-room rented shack unless the sun was out. They sometimes went without lunch, but Mama always managed something for breakfast and some soup or stew for dinner. Charley didn't realize how poor they were.

The folks she gardened for would sometimes let her take home anything that was overripe or what they thought was spoiled. Charley said whatever she cooked always tasted good to him.

My father, Bartholomew Tobin, was an Irish immigrant who couldn't read or write. He made his way to St. Louis sometime in 1819. He had no special skills and earned most of his livelihood by working as a common laborer. Tobin arrived in St. Louis with a small amount of cash and bought a lot with a house and a barn on North Church Street where he boarded a few horses.

Mama was industrious, a catch for my hard-drinking father. When he married her in 1822, she owned three head of meat cattle worth about twenty-four dollars. When she and my father married, both she and Charley were accepted by the close-knit Irish immigrants even though they weren't white. I was born a year later, in 1823. Two years later, my sister Catherine was born.

My father was a mean drunk, and my mother was conscientious and protective. It was a rare night that Tobin didn't stumble home late. I soon learned to make myself small and stay as far away from him as possible. Catherine was his favorite. Drunk or sober, he would hold her on his lap and cuddle her. If I was unfortunate enough to be noticed, he would find something I had done or was doing that irritated him. When he came for me, I had to keep Mama between us. She saved me from many beatings, but not all of them. By the time I was six years old, I learned to stay away from him.

I hated him and told Mama and Charley so. Mama said she was sorry but someday I might understand why she put up with him. I never did. Tobin also seemed to have it in for Charley, who also learned to stay away from him.

Neither Charley nor I ever went to school. He started running errands when he was seven or eight years old and working as a common laborer after he turned eleven. Like our mother, he was hardworking, intelligent, and industrious.

Mama told me that when he was twelve years old and muscular from the heavy lifting he was doing while working twelve-hour days, Charley intervened for the first time when Tobin was beating on her after coming home drunk. When Charley got home that night, he found Mama with her face bruised and Tobin passed out on the bed.

"Did he do that to you, Mama?" Charley asked.

"Yes."

Charley grunted and picked up a frying pan hitting my snoring father on the top of the head. Tobin woke up and grabbed Charley's hand. But Charley wrenched away and delivered another blow, this time to the right side of Tobin's face.

"You ever hit our mama again I will kill you, do you understand me? Answer me, you drunken fool!"

He just nodded and passed out.

It wasn't until the next year that Mama finally had enough of her abusive husband. She and Tobin legally separated and sold most of their common property for a hundred dollars. They divided the money, and Tobin took his belongings and boarded a boat going up the Mississippi River. I was more than happy to see the last of him. He didn't seem at all concerned about leaving us. We later learned he got off in Galena, Illinois, and after a series of misadventures, mostly the result of strong drink, he died a lonely, broke man.

Mama was on her own again, but this time she had three children to take care of. Charley took every job he could find, but he didn't earn much. To add to our woes, we were free niggers again. Most everyone looked down on us. Mama took whatever work she could find, including preparing the dead for burial by hiring out to wash and dress the bodies in shrouds she sewed herself.

For the rest of my life, I was determined to make enough money that no one would disrespect me again.

Chapter 2
Felipe Niero Espinosa

I was born in 1827 and given the name Felipe Niero Espinosa. My life was not always desperate, complicated, or dangerous. My father, Pedro, was the son of an Apache girl and the renowned priest Fray Niero Tomas Espinosa, the man who gave Pedro his name but never admitted his parentage to the public. I did not find this out until I was an adult.

In 1806, when my father was twelve years old, his mother died during a smallpox outbreak, and he was hired out to a branch of the Espinosa family who farmed irrigated river bottom and owned about forty sheep that they grazed on communal lands. My father's job was to herd the sheep.

Because it is important to the story of my life, I should explain about communal lands. The Spanish Conquistadores granted indigenous and mixed-race people parcels of deeded land, usually in river valleys, suitable for irrigation. The recipients of these grants banded together into pueblos for protection and community. The pueblo was also granted communal property extending out from the sides of the river valley. These lands were used to graze livestock, and they also provided firewood, lumber, and edible and medicinal plants.

The Espinosas were kind people and treated my father more as a nephew than a hired worker. They sent him to Fray Niero to learn to read and write. The family's daughter, Maria Gertrudis, was born in 1804. She and my father, ten years her senior, became close. The family also sent Maria to Fray Niero's school. My father continued his education beyond the basic lessons by reading any book Fray Niero would allow him to borrow. Maria and my father frequently huddled in the evenings and took turns reading aloud to each other. Their marriage in 1824 was no surprise. My mother soon gave birth to two babies, the first in 1825 and the second, a year later. Both died before reaching their first birthday. I was born in 1827, followed two years later by my sister. My brother, Jose Vivian Espinosa, was born in 1831.

I grew up in the pueblo of Abiquiu on the Rio Chama. Abiquiu was a small, quiet place where everyone knew each other. If a child did something wrong, the parents knew about it before the miscreant returned home. My mother said I was an easy baby. As I grew older, I was quiet and didn't cause problems. My father and mother rarely needed to correct my behavior, and then only with a word. I don't remember ever receiving a beating. My parents put great emphasis on learning, and my siblings and I received a good education. As soon as we were old enough, we attended Fray Niero's school, where we were encouraged to read anything of interest and learn to write so others could understand our thoughts. When I was about eight years old, my father started taking me with him after school. He gave me a practical education in making a living from agriculture.

Fray Niero taught that six years before I was born, Mexico managed to free itself from Spain. That same year, in 1821, the church hierarchy in Mexico City summoned the Franciscan, Dominican, and Jesuit priests from its provinces, replacing them with secular priests to maintain credibility in response to the political leanings of the new order. However, the church was unable to provide new clergy to every community, especially those most secluded. However, Fray Niero refused to leave his people. Without renouncing the priesthood but in danger of arrest by the authorities, if he conducted Mass, he continued his school, and with other expelled priests of like mind, he organized a lay fraternity of Roman Catholic men to further the teachings of Cardinal Baronius. He and his colleagues traveled to isolated communities throughout the region organizing 'The Brothers of the Pious Fraternity of Our Father Jesus the Nazarene'. These fraternities became known as Los Penitentes, Los Hermanos, or the Penitente Brotherhood.

From my reading, I learned that the concept of a single supreme being was fundamental to the religious beliefs of many of the indigenous people populating the Americas. Their legends taught that the God figure, male or in some cultures female, departed to an unknown place with the promise of returning to them. This had consequences when the Spaniards arrived. The concept of a virgin goddess was also frequently included in the native belief system along with the belief in a pantheon of lesser godlike beings, often unique to a specific tribe, physically capable of affecting the lives of the living.

These belief systems often included sacred places. The faithful were required to propitiate the sacred beings by penitential pilgrimages to a sacred site at regular intervals. These precepts fit well with Spanish Catholic teachings, so wise priests only needed to convince the natives that they were worshipping the same God and godlike beings, but with Spanish names. Knowing all this seems to have made me more of a believer.

Although many of the men in the Penitente Brotherhood were illiterate, some could read and write. The organizers adopted a written constitution formalizing the rules of the order. Communities of the Brotherhood formed in almost all the settlements in what is now northern New Mexico and southern Colorado.

Much later, my father explained to me that after Fray Niero indoctrinated him into the order, he embraced all aspects of the Brotherhood with enthusiasm and started fulfilling the various roles of leadership. I knew my father was active in the Penitente Brotherhood, but that was the extent of my knowledge of that secret society as a child.

Chapter 3
Tom Tobin

I was only four years old when Charley first went to the mountains in 1827. I had a feeling that I remembered when he left, but maybe I just remembered him talking about it on one of his infrequent trips home. According to Mama, all of St. Louis was abuzz with the news after General William Ashley came home from the Rocky Mountains with a fortune in beaver, fox, ermine, and bear hides. Charley heard that the general advertised in the St. Louis newspaper for fifty men to join a supply caravan to the mountains.

Charley went to the general's house and knocked on the door. A man's voice shouted for him to come in, so he did. The man sat at a table, writing in a large book. The room was cold, and he was wrapped in a wool blanket. The man held up his hand to stop Charley from talking. Charley stood there like an idiot until the man finally looked up. He asked Charley what he wanted, and Charley told him he wanted to go up the river and trap for fur.

The man told him the general was looking to hire men, not boys. Charley said he could do the work of any man. The man stared at Charley and then told him to wait while he went to talk to the general, who was upstairs.

A few minutes later, the general came into the room, walking ahead of the clerk.

He looked Charley up and down. "So, you think you want to be a fur trapper, young man?"

"Yes, sir."

General Ashley told him it was a hard life, living in the open. It was wet, cold work. "You won't always get enough to eat and could be attacked and maybe killed by Injuns." Then he added, "You say you're strong—let me feel your arm."

Charley flexed his arm. When the general squeezed, Charley flexed more. He wasn't going to let him know it hurt. The general took back his hand. "The job doesn't pay much. Someone like you, with no experience, would get one hundred dollars a year. Plus, you have to sign on for two years. After you reach the trapping grounds, you will split off with a few others to trap."

"What happened then?" I asked. I was completely drawn in, imagining myself having this adventure.

"He told me that his company would supply me with two shirts, two pairs of pants, a warm coat, four knives, an axe, two pots, a frying pan, five pounds each of salt, coffee, and flour, a pound of sugar, three plugs of tobacco, a flintlock rifle with powder, extra flints, a bullet mold, lead bars, and eight beaver traps."

"Did you really get all that stuff?" I asked.

"That and more, I also got a saddle, a packsaddle, a riding horse, and a pack mule. The traps, saddles, horses, and mules were on loan as long as he worked for the company, but if Charley wanted to stay in the mountains and wanted to keep them, he would have to pay for them in pelts at the going mountain rate."

"I told the general I heard he was paying men a hundred and ten," Charley said. "I wasn't going to let him take advantage of me. The general said that rate was for men with experience, and I didn't fit that mold. So, I told him a hundred would do, but could he pay my mama the salary here in St. Louis?"

Charley said General Ashley asked why, and he told him. "I reckon I can live well enough on all of that what you said."

The general said that was true unless Charley wanted to buy liquor.

"I reckon not, sir. My stepdaddy drunk enough for everyone in our family. I don't mind what others do, but I don't need no strong spirit. Saw what it did to Mr. Tobin."

The general then asked if Charley had any kin working as traders up the Missouri, and Charley told him he didn't know.

"Well, never mind," the general said. "There's a passel of half-breed Autobees on the river, most of them related in some way. You think you can handle the wilderness, son? Can you shoot a rifle?"

Charley told him he could shoot a scattergun—never shot a rifle, but he could hit a running rabbit with a slingshot.

General Ashley produced a paper from a pocket of his coat and asked Charley if he would be ready to leave by the twelfth of April.

"Yes, sir, but ah can't read. What do that paper say?"

"It says everything I told you about earlier and I will add that we will send the pay to your mother. One hundred dollars a year."

Charley was satisfied, so he spit on his palm and held it out to the general, who asked for his mama's name, and Charley told him.

"Sarah Tobin? I think I met your mother. She's a tall woman, mulatto, right? She came to this house and got my wife ready to be buried not long ago."

The general told Charley he would have to work for the company for a year before they could give Mama the wages. They couldn't pay for work that was not yet done.

Charley asked him if there was any chance he could give her some money after he'd been working for six months. "She's gonna have a hard time of it with my brother and sister to feed."

The general thought for a moment before a sly look crossed his face. "I'm considering running for governor and doing that might prove to be good politics. I'll give it to her every six months."

"Thank you, sir. You are a gentleman, and I take your word for it."

General Ashley asked if Charley could sign his name, and he told him he never learned. He pointed to a spot at the bottom of the contract. "My clerk will witness you making your mark there, and then I'll sign."

Mama did her best, but even with Charley's salary, we lived poorly. She continued to take in laundry, prepare the dead for burial, and, in the summer, work gardens for rich folks.

General Ashley was true to his word. Every six months he would send a man, each time a different one so the word of his largesse would spread, with fifty dollars to our house. With those resources and the few extra coins my mother earned, we managed to not starve or freeze.

One day I was playing with five other boys. We were kicking a can through the space between two piles of junk. Although I was the shortest and skinniest, I was also the fastest. I stole the can from George O'Leary, but he tripped over my foot and fell face-first into the dirt. I pushed the can around him with my right foot and kicked it through the goal with my left.

"You cheated," yelled George, still lying on the dirt road.

"Did not."

"Did so, you bastard. Don't even have a pa."

"Ah'm no bastard I have a pa, he just don' live here. My ma done kicked him out."

"Well, your ma's black, so you're trash, and you cheat."

I ran up to George who started to get up. "Don't you call me trash. You be the trash around here." I pushed him back to his knees.

George jumped to his feet and grabbed me around the neck. The other boys ran over and joined in. Soon I was lying on the dirt road, covering up my head while the boys punched and kicked me. Mama heard the commotion and ran outside to see what was happening.

Boys were flung away from me, and I heard Mama's angry voice.

"Get off! Get off! Stop it! You boys leave him be. Enough of this fighting, leave him be."

Two other mothers ran outside, protective of their own. Us boys stood off to the side, focused on the drama of the three women standing in the middle of the road arguing.

Mrs. O'Leary, a foot shorter than my mother, stood on her toes, bumping Mama with her ample bosom, her head thrown back, spraying spit into my mother's face.

"Don't you lay your black hands on my Georgie. You got some nerve to do so."

Mama gritted her teeth, stifling her anger, while clenching her fists. "So, when Tobin were still here beating me and my children whenever he come home drunk, I were equal to you? But now he's gone, me and mine are just dirt?"

"No one with your black face is equal to me, you bitch."

Mama decided to quit before she hit Mrs. O'Leary, then she turned and grabbed me by the shoulder. "Come, Thomas, I'm gonna clean you up. You don't need to play with this trash. You're better than them."

Although I looked no different than the neighbor children—in fact, my skin was lighter than many of theirs, and my features were clearly Irish—everyone in town seemed to know my mother was a mulatto. That put me in the same class with slaves and drunken Indians.

Chapter 4
Felipe Niero Espinosa

When I was seven, Fray Niero taught me reading, writing, and mathematics. My father reinforced this learning by insisting I read books borrowed from the Penitente Brotherhood where he was a member, or from the church. After we moved to El Rito, every winter after the Navidad, when there was little work to do in the fields, my father took all of his children to Abiquiu. The members of the Abiquiu Brotherhood housed and fed us while Fray Niero educated us.

"Why do we have to continue to learn from Fray Niero, Papa?" I complained. "You can teach us, and he is quite strict. When we make a mistake, he hits us with a switch. You don't hit us when we make a mistake."

"Life is not fair, my son. There is no permanent harm done by the switch of Fray Niero, and he has much to teach you. Soon you will become a man. I will not allow you and your brothers and sisters to be ignorant, illiterate peons. If you are to become real vecinos, who know their rights and are able to protect those rights, you must be educated. You must be able to read what educated men have written as a guide to what life should be, what the laws say, and what they do not say. We are protected by the laws, but only if we know what the laws are."

I was not happy with my father's reasoning when I was young, but I came to understand when I was older. My younger brother Jose Vivian always wanted to do whatever I was doing, but three years made a big difference. Failure frustrated him, and by trying harder, he made mistakes that irritated Fray Niero. When irritated, Fray Niero applied his switch with increased vigor. When Vivian saw unguarded items he wanted, he took them, unmindful of the actual owner. When he was caught in these transgressions, Fray Niero forced him to return the item and then punished him. At home, our father was less severe, administering no more than a cuff to the head when particularly angry.

It was difficult for me to understand why Vivian did these things, but I told myself I would not steal if it meant getting punished. That would change.

In 1838, when I was almost twelve, my father called our whole family together after a meeting of the Abiquiu Brotherhood and explained that the Alcalde of Abiquiu had told him about a valley not far from Abiquiu where the El Rito flowed before it emptied into the Rio Chama. With the approval of the governor, the alcalde was going to make a land grant for ten families to build and make their homes in this valley. They would develop the valley for irrigation. There was enough good land for each family to have about a hundred varas and share in the communal lands on both sides of the valley for as far as a man could walk in one day.

The alcalde and my father chose nine men and their families to go to this place and make a new pueblo. My father would be the Hermano Mayor and would have the first choice of land. He would measure off and mark each plot of land that would be deeded to a family. He would also be responsible for determining the boundaries of the communal lands. He and his compadres would promise to defend the land against the attacks of the savages or the Americans. They would be Abiquiu's first line of defense against attack. Father said the alcalde told him, "You will not be a rich man if you do this for me, Pedro, but you will be a vecino, a free man who owns his own land."

My father told us they had to supply their own tools and seeds, but the people of Abiquiu gave each of them a musket, powder, a shot mold, and lead. The Abiquiu Brotherhood also gave them five riding horses, five donkeys, and forty sheep, but they had to pay back ten percent of the annual harvest from their farms and ten percent of the wool from their sheep to the Brotherhood. It would take them ten years to do that.

Papa and the alcalde agreed on the nine other members from the Abiquiu Brotherhood who would form the new community: Jaime Bernal, his brother Salvador Bernal, Vincente Romero, Ignacio de Leon, Diego de Arguello, Melchor de Vargas, Jacinto Roybal, Ramon Congora, and Manuel Sanchez. The evening after they agreed to move to the new pueblo, they all signed the contract with the alcalde. Those recruited, including my father, were all peons, serfs, without land of their own. They had all been working as virtual slaves and were happy for the opportunity to own their own property and become vecinos.

I could not hold my tongue as I watched Papa make the preparations to lead his friends to start building their new home. "Papa, please let me go with you. I am almost a man, and I can help with the work. Please, Papa, you know I am not afraid to work hard."

Papa shook his head. "If you go with us, who will take care of the family? I am leaving you with that responsibility."

"Mama can take care of the family, and her family and brothers are right here. They don't need me."

Papa continued sorting the seeds he was taking for our new fields, saying nothing for several minutes while I bit down on my tongue to keep from pleading any more. He finally looked up at me. "Yes, Felipe, you are right, but the work will not be easy."

My heart raced, and I could not restrain myself. I went to him and gave him a huge abrazo. "Of course, Papa, I understand." I was determined not to let my father or the others down.

Two and a half months later, in early spring, the eleven of us left for the site of the new settlement. We took beans and flour. Each man had his smooth-bore musket, two blankets each, machetes, picks, axes, shovels, and seed for wheat, corn, squash, peas, and beans. I carried my share of tools and seeds and my own blankets but was not allowed a musket. My father also took a blank journal and pen and ink to record the survey.

We followed El Rito creek upstream until we reached the valley the alcalde had described. We went down into the valley and made camp in a small meadow of rice grass and water sedge. The fragrant aroma of wild onion filled the air. We built a fire of dead cottonwood branches, drank the sweet, clear water from our river, and feasted on two rabbits and a wild turkey brought in by the middle-aged Ignacio, our best hunter. We all felt the elation and anticipation of building a new pueblo of our own. All of us would be free, true vecinos. The next morning, my father, Jaime Bernal, and I used the cordel to measure the valley. Our cordel was a standard length of rope fifty varas long, each vara being equal to the stride of an average man. Starting from the site where all agreed the dam would be built, the cordel was stretched tight, parallel to the waterway. Each man was to receive one hundred and forty varas of waterfront and all the land extending on either side of the waterway for the width of the valley. We built a small monument of loose rocks on the four corners of each designated field, and each man drew lots for his allocation.

When they signed the contract with the alcalde, they had all agreed that my father would have his choice of location, and he took the fields at the widest portion of the valley. The men were satisfied with this arrangement since he was their Hermano Mayor and was at least partially responsible for each of them being included in the new pueblo.

On our second morning, we built two-wheeled carts under the direction of the Bernal brothers, who were experienced carpenters. The carts, pulled by our burros, would carry all the rocks and boulders each man cleared from his field to the site of the dam.

For the next six days, my father and I strode the boundaries of our communal lands, building rock monuments on each of the four corners. Papa entered into his journal the number of strides it took to reach each monument. We were to claim these communal lands based on how many strides it took in a day to reach a corner, in as direct a line as possible, using a compass, from the edge of our valley.

While Papa and I completed this task, the others built the dam and irrigation ditch. All this time we lived mostly in the open, with only canvas tarps strung between trees to keep the occasional rain off our bedrolls. Once the ditch and diversion dam were finished and water was flowing, leaving the stream a mere trickle, we fashioned rough wood plows, hitched the horses to them, plowed the fields, and planted our first crops, carefully flood irrigating the fields so as not to wash away the seed.

Then we started building our jacales. These were simple one-room huts not more than ten feet in diameter, constructed from poles cut from the ample supply of cottonwood. The poles were set as pickets abutting each other in a trench. Once all the pickets were placed, the trench was filled in and the space between pickets was plastered with dry grass and mud. The roof of the jacal was fashioned with small poles, and tree limbs and branches were laid in layers across each other. This was covered with six or eight inches of sod. The entranceway was short on purpose, less than four feet tall, so an invader would have to bend over, exposing his head when entering. Each jacal had window openings facing each of the cardinal directions. Later, once sheepskin was available, we covered the openings with parchment. The door was made of rough axe-split planks attached with leather hinges. Similar wood shutters protected the windows. Close to each jacal, we built a separate three-sided kitchen shed with a rock fireplace opposite the opening. We built a closed shed straddling a deep hole behind each jacal for a latrine. All of us, working together from dawn to sunset, were able to finish each of these small homestead projects in a matter of days.

After all was completed, Papa took me aside. "Felipe, I have a task for you. Tomorrow we will go back to Abiquiu to bring our families here to our new home. I want you to stay here, guard our pueblo, and irrigate the fields if there is not enough rain. Can you do this for us?"

Once again, I was filled with pride that my father had so much trust in me. "Of course, Papa, it will not be a problem for me." My heart was beating so fast and loud that I could hear it. Perhaps he could hear it too. He trusted me and treated me as a man, and I knew I could make him proud of me by doing as he asked. He smiled at me and gave me an abrazo, and tears filled my eyes.

Chapter 5
Tom Tobin

It was a warm evening in the summer of 1830 when Charley surprised us by walking through the open door of our shack. He tossed his torn and dirty leather hat onto the table, dropped his heavy, smoke-smelling pack, and set his rifle down carefully on the dirt floor.

"Hello, Ma. I'm home."

Mama, busy at the hearth, turned with a start and shrieked. Catherine, who was about five years old, was playing on the bed. She jumped off and ran to Charley. I was unable to move, frozen by seeing the brother I barely remembered, now a full-grown man. Catherine tried to crawl up his leg, and I finally ran over to hug him around the waist. He walked to our mother and gave her a hug, with brother and sister hanging on to him. Now close to eighteen years old, Charley was broad-shouldered, narrow-waisted, and well-muscled, and he acted as though he owned the world. The dark skin on his face, where not covered with the beginnings of a beard, was wrinkled from exposure to the elements. His thin lips lifted at the corners in an unfamiliar smile. He was wearing buckskin pants and a shirt, crusty with dirt and stains.

"Let me look at you," said Mama. "You left a boy and now you're a man. Look at you, taller than me and hard as a rock." She was laughing and crying at the same time and wiped the tears from her face with her apron.

During the rest of Charley's visit, he told us about his adventures in the mountains. "The boat we boarded was about seventy feet long and sixteen feet across in the middle. The cargo was loaded into the-four-foot-deep hold protected by a boxlike structure, with the deck on each side about three feet wide. There was room in front of the box and behind it where the men rested between shifts of pulling or working the poles. The mast came up out of the cargo box toward the front of the boat. A heavy rope was attached to the top of the mast and passed through a brass ring attached to the bow. Most of the time, about twenty men took two-hour shifts pulling the boat upstream against the current from the shore. Sometimes they had to flip that heavy rope over the brush along the bank. One man in the back of the boat guided it with the rudder."

"Did you make any friends during the trip to the mountains?" I asked.

"After my first time pulling," Charley said, "I was back on the boat resting when a fella, maybe a couple of years older than me, plunked his self down and held out his hand. I'm Charley Nadeau, he says. I'll be damned, I say, I'm Charley too, Charley Autobees."

Mama asked Charley if he made any other friends.

"Well, the general told us there were six men in the group who had been to the mountains before. Each one of them was assigned to be the sergeant of a small group of newcomers. The sergeants handed out our supplies and were also responsible for our conduct. They enforced order and relayed the commands of the general or his lieutenant. I sort of made friends with my sergeant."

"What happened after you all left the boat?" I interrupted.

"Each of us was gave a horse to ride and two mules to use. Each mule had a packsaddle, a saddle blanket, and a bearskin or buffalo robe to cover the packs. Once we started out for the mountains, we followed rivers, except when we cut across country to avoid large bends or to cross to a different river. Our camps were organized into a large square with one side protected by the river or lake. The square had to be large enough to allow every animal at least a thirty-foot circle to graze. When we were in a dangerous country, five or more men would be assigned scout duty. At daybreak, these men would mount up and scout out any ravines, woods, hills, or other places where savages might be hiding. After they returned and reported everything clear, the rest of us would leave our breastwork, get breakfast, and break camp. The scouts would ride ahead several miles to make certain the way was clear. Additional scouts would ride no more than half a mile on either side and behind the column to guard against surprise attack."

"I heard the general came back here, didn't go all the way to the mountains," said Mama.

"That's true. He was sick, so he told Bruffee and Scott, his lieutenants; they were to take the company to the rendezvous in the Sweet Lake Valley.

My partner and I decided we would prove our worth by taking on all chores and getting them done fast and right. The experienced hunters in the group took us along on their hunts, and we soon learned what was necessary to survive in the wild. Whenever trouble came—a slipped pack, an unruly animal, someone injured in an accident or kicked by a mule—we made sure we were among the first to help out."

"Who was the sergeant of your mess, Charley?" I asked.

"His name is Jim Beckwourth, and he's a mulatto so him and me got pretty close. He's the one who taught us the most. I remember he rode up next to me one day and pointed out some sand hills up north. He said the wind blew them hills up from the river valley, and the Platte was named that by the Frenchies because it be wide and flat. He said in most places the water's not more than a foot deep, but probably deeper under the sand, and there's a lot of quicksand you got to watch out for. It was also bad Injun country, four different families of Pawnees—the Gran Pawnees, the Republican Pawnees, the Tapage Pawnees, and the Pawnee Loups. Jim said they be friends of the Mesicans, but not us. They're a mean bunch, warring with other tribes and hitting us if they thought they got the odds in favor. Jim was scouting ahead, and Mr. Bruffee told him he could take me along to show me the ropes."

Charley said they left camp the next morning heading west and a little north. "On our left, the Platte River spread out almost three-quarters of a mile wide. Beckwourth told me the river was plenty long, maybe a thousand miles or more. The North Fork starts out in the mountains at North Park, flows northeast, and curves around through a red sandstone canyon, then flows southeast to join up with the South Fork not too far from here. The South Fork comes from South Park where we're headed. It comes east, then north along the east slope of the Rockies, then northeast to join the North Fork. The whole thing eventually empties into the Missouri. It flows wide and shallow most of the way. Lots of willows and cottonwood and berries. You can see the waters run fast and hard, but most of the route is through sand, so it just picks up sand in one place and puts it down someplace else. The damn thing's so shallow a man can't float a boat of any kind—even a bull boat doesn't float in most places. Then he tells me to head up and check out the ravine off to the right. He said if I saw any Injuns, I should shout out, and he'd come up fast. He told me I should hold my ground if they saw me, and don't do anything until he got there."

They didn't find any Injuns that day or for the rest of the trip. But Beckwourth told him about the Injuns they could expect to find at the rendezvous and afterward.

"First," Beckwourth told them, "you'll get them that'll prolly be friendly enough, except you got to know any of them will steal anything left untended, just what they do. They be stealing horses whenever they can get away with them clean. Don't mean nothing, just their nature. You have Piegan, they call themselves Pikuni. They are a Blackfoot tribe, but a separate family of Blackfoot, and usually friendly. You got the Crows, call themselves Absaroka. They are mostly friendly to us mountain men. Then there's the Shoshones, some call 'em Utahs, but they ain't, and the Flatheads, then two other tribes, the Salish an' the Nez Perce, they call themselves Sahaptin. That's all the friendlies. Might any or all of them be at the rendezvous. Then there are the mean and ugly Blackfoot—the Siksikau are the biggest tribe of them—and the Bloods; they call themselves Kainah, and the Grosventures. Them's the most hostile of any of them. But they're friendly with the Arapahoe so that lot tend to be hostile too."

Charley told us he asked him how you know which is which, who's friendly, and who ain't. Beckwourth laughed and told him, "You don't until one of them sticks a tomahawk or a knife in you."

The next evening, Charley continued telling us about his travels. "We passed through lands where rocks were shaped by wind, rain, and flowing water into all kinds of weird forms. One they called Chimney Rock. We got to where the Laramie and North Platte rivers join. Traveled over six hundred miles to get there. That's where we finally got into the foothills of the Rockies. About eight hundred miles out, we forded the Platte again, and about forty miles further on, we reached Independence Rock. Several men climbed it and scratched their names on it."

I was full of questions. "How long was it before you got to the rendezvous?"

"It was early June. The valley spread out in front of us. The greenish-blue water of Sweet Water Lake shimmered in the breeze that came from the northwest. The valley was at least a dozen different shades of green with scattered groves of trees and a line of willows and cottonwoods following the water draining out of the lake."

"Were other people there already?"

"Yep, they were scattered along both sides of the creek, groups of buffalo skin teepees, an occasional dirty white canvas wedge tent. Everywhere were campfires, their smoke drifting off with the breeze. Most fires were surrounded by buffalo robe-covered bedrolls laid out or rolled up. All the camps had stacks of equipment and packs of pelts covered with buffalo robes."

"Were other trader companies there, or just yours?"

"There were two other traders who had already set up shop. They had big canvas tarps roped out lengthwise between trees at the four corners and positioned higher in the front, sloping down to the back so the merchandise for trade was at least partially protected. Bruffee and Hicks had raced ahead that morning, and we spotted them motioning us to the spot where they intended to set up their store. They were in a small clearing stacked with equipment and bundles of pelts—the other partners, Jackson, and Sublette, were successful with their fall and spring hunts. Off to the west, a flat, grassy meadow was being destroyed by at least fifteen men on horseback madly racing in a long, wide circle. Nadeau and I couldn't tell if they were Injuns or trappers."

"Why were they racing?" I asked.

"Nadeau reckoned the winner would collect the large pile of pelts, jewelry, guns, ammunition, and other valuables stacked up behind the cheering folks watching."

"Who were the ones cheering?"

"A bunch of native women dressed in beaded, fringed buckskin, with flowers and beads braided into their long black hair. Their necks, arms, and wrists were covered with all sorts of ornaments. Some had babies in decorated carrying boards strapped to their backs. I thought all of them were standing too close to the path taken by the racing horses and expected at least one of 'em would get run over while we watched."

"Did any of 'em get run over?"

"Nope, the winner claimed his reward. His woman was holding his arm and jumping up and down as he loaded the loot onto his pony. The other riders led their mounts away, their women following with their heads down."

"What happened after that?"

"Beckwourth introduced me and Nadeau to most of the free trappers who had been roaming since the previous year's rendezvous."

"What are free trappers?" I was still full of questions.

"They don't work for a company. They trap in the fall and spring and hole up in the winter. Some winter in an Injun village and take a woman as a wife. Many of 'em have Injun wives. It's a mark of pride to have the woman with the fanciest gewgaws. The free trappers and Injuns make the rounds of the company stores trying to get the best prices for their packs of furs. The smartest ones wait to start drinking until after they make their best deals, trading for the equipment and supplies they need for the coming year, or for credit with a company that they can draw on. The booze gives the traders a huge advantage. The once-a-year binge for both Injuns and trappers results in brawls—sometimes some men get killed. There's gambling of all kinds, and they all want to treat their friends to more drink and bad behavior. The drunks usually trade their furs at ridiculous high prices for supplies and more whiskey. Many of the free trappers leave the rendezvous in debt for the supplies they need and then have to do business with those they owe. Most of the company trappers use up their wages purchasing the whiskey at what they call mountain prices."

"I told Nadeau it appeared those men would be a lot better off if they left off the whiskey. Nadeau agreed but said drinking liquor ain't all bad."

"Makes you feel good. You can break loose and have some fun. Look at them boys, they be having a grand old time."

"I told him he could do what he wanted, but it ain't for me."

That night after dinner, our family huddled together in the shack. Little Catherine sat on Charley's knee as he continued to tell us about his adventures.

"What did you do after the rendezvous?" I asked Charley.

"After the rendezvous was over, Mr. Sublette came back to St. Louis with all the furs they traded for, and I went with Mr. Jackson and forty men to trap the mountains north and west of Bear Lake."

"What animals did you trap?"

"Beaver, mostly. They live in water most of the time and eat twigs and bark and such. They're smart. They build a dam to make a pond in a creek, then they build a house and live inside the dam. The only way to enter the house is from under the water. They have a big flat tail that they slap the water with when there is danger. The tail makes some good eating." Charley smiled.

Catherine squinted her eyes and made a face. "You eat the tails? What do you do with the rest?"

"We skin the animals—it's their fur what's valuable—then we eat the meat. Kinda tastes like squirrel."

"If they're in the water most of the time, how can you trap them?" I asked.

"We use steel traps. The jaws stay open like this," he said, showing us with his hands. "The traps got a big spring, and when the beaver steps on the part that releases the spring, he's caught." Charley slapped his hands together, and Catherine and I jerked away.

"We put the trap under the water where it looks like a place the beaver comes and goes and put a nice juicy twig near the trap. The trap has a chain that's held with a stick we pound in the bed of the creek. When everything is well hid, we put some castoreum on it."

"What's castoreum?"

"That be some stink we get from other beavers from glands under their tails," Charley said. "We put it on the bait stick, so the beaver don't suspect nothing. Then we walk away, staying in the water for a ways, so the beaver don't know we been there. When the beaver sees that nice juicy twig and goes for it, he steps on the trap."

Charley slapped his hands together again. That time Catherine jerked, but I didn't.

"We set traps early in the morning and check on them that night or the next day. If we catch a beaver, we put the trap in a different place to catch more."

I didn't know how much of all this to believe. "What's that stuff you put on the twig smell like?" I asked.

"It stinks," he said, "kinda like skunk, but not so strong or nasty."

"How do you get it?"

"We squeeze the glands under their tail and milk the stuff into a container made from the tip of a buffalo horn."

Catherine wrinkled her nose, hid her face in Charley's shirt, and soon fell asleep. Charley continued talking late into the night. He described his new life—skinning the animals, scraping the hides, stretching them to dry, then putting them into bundles for storage and transport. He explained how to build a cache. He showed us how he used a mold to make bullets. He emptied his shooting bag and showed us the tools needed to make repairs on his rifle, and the wire and brush used to keep the touchhole open. He showed us his bullet mold, lead balls, a piece of tanned leather to cut off patches for wadding, extra flints, and spare parts necessary to keep his rifle operating. He showed us his powder horn and a piece of elk antler drilled out to hold just the right amount of powder. He called that his powder charger. He showed us other survival tools: a patch knife for cutting patches from a piece of leather, a sheath knife and sheath, a tomahawk, a flint, and steel for starting a fire, a spoon made from a buffalo horn, and a pot for cooking.

I whispered to Charley. "Did you kill any Injuns?"

Charley put a finger to his mouth and shook his head, gesturing with his chin at our mother. "I'll tell them stories when we be by ourselves," he whispered back. I was disappointed; I wanted to know about the Injuns, not about a cooking pot. But it was late, and my eyes kept closing. Mama said it was time for all of us to go to sleep.

The next day, Charley told us about traveling through mountains that reached way up in the sky, most with snow still on them even in summer. He told us the sky's a color blue you never see anyplace else, the clouds pure white. He said the trees, the grass, and the bushes were maybe ten or twenty different kinds of green, and the mountain water was all kinds of blue and green. Then he got misty-eyed and stopped talking, lost to us, back in those mountains.

I almost split a gut waiting for him to tell us more. I jiggled my legs, but he ignored it. Finally, I poked him in the ribs. He was still lost. After a while, he shook his head and continued. "We got to the Salmon River, to the south of Bitterroot Mountain. Followed it upstream for a couple of days. Mr. Jackson sent three or four men up each creek that emptied into the Salmon to scout for signs of beaver. Then we circled around to the west and scouted every river we came to. After about another month of exploring, we circled three-quarters of the Bitterroot range and came to Lolo Creek. We traveled about fifteen or twenty miles a day, and Mr. Jackson reckoned we covered more than a thousand miles. We made note of all creeks with good beaver sign to come back to when it was cold. It finally started getting cool in the evening, and Mr. Jackson took us around to the east side of the range to the Bitterroot River Valley. He told us we should come there to gather for winter camp. There was plenty of wood to build shelters and fires, grass for the horses and mules, and plenty of buffalo and elk for food. Then he split us into small groups, and we went out for the fall hunt. He told each group which streams to trap and said he would come around every now and again with supplies and to bring their pelts back to the main camp."

"How many in your group, Charley?" Mama asked.

"Nadeau and me be pilgrims, greenhorns, so Mr. Jackson put us with Carlos Beaubien, Old Bill Williams, Tom Fitzpatrick, and Pete Simmons. All of 'em are old hands. Old Bill be some strange. He talks out loud, preaching at the mountains and the rivers and such, but hardly ever talked straight to one of us. But if you just watch what he does, you can learn about being a real mountain man."

I frowned. "You learned just by watching?"

Charley slapped his knee, laughing. "No! We learn by doing. The old hands taught me and Nadeau how to keep camp for them. They called it our initiation. They do it to all pilgrims. They gave us lots of stupid chores, but they also taught us to skin an animal right, scrape the inside clean, and stretch out the pelts. They would come in from their trap lines and dump the dead critters and leave us to prepare them. Every now and again they would shoot or trap a mink, fox, or wolf, or some critter with a good pelt, and one of us would skin it out. After a bit, they taught us how to trap beaver. Even after we got to be good enough at trapping, we still had to do all the cooking and skinning and such. It was all part of becoming a mountain man. When we got all the beaver we could from a place, we'd move on to find more beaver sign and make another camp."

"How long did you do that for?" Catherine asked.

"Well," he said, "after a bit, it got colder and colder at night and the snow started. Wading in icy creeks got awful old, so we packed up and headed for the winter camp in Bitterroot Valley. When we got there, we found a fair-sized tribe of Nez Perce and another of Flathead Injuns camped nearby. Both of those tribes be friends between them and with us. It was a comfortable winter. The Injuns taught me and Nadeau some of their lingo, and with sign, we could get along good with 'em."

"What sign, Charley?" I asked.

"That be using hand signs to mean words. This be the sign for a horse." He held his left hand, fingers straight out, in front of his chest and put the first and second fingers of his right hand over the top of the straight fingers. Then he held his two hands up next to his forehead and said, "This means buffalo."

"Oh," I said, thinking about how much I wanted to share in those adventures. "Charley, are you going back? If you do, will you take me with you? I'll do anything you tell me to do. Please!"

"How old are you now, Sprite?"

"Seven."

"Well, I'm going back for certain, Sprite, but you won't be old enough or big enough to come along this time. You need to stay here to take care of Mama and your sister. When you get big enough, I'll take you with me."

"Promise?"

"Yeah, I promise. It's a good thing living in the mountains. In that country, Injun or white man don't care about your skin color, who your papa or mama be, or what you done before you come to the mountains. Every man is judged on how good his word is, how good he can shoot and trap, how hard he works, how reliable he is, how brave he is, and how willing he is to risk his own life for his friends."

I couldn't wait to grow up. From that day on, all my dreams were about what life would be like once I left St. Louis. I would leave behind everything that made me feel not as good as other boys just because my mama was black.

"Will you teach me to shoot a rifle, Charley? Please?"

"When the time comes, Sprite. You're too small now. My piece would set you on your butt for sure."

The following day, Charley and I took a walk to the docks.

"Did you fight any Injuns, Charley?"

He leaned in close. "You seen that notch on the barrel of my rifle?"

"I did. You put it there on purpose? What do it mean?"

"Whenever a mountain man kills an Injun, everyone expects him to put a notch on the barrel of his rifle."

"Why?"

"I don't know, exactly, but everyone does it."

"So, what happened? How did you kill the Injun?"

We arrived at the docks and stood watching some men loading a boat. "Me and Nadeau were sent out for the spring hunt with Pete Simmons. Pete is a Dutchman, always has his pipe in his mouth. One day, all three of us were on the same creek, maybe three or four hundred strides apart, setting traps. Our horses were hobbled and grazing off a ways. The pack mule was back at our camp, staked out to graze. The mule suddenly started to bray," Charley said. Then he put a hand on my shoulder. "Mules be a lot smarter than horses, Tom. That mule, he smelled Blackfeet. Old Pete, he lets out a whistle and jumps up on the bank, grabs his rifle, and hightails it full speed toward camp. We followed as fast as we could. About three hundred feet from camp, Pete signals us to git down behind some brush and shush. Then he circles around and spots three Blackfeet going through our stuff and another leading off the mule. Pete starts laughing and shoots the one leading the mule. Nadeau and me both fired at the same time, and one of us hit an Injun in the back of his head. He was dead before he hit the ground. The ones going through our stuff drop everything they's holding and takes off running in different directions. Old Pete is on the tail of one of them, reloading while running, still laughing. Then he drops to one knee and shoots him."

Charley continued, explaining that he and Nadeau had trouble reloading their rifles while running. "We finally got our rifles reloaded and squeezed off shots. Nadeau missed, but I hit the savage in the back, and down he goes. We go over to him. His eyes are open, looking at us, but he's not saying anything. Old Pete comes up holding three scalps with blood dripping from 'em, still laughing. He asks me if I got this one and tells me to finish him off because if he lives and goes back where he came from, we'd be swamped with the devils in no time. Pete says, 'Don't waste powder or lead on him though, slit his throat.' I didn't want to do it and I told Pete so."

"Pete says if that was me lying there and the savages were us, they would take me back to their camp and torture me until I died, but nice and slow. It might take days. He said if I cut his throat, I'd be doing him a favor because he's expecting me to torture him. So I unsheathed my knife and reached for him, but he kinda gurgled and died before I got to him. Old Pete scalped him and added the scalp to a bag of them. Nadeau and I decided we didn't need to be collecting scalps. When we got back to the company and found a file, we both put a notch in our rifles. The code of the mountain man is that you can only count the ones you know you killed. We took the four Injun ponies—one each for Nadeau and me and two for Old Pete. Mine are waiting for me back in the mountains."

I was both fascinated and confused by the story. I couldn't believe Charley could be so calm and matter-of-fact about them killing four people, even Injuns, but I was kind of proud that he had refused to cut the injured man's throat, but the Injun died, and he didn't have to.

The next evening, we were all gathered at the table with the dinner bowels washed and put away when Mama said, "Well, son, last night you told us what happened to you the first years you were in the mountains. What happened to you after that?"

Charley explained how Smith, Jackson, and Sublette had agreed that Smith would probably be gone for two years. Sublette would take their furs back to St. Louis, then return with supplies for Jackson's party at the '28 Rendezvous, again at Bear Lake. "Me and Nadeau trapped with the Jackson party during the fall and spring hunts following the '28 Rendezvous. The three partners were supposed to meet in the Snake River valley at the base of the Teton Mountains in the summer of 1829."

"We wintered in Jackson Hole," Charley told us that valleys enclosed on all sides by mountains were called holes. "That spring hunt was really good, and we kept following the beaver further and further away until it was too late to get to the rendezvous. Sublette arrived with a massive shipment of supplies, but none of us trappers made it. He traded some of the merchandise for furs and sent them back to St. Louis with some trusted men. Then he took what he had left and went searching for Jackson and Smith. He found Jackson and us on the Snake River, and we all took off to search for Smith. We crossed the mountains into Pierre's Hole, where Sublette stayed while Jackson took Nadeau and me and a few others, with some supplies, to the Flathead country where we found Smith and his men. They had been through a bunch of disasters and would have returned empty-handed from their travels, except Smith was able to sell the furs they collected in California to the Hudson Bay Company. That was lucky 'cause they lost all their horses and pack animals. No way to carry the furs. Smith got Hudson Bay Company papers for the value of the furs and carried the paper next to the skin on his chest."

I was having trouble remembering all the names but couldn't get enough of listening to his adventures. "Then what happened?" I asked him.

"Well, me and Nadeau's contracts with the company were done, but we agreed to stay on with them through the fall hunt in exchange for a horse, a pack mule, and supplies. We both still had the Injun ponies we took from the Blackfoot warriors. We had everything we needed to stay in the mountains and start being free trappers the next spring. I also arranged with the company to transfer almost all the money I would earn to their St. Louis office for Mama to draw on."

"And that has saved us, son," Mama said, then went over and kissed him on the forehead.

Later, when he and I were alone, Charley continued the story. "After we started free trapping, we come across some mountains between the Gallatin and Yellowstone Rivers. We came up on a big band of Blackfeet who reckoned they'd take our horses and mules. Old Tom Fitzpatrick, he was the Booshway of our group, sounded the alarm, and the Injuns found they made a miscalculation. We beat them off fair and proper."

"What's a Booshway?" I interrupted.

"That's the captain of the group of free trappers who all agree that he is in charge. Anyhow, me and Nadeau be with Old Tom, and it don' take long before Pete Simmons is laughing, and we're all spreading hot lead around. Two of our boys got themselves killed. I don't know how many Injuns because they always take their dead when they can. The fight was spread out over that big valley, us shooting and riding for cover because there was more of them than us." Charley was again lost, this time in the fight. I didn't interrupt, afraid he would not continue. "Me and Nadeau followed Jim Beckwourth because he was the most experienced hand close by. We made it to a grove of trees and hid out until dark, then we got out of that place fast. The company didn't get all together again until we got the Big Horn basin."

Charley stopped talking then and stared into the distance. I stayed quiet until he shook his head and continued.

"From the Big Horn, the whole outfit turned south with all the pelts we saved. It was too late to take the furs back to St. Louis, so we cached them in the riverbank, and everybody agreed to rendezvous at that place come summer. Mr. Sublette took one man and hightailed it for St. Louis just after Christmas. I heard they made it here in early February. That was some feat, traveling in winter. He did it so the company would have supplies at the rendezvous that summer."

Charley went on to explain that the firm of Smith, Jackson, and Sublette sold out to the Rocky Mountain Fur Company, which included Thomas Fitzpatrick, Milton G. Sublette, Henry Fraeb, Jean Baptiste Gervais, and James Bridger.

"They were all good hands in the mountains, but me and Nadeau didn't know if they would be good at business. Anyhow we didn't drink whiskey, so we did some hard trading. We ended up trading pelts to a different outfit, the American Fur Company, not the Rocky Mountain boys. I got a hundred and eighty dollars for my pelts. I kept fifteen, but they were supposed to pay Mama a hundred and sixty-five. Did they do that?"

"Yes," I told him. "Mr. Chouteau sent a man and told us Mama got an account with them."

Charley explained how he and Nadeau then joined a large company led by Fraeb and Gervais. They went south into the mountains of Colorado, an area where neither of 'em had been before. They hunted that fall and wintered in the San Luis Valley, finding some virgin streams where beaver abounded. After the spring hunt, the two of them made their way to the Platte, then all the way home to St. Louis.

"Nadeau and I done really good this spring, and Mama's account with Mr. Chouteau is now close to three hundred dollars."

I was so proud of Charley.

Chapter 6
Felipe

During our second year in El Rito, in 1839, the irrigation ditches were improved, and additional fields were cleared, plowed, and planted. After the plots of wheat, corn, beans, squash, peppers, and herbs were in the ground, there was time for other activities. Papa and both the Bernal brothers went to Abiquiu to take delivery of the thirty-eight ewes and two rams promised by the Alcalde of Abiquiu. They drove the sheep back to El Rito where Vivian and I, and the sons of the other vecinos, took turns herding the sheep, horses, and burros as they grazed on the mesas abutting the valley. The following spring, lambs were born, and it wasn't long until the herd numbered almost two hundred head of ewes. The male lambs were castrated then used for meat.

After the spring planting, all ten men gathered their families and started making adobe bricks using straw saved from the wheat harvest. We mixed mud with the straw and formed the paste into bricks using wood molds. These were set out in the sun to bake dry. The parents instructed the children in this work, then left us to make bricks. Vivian and I, as the eldest male children in the village, oversaw adobe brick manufacturing. All the vecinos treated me as an adult, and I felt I was.

While we continued to live in the jacales, work parties traveled to the forest to harvest large trees to saw into boards and straight poles that would become beams and rafters, what we called vigas. These were necessary for the construction of our casas. To saw the boards, we dug a pit deep enough for a man to stand in and built a scaffold over the pit. Each log was placed on the scaffold, with the length running the length of the pit. One man stood below, the other on the scaffold, and the two sawed thick planks from the log. It was hard work and required skill with a file to keep the saw sharp, but the work progressed. Gradually, the supply of timbers and boards grew until there were sufficient vigas for the roofs of ten houses and the required doors, shutters, and furniture. The bachelor Bernal brothers were skilled carpenters and furniture makers, and they traded these skills for clothing, blankets, and other items they could not make for themselves.

The second winter was spent building ten adobe houses. Near each jacal, the owner selected an area of ground. We all worked together to level and smooth each spot with pickaxes, shovels, and rakes. We laid out the houses, usually two rooms, each ten to twelve feet square, by running a string tied to stakes driven into the ground at each corner. Measuring with a string across diagonal corners allowed us to make certain the layout was square. Poles were substituted for the stakes, and strings were strung from pole to pole. After first laying the corners, we positioned the guide strings to allow the men to build walls that were straight and square. No mortar was used. When necessary, we shaped the adobe bricks to fit tightly using a machete. The walls were a hand's width taller than my father, the tallest man in the pueblo.

After each man held a long consultation with his spouse or his entire family to decide where to place the openings, we framed windows and doors. The vigas were set over two extra courses of adobe bricks on top of the front wall of the house, thus sloping down from the front to the back. Four more courses of adobe brick were set around and over the vigas to secure them. Next, we lashed smaller poles across the vigas for the roof. These poles were covered with branches, then pine boughs, and finally, large chunks of sod. The final step was to smear mud over the walls, inside and out. The younger children plastered the lower portions of the walls, the older children the higher sections. Ten men, eight women, and scores of children worked on each house. We completed all ten houses in two months. The community became even more cohesive and efficient with this time spent in common pursuit.

The communal lands were rich with good pasture, firewood, and several varieties of timber suitable for lumber. We left the edges of the valley, outside the irrigation ditches, in native grasses and harvested these for hay to feed the animals when the weather prevented taking them out to pasture. Corrals for the livestock were built next to the trails leading to the mesas, with adjacent sheds for saddles, bridles, animal medicines, and hay storage.

When all the families had moved into their houses, it was time to start construction of the Morado, the community house of the Brotherhood. Papa told me the Brotherhood spent more than an hour debating about where to put it and finally decided on the base of a small hill near the south end of the valley. It was fourteen feet long and thirty feet wide. Vigas sixteen feet long were required, and it was necessary to build a hoist to lift each end of the logs into place. When finished, the building had a door at each end and two windows front and back. The Brotherhood now had a home where they could conduct their rites and hold their services. It also functioned as a general meeting house, a church if a priest happened by, and a fort if the community ever came under attack. A small library was kept there, as well as the paraphernalia necessary for the Brotherhood to perform its rituals. The latter were locked away in a small attached storeroom.

My family mostly lived in our two-room adobe house and adjacent jacal, but my brothers and I each had our own beds in the jacal. We swept the dirt floor daily, but spiders and other critters frequently dropped from the sod roof. Each of us had two heavy blankets, a buffalo robe, a straw-stuffed canvas mattress, and a straw-stuffed pillow.

In the adobe house, tanned lambskins, scraped so thin that only diffuse light forced its way into the interior, covered the windows. Our mother and father shared the privacy of the back room in a bed barely wide enough to accommodate them both. The Bernal brothers built them a chest with two drawers in which they stored clothing. All our furnishings were built by the Bernal brothers, who continued to acquire more sophisticated tools and additional skills using them.

A large cupboard dominated the main room. Two beds hugged the wall away from the door, one for each of my sisters. Set into the wall near the foot of each bed were four pegs hung with each girl's entire wardrobe.

In the middle of the room sat a rough wood table. On either long side of the table were benches that sat three people to a side. Our father had a chair with arms at the head of the table; our mother an armless chair at the foot. On the table was a box with candles made from tallow, a half-burned candle in a holder, and almost always a book borrowed from the small library of the Brotherhood. It was our habit to read aloud to each other at night before going to sleep. The dirt floor was hard-packed from a daily sprinkling of water, the constant tread of bare feet, and daily sweeping.

My family prospered. Each year our irrigated fields produced more than we could use. We sold the surplus at the market in Abiquiu, with ten percent tithed to our Brotherhood. The funds reserved for the Brotherhood were kept safe for future needs or emergencies. Our community was also repaying the loan from the Abiquiu Brotherhood. The pueblo's common lands proved profitable. Each fall, after the harvest, we felled trees and cut them into wood planks. We purchased a wagon and two draft mares and hauled the lumber to Taos, where it was in big demand. The pueblo acquired more sheep, cattle, horses, and manufactured goods, such as iron nails and steel tools. We bred the mares, including the two draft mares, to our jack burro to produce mules. We had three young mules, and all our mares became pregnant again.

The pueblo's sheep herd now numbered almost two hundred. We also owned a dozen cows and one bull. Castrated male lambs, calves, wheat, corn, squash, peppers, and other vegetables produced cash. Each family in the pueblo had at least one riding saddle and one packsaddle, bridles, and other tack. The pueblo also had a good supply of tools for every purpose and a rudimentary blacksmith shop. The men, including all boys over the age of twelve, had rifles. Their fathers made certain the boys knew how to use them.

It was early spring of 1839. I awoke to the sound of light rain and the filtered gray light of dawn. I roused myself and rushed to dress. I heard the slap of my mother's hands patting out the tortillas for our breakfast and inhaled the warm smell of frijoles mixed with the leftover lamb stew from last night. Perhaps there would be some early spring melon from the garden. I went over to where Vivian was still sleeping and shook his shoulder.

"Time to get up," I said.

It was our week to take the animals to pasture and stand guard over them. We would take the herd east up toward the Ortega Mountains to take advantage of the spring grass. We would be gone for the whole week, camping on our own. For the last several weeks, the animals had been grazing on the mesas to the west of the valley. Those flat mesas now needed time for the grass to recover. The Roybal brothers, who had overseen the herd the previous week, had returned to the valley with all the animals now crowded into the corrals.

Both Vivian and I squatted close to the fireplace at the back of the kitchen shack to keep warm. As we ate our tacos, we talked to our mother. I had brought out our bedrolls and packs to lean against the outside wall of our jacal. Our heavy wool serapes formed a tent around each of us as we ate.

Mama gave us a canvas bag with our lunch—flour, beans, and dried chilies. We would hunt for our meat. After we finished eating, we saddled two horses and affixed our packs to one of the burros. Vivian mounted and herded the animals to the trailhead as I opened the various corral gates to let them out. We left behind eight horses for the use of the pueblo. Those horses stood close to the corral fence, neighing to their mates as the herd moved away. I mounted, and we herded the animals north to the dam with its impounded lake so the animals could drink.

After the animals were finished at the lake, we moved them toward the trail going to the east, following a path parallel to a small stream originating from the Ortega Mountains. My mare, a bay with white stockings on all four limbs, remembered the lush spring grass in those mountain pastures and pushed herself into the lead. The herd followed the well-worn paths. Since our arrival, the pueblo's livestock had moved up and down these trails many times. After an initial steady grade, the path, originally built by hard work with shovels and pickaxes, became a series of five switchbacks climbing the steep slope. At the top, the animals spread out and were soon grazing an area containing scattered juniper and pinion trees as well as a profusion of lush spring grass.

"Should we let them stay here for a while or move them?" Vivian asked.

Spanning out from the little mesa were paths to the north and south that circled around the mountain and led to some small valleys where the snow would have collected and now melted.

"Let's save this area for later and move them around to the north. You know that small valley that's only about a thousand varas to the north and then east?" I said.

"Yes, I know it."

"There's a good place to camp there. When I was hunting with Ignacio last fall, there were deer and plenty of rabbits. We could use our slingshots to kill the rabbits."

"Good, let's go."

We circled the herd in opposite directions and started the animals in the chosen direction, following the trail from previous years. It wasn't long until we arrived at the little valley. A small stream flowed with fresh snow water, cold and clear, trickling over smoothed rocks and small waterfalls. There was a small pool of water at a spot where the ground flattened. The trickle of a shallow creek drained the pool and wound its way through the meadow, which was filled with pale green spring grasses and a profusion of early-blooming wildflowers. The meadow was ringed by hills that rose to the nearby mountain peaks another eight hundred to two thousand feet above us. Spruce and black pine covered the hills and mountains, except for the rocky peaks.

"This is good, no?" I remarked. "There is grass enough here for all of them for at least two or three days, don't you think?"

"Yes, I agree," Vivian replied. "Where should we make our camp?"

"I think that spot on the far side of the pond." I pointed to a small clearing containing the remains of a lean-to. "Let's hobble our horses so we can catch them if we need to. They will be able to graze with the rest of the animals. The herd won't start to wander from here for at least two days. Then we can move them."

It didn't take us long to make a camp. We spread fresh pine boughs on the ground under the skeleton of the lean-to built the previous year. We repaired the lean-to with more layers of pine boughs, forming a relatively watertight roof and two sides; the front was open to the rock fireplace we rebuilt. We spread out our bedrolls and unpacked our supplies.

"Did you and Ignacio see any sign of bear when you passed through here in the fall? Should we hang the food up high in this tree?" Vivian asked.

"We didn't see any bear sign, but we should throw a rope over that large limb and raise the food bag high enough to keep it out of reach of any bears wandering through."

That evening, at dusk, I led Vivian through the woods to a very small meadow just over the ridge to the east. I thought we might find some deer there. We moved quietly to a vantage point and spotted three does grazing in the meadow. At frequent intervals, one of the three raised her head, ears, and nose twitching, intent on discovering hidden danger. I took careful aim and brought down one of the does with a shot to the heart. The other two does scattered into the trees.

Vivian did not fire his rifle. The signal for an emergency was two shots in quick succession, followed by a third in a minute or two it took to reload. That signal would echo through the mountains and be clearly heard in our pueblo. The men would drop everything and come as fast as they could.

That evening after a dinner of deer loin roasted over the fire, we worked on the deerskin. We had soaked it in the water coming out of the pool and now took turns scraping the inside. It was nowhere near clean enough to pass inspection by Ignacio. We scraped it until we were tired of the task, then stretched it out.

"When we go back to the pueblo," I said, "I will soak it again in hot water, scrape off the hair, then tan it with the brain. I've watched Ignacio do that. I will split the skull and get the brain out in the morning. I'll save the brain in the cold water from the pool until we use it. Mama is very good with scissors and needles. Maybe we can get her to make something for each of us from the skin."

Just before dawn, I woke up to a noise I couldn't identify. Then I heard it again, the bleating of a sheep in terror. I threw off my blankets, reached for my rifle, and shook Vivian awake.

"Something has attacked the sheep," I whispered. "There, do you hear that? It's being dragged away."

"Yes, I hear."

"Follow me. I'm a better shot, so let me shoot first. Be quiet. Maybe it's a cougar."

We moved quietly through the herd, bent over at the waist with rifles held out in front, cocked and ready. Our powder horns and bullet bags, strung on leather straps around our necks, bounced off our knees as we moved. When we reached the woods on the opposite side of the meadow, Vivian pointed to a spot where something had pushed through the dense undergrowth. I nodded to show that I saw it and pushed through to follow the trail. We followed bent and broken brush through the trees for about a hundred varas; then we heard something moving directly ahead. We stopped, motionless. The sun peeked over the eastern ridge, warming our skin.

I motioned to Vivian to follow me and moved off through the trees to my right. We quickly circled around until I dropped. Vivian did the same. Lying on the ground, we peeked through the underbrush and saw two men. One was leading our horses with braided rawhide ropes made into crude halters consisting of one loop around each animal's neck entwined with another around the nose. The second man was dragging the carcass of a ewe, heavy and probably pregnant with twins, its throat slit. I thought they might be Apache, the tribe that Ignacio told me sometimes hunted in this area. They were both squat and heavily muscled, wearing only breechcloths and moccasins despite the early morning chill. Their long, dirty hair was held away from their faces by filthy bandannas tied in the back. Their bows were slung across their chests diagonally, and each had a quiver holding eight or ten arrows hanging on his back.

Shaking with excitement and fear, I took aim at the man leading the horses. I fired, hitting him in the right shoulder, far from his heart where I was aiming. The horses reared, pulling the ropes from the man's now useless hand. Snorting with fear and the smell of blood, the horses turned, crashing through the trees and underbrush back to the herd.

Vivian was unable to hold his rifle steady, but he squeezed off a shot. The ball whooshed well over the head of the second Apache, who dropped the ewe, got his bow free, and strung an arrow all in one continuous motion. He looked around wildly for where the shots had originated. His companion, grunting in pain, was moving quickly off to the north. The second Apache, his bow pulled and ready to fire, crouched low, turning in jerky movement to all sides, listening intently. He sent an arrow in our general direction, then hurried after his companion. Shaking, we hurried to reload, and I finally sent another round after the fleeing Indians, knowing the shots would bring the men in the pueblo to our aid.

In my mind, I could visualize the pueblo suddenly coming to life as the rumbling reports of our rifles echoed down from the mountains. After the third shot, the men would be on the run for the corral, their wives following with their rifles, powder horns, and bullet bags. The men would catch horses, affix bridles and saddles, and mount, then reach down to take everything from their wives. Ignacio, who would certainly be the first to mount, would go up the trail as fast as he could; the others would follow. Those who had arrived too late to get a horse would follow on foot, trailed by any boys who could get away before their mothers stopped them. Ignacio would follow the fresh tracks of the herd and would soon deduce where we were. Our father would be close behind Ignacio, pushing his horse hard, his rifle in his right hand held high for balance. When they broke into the meadow, the herd, by then grazing calmly, having recovered from the excitement, would scatter away from the onrushing men. Ignacio would glance at our empty camp, then search the periphery of the meadow for signs. He would spot the two horses with trailing lariats still around their necks and surmise what had happened. "Indians," he would tell my father. "They tried to steal the horses, and the boys must have tried to stop them. Let me circle the meadow and find where they went."

Ignacio heard Vivian and me as we returned the way we had come. I was elated to see him and Papa, not really believing they could get to us as fast as they did.

They greeted us with shouts and hugs, everyone wanting to know what had happened.

"There were two of them," I said. "I think that's all. I shot at one but missed his heart and hit him in the right shoulder." I looked at Ignacio. "It was a very bad shot. I was very nervous and shaking. It was not the same as shooting a deer or elk."

"Yes, I understand," he said, smiling. "It is difficult to shoot a man." Then he looked at Vivian.

Vivian shook his head. "I missed completely. I think my eyes were shut. The one I missed was dragging one of our ewes. They had cut its throat, but we heard it bleating when they first dragged it off. The one Felipe shot was leading our horses." He looked around at the herd. "There they are, with the ropes still on them."

"The third shot?" Papa asked. "Were you able to hit either one with the third shot?"

"No, they were gone by then, into the woods," I answered. "I just fired in the direction they went. I did not think it would be wise to follow them."

"That was smart," Ignacio said. "If you had tried to follow them, they probably would have killed you both. But you did well. You protected the herd."

I looked at Ignacio and smiled. Any praise from him was something to be treasured.

"We heard a single shot yesterday. What was that?" Ignacio asked.

"I killed a deer. We have plenty of meat. Maybe everybody is ready for breakfast?" I was grinning broadly now.

My father smiled at me. "Yes, you are a good host. I think we should all have some breakfast. Ramon Jose," he called to one of the Congora boys, "go to the pueblo and let the women and children know everything is good. They will be worried. I'm certain they will feed you well there."

"Yes, Señor. I go."

The others gathered around the fire that Vivian built up from the coals. Ignacio cut thick steaks from the deer carcass, and each man and boy roasted the meat over the fire after skewering it on a green branch. Most of the meat was seared black on the outside and dripped blood that ran onto our chins as we ate.

"After we finish eating, I want you to show me and your father the place where they left the dead ewe," Ignacio whispered to me. "We will follow their tracks and make certain there are not more in the vicinity. If there were only two of them, you wounded one, and they won't stay. They were probably just out stealing horses and took the ewe for something easy to eat. They don't want to kill us. They want us to stay and prosper so they can come and steal from us our horses, cattle, and sheep. It is an easy way for them to survive, especially during a hard winter. It is much easier than finding food in the wilderness. They would take our horses to another pueblo and trade them for flour, beans, and whatever they could. It won't be long until they come to us with something they have stolen from others to trade for food. It is their way."

After all the others returned to the pueblo, Vivian and I led Ignacio and Papa to the dead sheep. Ignacio kept us back from the site as he circled around, studying the ground. He touched the blood on a branch the Indian had brushed against, then crouched to examine the dead ewe. Finally, after asking us to show him where we were when we managed to ambush the Indians, he searched and found the arrow shot in our direction. He extended the arrow and showed us the characteristic markings.

"Yes, these men were Apache. Felipe, you and Vivian go back and tend to the herd. Your father and I will follow these two and make certain they have left the country."

After they left, I turned to Vivian. "I think we did well," I said to him.

"Yes, I am of accord. Both Papa and Ignacio appear to be pleased with us," he responded.

My heart was still beating faster than normal from the excitement, but I was proud that my brother and I had done what we did. I felt very close to Vivian. I reached over, put my arm around his shoulder, and drew him in close. "Yes, my brother, we did very well."

Chapter 7
Tom Tobin

Charley stayed with us that fall and winter. His friend Nadeau was a frequent visitor. They both got jobs with the fur company that acted as Mama's bank because the owners knew neither of them drank and both of them were hard workers. I had my eighth birthday that winter, and Charley made me a slingshot and taught me how to use it. I slept with that slingshot and still have it. The following spring, the two signed on to help transport the American Fur Company's goods to the rendezvous.

It was six long years before Charley surprised us again by walking into the shack while we were eating dinner. This time, he was travel dirty but well dressed, now a fully grown, mature man with a full beard. Everything I am going to tell you now was told to me around a campfire after Charley finally took me with him.

"In the spring of 1837, me, Nadeau, a new recruit named Livernois, and Jim Beckwourth were trapping tributaries of the Salmon River when a small group of Blackfeet attacked our camp. We were in Blackfeet country, so we took the time to fortify the camp with logs stacked two feet high. During the fight, we took turns shooting at any warrior we could see while the others reloaded. Our long rifles kept them Injuns out of range with the three smooth-bore muskets and bows and arrows they had. Toward dark, a lucky shot from a musket hit Livernois in the right eye and he were dead. A bit later them warriors must 'ave decided they weren't makin' headway in the fight and took off. We buried Livernois next to the creek running past our camp and named the creek after him."

"Summer me and Nadeau wandered west to visit the Flathead Indians while Beckwourth went to spend time with his Crow wives. We went with a band of Flatheads to the rendezvous at Pierre's Hole, where we both took Flathead wives."

"What?" I shouted. "You have a wife?"

"Not a legal wife. I gave her gifts, and she agreed to live with me. Nadeau did the same."

Charley continued to deposit most of his earnings into an account with the American Fur Company so Mama could have access, but he told me he wasn't able to resist the urge, shared by his mountain man companions, to spend some money for cloth, sewing thread, needles, heavy blankets—what he called gewgaws for his new bride.

"After the fall hunt, me and Nadeau were in winter camp with our band of Flatheads, our wives, and my three-month-old daughter."

"You have a wife and a daughter? What are their names?"

"I call her Elisa, but both her and her Ma have Injun names you won't be able to say. If you wanna hear about what all I been doin, ya gotta stop interrupting. While we was with the Flatheads, Nadeau was on guard duty. A Blackfoot sneaked up close and let loose an arrow that nicked his ear and stuck in the side of the tipi where me an' mine were asleep. Nadeau woke the whole camp, but nothing else happened. At dawn, I left the camp to scout and found the valley was fulla them Injuns. I went back and managed to talk our warriors into attacking right away and not waiting for them to attack us. We fought 'em 'till late afternoon and some were killed and a lot more wounded on both sides. I put a ball into a warrior with a lot of feathers and war pain who kept pushin' to the front of every attack. When he went down them Blackfeet started hollerin' 'Nick-oose, Nick-oose' so I reckon he was some sort of chief. Then they broke off, took their dead and wounded with 'em, and runoff. We didn't bother to give chase."

"Over the next two years, me an' Nadeau kept movin' about and showed up at each rendezvous with many pelts. Our wives were experts at preparing them pelts, tanning deer hides, making buffalo and bearskin robes, and sewing buckskin clothing an' we did good sellin' 'em. Because me an' Nadeau were teetotalers, and I didn't gamble, 'though Nadeau did a bit, I could send money home and still get some gewgaws for my sqwaw."

"We trapped in the spring and fall and lived with the Flathead band in the summer and winter. But I got to be unhappy and my sqwaw got to be more of a pain. She knew I was sending most of what I made to support Mama, you, and Catherine. I went hunting for food on my own or with Nadeau but during those winters I spent with the tribe, there were times when there was very little to eat. Them Injuns were usually too lazy to hunt when it were hard to find game and just decided hunger was part of their life."

The price for beaver pelts was not as good as in previous years because the price of pelts traded in St. Louis had fallen and was expected to fall again. Charley met a man named Nathaniel J. Wyeth at the rendezvous. Wyeth had made a contract with the partners of the Rocky Mountain Fur Company to supply them with goods. When he returned to Boston, Wyeth convinced his partners to outfit a ship with trade goods and send it around the horn and north to the Columbia River. The plan was to go overland, meet the ship, and conduct trade in the Columbia basin. After emptying the ship, he would fill it with salted and smoked salmon to be sold in Boston. He arrived in St. Louis in early March and hired seventy men, but he had to offer them higher than usual wages because three other companies were competing to supply the rendezvous. The Wyeth party left St. Louis, but in Independence, he found the competition for horses and pack animals had driven up their price significantly. He was late getting away.

One of the principals of the Rocky Mountain Fur Company was William L. Sublette. His brother Milton was traveling with the Wyeth party. Milton became ill and turned back. Wyeth was concerned about the contract, fearing that without Milton at his side, William, who was pushing hard to arrive before him, would prevail upon the fur company to break their contract. Wyeth's fears came true. When he reached the rendezvous site, the Rocky Mountain Fur Company was in grave financial trouble. Because of competition with other trappers, attacks by Indians, and a general decline in the number of beaver pelts, they had only enough furs to pay off their men. The partners dissolved the company and formed a new firm with Fitzpatrick, Sublette, and Bridger as partners. The new firm refused to honor Wyeth's contract, and the now-defunct old firm even refused to pay the interest on the forfeit, part of the terms of the original contract. Wyeth was angry and frustrated, but there was no way for him to enforce his contract with those tough men. He had a large quantity of goods, and there was no market for them. But he was resourceful. He left the rendezvous with forty-one men, well over a hundred riding and pack animals, his merchandise, three cows, a group of scientists, and a group of missionaries who had attached themselves to his party. Charley and Nadeau sold their furs at the Green River rendezvous, and with their families, joined Wyeth's company for protection on the trip back to the tribal lands.

"Wyeth told me and Nadeau that he intended to set up a fort and trading post on the Snake River in the country of the Nez Perce and Flatheads. He wanted to do all he could to create problems for the former Rocky Mountain Fur Company's trappers. We got to the Snake, he selected a site and started building his fort that he called Fort Hall, I think that was the name of one of his partners. By August, he felt the post was far enough along for him to leave Mr. Evans in charge of eleven men, fourteen horses and mules, and the three milk cows and Wyeth left for the Columbia basin. But before he left, he hired me as an interpreter for a year, to start in January, at a salary of three hundred and eighty dollars. That was easy money. Me and Nadeau did a fall hunt, but the country was over-trapped, and we didn't get many pelts. In January I joined Wyeth's outfit and started my interpreting job, setting up a camp just outside the fort."

"A bit after starting the interpreter job, I told Nadeau that I wanted to cache my pelts until the following year. I was tired of how hard getting good pelts was and the price we were getting was hardly worth the effort. I was also not happy about living with the tribe anymore. I told him once I finished the job with Wyeth, I wanted to travel south to Taos and find a new way to earn a living. Nadeau agreed to join me if the price for their pelts didn't improve. We heard the price of pelts was even lower than the year before, so we got our furs, I bought a blanket, some cloth, a looking glass, and some buttons as farewell gifts for my sqwaw and with some men from the fort who lost their jobs we went to New Mexico."

"What about your daughter?" I asked him. "Have you seen her since you left?"

"Nope. We left Fort Hall and traveled to the Green River. Crossed it and found the Old Spanish Trail. We followed that to the Colorado River, crossed that, and climbed into the San Juan Mountains, arriving at Abiquiu where the trail continued to Santa Fe. Then we followed the Rio Chama, crossed the Rio Grande del Norte, and got to Taos."

"Did you find work in Taos?" I asked.

"Just hold on, I'll tell my story my way," Charley said. He described how the Rio Hondo flows through the center of the Arroyo Hondo, forming a deep canyon about seven miles north of Taos. Fur trappers coming and going to

Taos from the Colorado Rockies made the Trappers Trail. Where it crossed the river, the valley was level for about a half mile on either side of the stream. A small pueblo called Santa Dolores Plaza was about two miles downstream.

The next night, Charley told me about the man who changed his life.

"Turley bought somethin' over a thousand acres along the floor of the arroyo on either side of the Rio Hondo just west of where the Trappers Trail crossed. Stands of native tall-stemmed Taos wheat were already growing on that land. Then he hired a stonemason named Dye. He wanted to build a two-story grain mill and distillery as well as a store and cantina. He also wanted houses for his family and his hired help and a dam at the narrows with a gated flume going into a ditch that curved over and back into the Rio Hondo. He pointed out the locations he wanted for each of the building projects."

"He and Dye sealed their deal with a handshake, and Turley paid Dye seven hundred dollars, plus an extra hundred for getting the mill and distillery done before the new year, an additional hundred for each worker's house, a hundred and a half for the store, and two hundred for Turley's own house that was much bigger than the others. He hired more men to build the dam and canals and he supervised that work himself."

"The mill and distillery were built like a fort. The first-floor walls were stone, with a three-foot-wide stone foundation. The walls were twelve feet high, but the second story was done with adobe bricks."

"Turley fell in love with a widow who had two children, but the Catholic Church controlled all legal marriages in Mexico. You have to convert if you wanted to be married plus pay some fees. Turley wasn't willing to do either, so Maria Rosa Vigil became his common-law wife. Every couple of years, Maria Rosa presented him with a child until there were seven children with the surname of Vigil. Turned out to be a happy, rambunctious gaggle of kids that spilled out of his house and a smiling Madonna who welcomed all visitors."

"When I arrived in Taos, Turley's businesses were all doing good. His way of doing business was to get the trappers drunk selling them whiskey cheap while negotiating for the pelts they brought with them. When I started negotiating for my pelts, he found out that I not only didn't drink, but I knew how much my pelts were worth. I came to the mountains to make money. It didn't take long for Turley to hatch another idea that meant I would settle in Mexico and go into business with him. He didn't have all the details thought out but reminded me that since 1832, it had been illegal to bring liquor into the

Indian territories. Ain't stopped it," I said, "but he told me he knew the trading posts were having a difficult time getting the liquor they needed to trade with the Indians. His idea was to supply pack mules and equipment, including flat kegs that fit on either side of the mule's pack. I could buy the liquor from him for three dollars a gallon and sell it to the trading posts at four dollars a gallon, or more if I could. He told me my furs would buy me three hundred dollars of credit. I asked him how much it cost him to make a gallon of liquor."

"How did you know to ask him that?" I asked.

"It's business, Sprite. You'll learn."

They negotiated and finally agreed that Charley would buy the booze for two and a half dollars a gallon. Charley figured the liquor cost less than a dollar a gallon to make, including the cost of the mill, since Turley grew his own wheat and corn. The traders would dilute the whiskey several times once it was in their hands, so whiskey was a profitable business for everyone. Since Turley was able to sell his liquor to the trappers so cheaply, but still more than triple what it cost him to produce, his trading business was growing. He had a large store of furs in the warehouse portion of the mill and distillery.

In the fall of 1836, Charley headed north and east with mules carrying a hundred and twenty gallons of almost pure alcohol. He first called at Fort Lupton, about twenty-five miles north and east of where they were building the new town of Denver, on the south bank of the South Platte River. Then he went to Fort Vasquez seven miles north. The traders were mighty happy to see him. They eagerly traded beaver pelts and buffalo robes, the robes fast becoming more valuable than beaver, at mountain prices for the Taos Lightning at four dollars a gallon. Charley told me they cut the alcohol in half with water, and added a small plug of tobacco to each gallon for color and traded it for ten times their cost. They cached most of the liquor to protect and hide it from any government inspectors. By the time Charley got back to Arroyo Hondo, the mules were struggling under huge loads of furs and robes.

The rest of that year Charley worked for Turley at wages of twenty-five dollars a month plus keep. He quickly learned to mill grain and make whiskey. Many of Charley's friends from the mountains, on the loose for winter, stopped at Turley's store and cantina to meet old friends and drink significantly cheaper whiskey than they could in Taos. Charley learned about new trading posts being established throughout the plew gathering areas and he expanded his whiskey route.

"In late spring of 1837, Turley offered me three hundred dollars to deliver all his beaver pelts and buffalo robes to Missouri and return with equipment for the mill and goods for his store. He supplied the mules, packs, and five Mexican hired hands. We left Arroyo Hondo and traveled to Bent's Fort, almost two hundred miles away."

"What's Bent's Fort?" I asked.

Charley laughed. "I was just going to tell you that. Give me a chance, Sprite."

"Ceran St. Vrain and three of the Bent brothers, Charles, George, and William, built Bent's Fort in 1833, finishing in 1834. It was made of adobe bricks made on the site. The fort was about sixty yards long and forty-six yards wide, with walls ten feet high and a second story. Two round towers on the southwest and northwest corners provided a complete line of fire along the outside walls. It also has an adobe walled corral, eight feet tall, across the entire length of the southern end. Inside the fort is a large room for trades, blacksmith and carpenter shops, and quarters for the Mexican workers, who worked to maintain the walls and buildings. Inside there are warehouses, rooms for visiting mountain men, a kitchen, a dining room, a cook's room, a wash house, clerks' quarters, a powder magazine, and four rooms set aside for visiting big shots. The second-floor rooms are for the owners. There's even a fully equipped billiard room and bar. It's the only well-stocked trading post between Independence and the Pacific Ocean. It supports the Santa Fe trade and is a landmark, an oasis, and a supplier of needed goods to all those in the area or passing through."

"We set up camp outside Bent's Fort and waited. Before long, traders arrived, some with only one wagon, others with several. Some wagons looked to be empty but left deep ruts in the trail. They were carrying Mexican silver, hidden in false bottoms. Most of the wagons were full of fur pelts and buffalo robes. James and Samuel Magoffin came in fresh from trading in Chihuahua City. Then there were enough of us to discourage any attacks from hostiles. We joined up and two months later arrived safely at Independence. I arranged for a place to pasture the horses and pack mules, leaving them in the care of the hired hands. I left them men with plenty of food and a small part of their earnings to explore all the city had to offer. I got Turley's pelts and robes loaded onto a steamship, and it wasn't long before I got back to you all."

Chapter 8
Felipe

The sun warmed the late afternoon of an early fall day. I crept up behind my mother. She was standing in the kitchen shed, working at the tall plank table, her back to the opening. I put both arms around her middle, nudging aside her long thick braid with my chin.

"Mamacita, what are you cooking? It smells wonderful."

"Stop, you naughty boy! Act your age, Felipe. You are not a child," she scolded, but her voice was not angry.

I reached around her to snatch a chunk of meat out of the pot. She smacked my hand, and I dropped the meat back into the pot, then licked the sauce from my scorched fingers. "Is that the deer meat Ignacio and I brought in yesterday?"

"Yes, I am making chile colorado with jalapeños, and other chiles we dried out from this year's harvest. We also had a good crop of onions. With beans and tortillas, it will be a good dinner."

"It always is, Mamacita. You are the best cook in all of El Rito."

"Never mind, you will not get anything to eat until dinner. Off with you."

Jose Vivian joined us and also tried to snatch a chunk of meat but got his hand whacked with the same spoon.

"Out, out with you both. Go find your father. He will find some work for you to do."

We left, Vivian matching my stride step for step.

That evening, after the family had finished eating, my father took me by the arm. "Come with me, son. I want to have a talk with you."

We walked out into the clear night, the stars and moon providing the only light.

"You are almost a man, Felipe, and it is time you took your place as a man. What do you know of the Brotherhood?"

"I know nothing about what the Brotherhood does, Papa. Neither you nor Ignacio will answer my questions. I know that everything concerning the Brotherhood is secret. I know in the spring before Easter, you come home from meetings with wounds on your back. I have seen them. Then at Easter, some of the men carry a wood cross from the Morado to the little hill south of it, and one of the men is hung from the cross with ropes. I even saw you suffer on the cross once. I also know that if someone is ill or hurt or has had a bad harvest, the Brotherhood takes care of that man and his family. That is good, but I do not understand why or how these things are decided."

"Well, some of these questions will be answered for you if you want. You know I am the leader of the Brotherhood in El Rito. If you are willing, I will take you to our meeting next week. We will instruct you in the duties and obligations of a novice. We will not tell you all our secrets until you have learned everything necessary to become a full member. If you make that decision, it is a decision for the rest of your life. I will always be your father, and I will accept what you decide to do, but if you join us, I will be very proud and honored."

I attended the meeting, became a novice, and was taught the history, and duties of the various officers, and what it means to be accepted as a brother into the order. I was proud that I was able to learn everything in a short time. The following spring, I silently and almost with pleasure endured the taste of the scourge, a whip with seven strands of knotted leather thongs. On Easter morning, I dragged a heavy wood cross from the Morado to the summit of the small hill where a hole was prepared to accept the base of the cross. The brothers tied me to the cross, raised it, and set it into the hole. They packed dirt and stones around the base of the cross, and I hung there until the sun began to set behind the western mesa. All day, the members of the Brotherhood kneeled and prayed before the cross. The women and children came and went during the day, offering their prayers. I silently endured, without food or drink. The coarse ropes chafed my wrists, arms, and ankles raw. Despite the discomfort, I did not falter. Just before sunset, they finally brought down the cross and released me. I was dizzy and disoriented. My mouth was dry, my tongue thick. I tried to stand and fell to my knees. Papa gave me a sip of water and told me to recite three Hail Marys. I struggled but managed to complete the task, and after I did so, I felt a flush of happiness in my heart.

The pueblo of El Rito functioned according to the seasons of the year. We endured, as all farmers do, too much or not enough rain, heat, or cold, but our ability to irrigate the fields mitigated the effects of the seasons. Vivian and I worked our family's fields side by side with our father. Each spring, we plowed and planted. All summer we irrigated the crops. All of the children in the pueblo hoed weeds as soon as they were old enough to manage it. When the crops matured and ripened, we were busy with the harvest. Vivian and I took our turn guarding the herds and flocks grazing on our communal lands, moving the animals to fresh pasture as needed.

The pueblo prospered. Our flock of sheep, herd of cattle, and numbers of horses, donkeys, and mules grew. Surplus produce and grain from our fertile river valley and the sale of wool, male lambs, and calves enabled us to purchase manufactured goods, making our lives more comfortable. We purchased better saddles and bridles, better rifles, warm winter coats, and even a few luxuries. My sisters and our mother were even able to purchase cloth to make dresses. They also bought combs, lace for shawls, and other minor luxuries. We still lived in our adobe house and jacal with dirt floors. Our diet was wholesome. We ate tortillas, frijoles, stews, fresh vegetables and fruits in season, meat from lambs, and wild game that Ignacio and I hunted. Our mother flavored our food with several types of chile peppers, used fresh in season and dried for the rest of the year. At times, we were able to splurge on sugar and chocolate.

I became the regular hunting companion of Ignacio, whose wife had not been able to raise any children beyond infancy. When we first went hunting, we rode bareback out of our little village in the morning darkness, leading a pack mule. We hunted the closer mountains early enough to greet the rising sun. Longer trips took us north to the valley of the Rio Conejos. Close to home, we hunted rabbits, other small game, and deer. Some trips took us even farther north into the San Luis Valley, where we hunted elk and buffalo. In keeping with the communal nature of the pueblo, we shared the meat, and keeping ten families supplied with meat was not a trivial task.

One early morning, in the darkness of the first fall frost, Ignacio stood outside our jacal, his breath forming into a cloud of mist. He called out in a hoarse whisper.

"Oye, Felipe, are you still asleep?"

I ducked through the door, pulling on the heavy wool coat my mother had just finished.

"I am here and ready, Señor." I looked with astonishment at the three animals Ignacio was holding. "What is this? You have two new saddles and a new pack saddle as well. Where did these come from?"

Ignacio chuckled. "I traded furs and robes for them. You know I always save and tan pelts from the animals we kill. Those hides are worth something in Taos. These are nice saddles, no? Here, let me show you how to adjust the stirrups for your long legs."

I was already two inches taller than the squat hunter who was my maestro.

"Did you clean your rifle last night, and oil it well?" Ignacio asked.

"Si, Señor."

"Did you bring some flour and beans and your blankets?"

I held up a homespun cloth bag, then ducked back into the jacal to grab my bedroll.

"Bueno. Vamanos," said Ignacio.

"Where do we go that we need all these supplies?"

"We go north to the Rio San Luis and perhaps beyond. I want to get at least two buffalo, perhaps some nice fat cows. The meat will keep in the cold, and it should last the pueblo for some days. We may be gone for five or six days, maybe more. I told your father of these plans. Did he not tell you?"

"No, he said nothing, just what I should have ready. I suppose he meant for it to be a surprise. It will be fun, no?"

"Yes, it will be fun, but also it could be dangerous. We must keep a close eye out for savages. Do you understand?"

"Yes, of course."

"Just do what I tell you, when I tell you. No unnecessary conversation, you understand?"

"Si, Señor."

As we traveled, Ignacio occasionally pointed out edible plants, identified animal tracks, and quizzed me over the wilderness craft he had been teaching me. Often we were silent, content to be so.

We made camp the first night next to a mountain stream, just east of the Sangre de Cristo Pass. Without words, I helped Ignacio build a shelter of pine boughs to mitigate the icy mist and snow flurries. We affixed a rail made from a sapling between two trees, then laid thick layers of pine boughs over the rail, driving the cut stems into the ground. We built a large fire in front of the shelter and covered the ground inside with more pine boughs. We were far from warm during the night, but I managed to sleep while huddled in two blankets and wrapped in my buffalo robe.

The next afternoon, we found a small band of buffalo. We slowly circled, stalking, keeping the wind blowing into our faces. The musky smell of the quietly grazing animals filled my nostrils. I killed my first buffalo cow with one well-placed shot from a little over a hundred varas. Shooting at almost the same time, Ignacio killed another. We spent the rest of the afternoon removing the contents of the buffalos' abdomens and thoraxes, skinning them, and butchering them.

"The mule and horses cannot carry this much meat and hides," said Ignacio. "We will build travois for them to pull."

I went searching for two long, straight saplings, a hatchet in my hand.

That evening we ate our fill of buffalo tongue and hump.

The next morning, after we had been on our way for about an hour, Ignacio stopped his horse and held up his right hand, pointing to a grove of aspen to our right. He dismounted. I did the same and followed him into the trees, leading our horses and the mule with their loads of buffalo. He knelt behind a fallen log, holding his hand over the nose of his horse. I got to my knees beside him as he gestured for me to do the same.

"What is it? What did you see?" I whispered.

He put a finger to his mouth and then pointed down the valley. I followed his finger with my eyes but could see nothing.

He held up his hand to keep me silent, then held up four fingers.

I looked again where he had pointed and saw four mounted Indians riding in our direction. Breathing as silently as I could, I watched as they got closer and closer to us. They stopped. One of them pointed at the tracks of the travois, then to where we had moved into the aspens. Ignacio got to his feet and motioned for me to follow him.

"They are Ute," he said. "I will talk with them. You say nothing."

The four sat still on their horses as we approached. Ignacio spoke some guttural words to them, and one of them answered. Ignacio nodded, turned, and took two haunches of buffalo off the travois and carried them to the warrior, who again spoke to him in that same harsh language. The warrior Ignacio spoke with tied the two haunches together at the hoof, and they were slung over his pony's back. After a short conversation with the same man, Ignacio pointed north, and the four warriors rode off in that direction.

"They are also hunting buffalo. I told them where we found the herd. We were lucky they were Ute," said Ignacio.

We did not encounter any other bands of Indians but killed two deer, and were back in El Rito in three days. A fiesta of thanksgiving for the welcomed supply of buffalo and venison followed.

Vincente Romero was one of the original El Rito settlers. He married late, and his wife, a kind and caring but plain-looking girl, bore him a child almost every year of their marriage. There were six children when we moved to El Rito, but none after that. I overheard my mother telling Ignacio's wife that the last baby Señora Romero bore had torn her badly, and it was unlikely she was able to accommodate her husband. It was rumored that this made him brutish. It was no rumor that his wife and children frequently suffered his blows, and although he was a brute, he was devout. Every time he beat his wife or his children, he repented and flagellated himself without mercy in the presence of the Brotherhood. I witnessed him doing that.

My sister Maria was only thirteen. Everyone in the pueblo agreed she was beautiful. Her raven hair reached the small of her back. Her eyes sparkled, and her lips were fixed in a perpetual smile. When she walked, she seemed to glide over the ground, spreading happiness as she passed.

One morning, she was alone, hoeing weeds in the family corn plot, when Vincente passed by. He sneaked up behind her, wrestled her to the ground, and took her. He left Maria sobbing on the ground.

When I got home that evening, I found Mama seething and Maria rocking in a corner of the house with red, puffy eyes. Neither would tell me what was wrong.

That evening after dinner, Papa took my mother aside and whispered, but loud enough for me to hear, "What is the matter with your daughter? She didn't eat and cried all evening."

"I will not tell you with all the children here."

"Felipe, you take everyone outside. Maria, you stay."

Once we were outside the house, I heard Papa roaring. "What do you say? Vincente Romero? He is stupid and mean, but rape our Maria? She is only a child."

I moved closer to the house to listen and heard Mama saying, "She is thirteen but has been a woman for the last half-year. You are oblivious to most of what happens in this family. You are too busy with the problems of the pueblo."

"Nonsense! I am aware," he shouted. "Vincente Romero! I'm going to kill that cabron this moment!"

I imagined Mama putting a hand on Papa's arm. "No, my husband. Killing him would be too swift, too easy for him. Think a moment. Think as the leader of this pueblo. How can you make the punishment much worse for him?"

I could hear Papa stomping as he paced. "You are right. I must think of a worse punishment for that defiler of children. Something that hurts him without hurting his family. He punishes his wife and children enough already."

The next morning Papa called an emergency meeting of the Brotherhood. As the Hermano Mayor, Papa was the first to enter the Morado.

One by one, each member of the Brotherhood knocked on the door and said, "God knock at this Mission's doors of his clemency."

Those inside replied, "Penance, penance, he who seeks salvation."

The person seeking admittance answered, "St. Peter will open to me the gates, bathing me with the light in the name of Mary with the seal of Jesus. I ask this fraternity, who gives this house light?"

Those inside replied, "Jesus."

The person seeking admittance next asked, "Who fills it with joy?"

Those inside replied, "Mary."

The person seeking admittance asked, "Who preserves its faith?"

Those inside replied, "Joseph."

The person then entered the Morado, crossed himself in front of each of the three wood statues of St. Francis, St. Thomas, and the Virgin of Guadalupe, and said, "My Lord Jesus Christ, I am a sinner come to perform my devotion." He then turned to those already in the room and said, "Pardon me, my brothers, if in anything I have offended or been guilty of scandal."

Those already in the room replied, "May God pardon him who is already pardoned by us."

The person then fell to his knees and walked on his knees to everyone in the room asking for their blessing, kissing their hands and feet.

Soon everyone had entered, and I noticed that the back of Vincente's shirt was wet with blood.

Papa stretched out his right arm and pointed. "Romero, do you have something to confess to this Brotherhood?"

Vincente asked innocently, "What do you mean?"

Papa scowled. "I have learned that you have a mortal sin to confess. What have you done?"

Vincente pulled his shirt over his head and turned his back to each of the men inside the Morado. The act of removing his shirt tore away fresh scabs, and his back bled anew. "I repent and I have flagellated myself. I will continue to do so daily for the next week. There are no priests here, so I cannot confess my sin."

"Nonsense," Papa spoke slowly and quietly, and we all bent forward to hear him. "When we gather as a Brotherhood, we are all priests. Confess to what you have done!"

Romero fell to his knees and made the sign of the cross. He bent over, his forehead touching the dirt floor. "I took the daughter of the Hermano Mayor in his cornfield," he whispered.

"What?" Papa shouted. "Nobody can hear you. Confess aloud, cabron!"

Romero raised his voice. "Mary, mother of God, forgive me. I took the oldest daughter of the Hermano Mayor yesterday afternoon in his corn field." Then he whispered, "I am truly sorry and repentant."

The room filled with the sounds of questions and exclamations. I remained quiet but grimaced. Outside the Morado, some children were playing a game and the noise of their cheerful play made the revelation of Romero's perfidy even more of a shock. I grasped the handle of the knife in the sheath on my belt. Papa reached out and grabbed my arm, stopping me from pulling the knife.

"You confess then to raping my oldest daughter," Papa said. "You confess this sin in front of all of us?"

"Yes, Señor, I confess. I repent. I promise to flagellate myself daily for as long as the Brotherhood deems proper. I am truly sorry."

"It is not enough!" Papa looked at each of us in the room. "I think you should be banished from this pueblo. I don't care where you go or what you do with the rest of your miserable life, but you will not set foot in this pueblo ever again. When your oldest son comes of age, he will inherit the deed to your irrigated lands. Until then, the Brotherhood will help your wife. We will till your fields and make certain your poor, innocent wife and children do not suffer because of your misdeeds. Does anyone here disagree with this judgment?"

"We should castrate him like we do the male lambs," I said.

Several men in the room voiced their agreement, but Papa remained calm. "No. To do that, or to kill him, would make his suffering too short and cause his family to suffer for his crime. He should repent and think about his sin for the rest of his life. And I hope he lives a long time. I turn my back on him. If you agree, all of you should do the same."

Papa slowly turned his back to the kneeling, blubbering man, and each of the other men in the room did the same. I was the last to turn, shaking my head with frustration. We were letting him off too easily.

We listened as Vincente shuffled out of the Morado, shutting the door quietly behind him.

Papa turned again to all of us in the room. "This will be a secret of the Brotherhood. Your families and his wife and children need know nothing about what has happened. He will be gone, and your wives and children should only have pity for the family he will abandon. Agreed?"

He looked at each man, one at a time, and each nodded in agreement. Last, he locked eyes with me.

I stood still, silent, for a long time and finally gave my agreement. But I was still frustrated and angry. How would this action ease the suffering of my sister?

Nine months later, a boy was born to my sister. The men of El Rito knew the truth, but they ignored the mumblings and questions from their wives and older daughters. We took the baby to Abiquiu where he was christened Jose Vincentes Espinosa. Mama pretended to be the infant's mother. The priest acted as if he believed the charade but did not act at all surprised when the infant started to cry in hunger and milk leaked from Maria's nipples.

Papa raised Jose Vincente as his son. My sister, unwilling to separate from her son, refused all proposals and opportunities to leave the family. She was content to be the oldest sister and secret mother to the infant.

I tried to ignore the baby. I was unable to look at him without seeing the sin, but with time, and with the joy that all babies bring to a loving home, I started to take my turn to hold and cuddle the laughing, happy infant. Each week I saw more of my sister and less of his father in the child. It was impossible not to love this baby—he was so happy. I would come to think of him as a brother, not a nephew, and certainly not the offspring of Vincente Romero.

Shortly after Jose Vincente was born, Vivian was initiated into the Brotherhood. Then Padre Antonio Jose Martinez became a regular visitor to El Rito. At least once a month he arrived to say Mass in the Morado. The whole community gathered for these events. He was happy to learn that both Vivian and I had insatiable appetites for learning. He made it his mission to bring us books each time he visited and spend time after the evening meal in our jacal discussing the books he loaned us.

On one of those evenings, I spoke about the church's teaching about violence and wars. "Padre, I have been troubled for some time," I began. "The Bible tells us to kill is forbidden, but the Bible is full of descriptions of wars and killing and even instructions for how to win battles. I find this very confusing."

The padre's face became very serious. "This is not a new question, Felipe. Many generations have asked it. The answer is that the Bible forbids us to kill except in defense of the faith or to protect ourselves or our families. The church is constituted by the baptized who represent the Body of Christ. When the life of the church is threatened, the Body of Christ must fight and kill, if need be, to protect the church."

"So, if the church is threatened, we have the right to kill those who threaten it?" I asked. "How severe must the threat be?"

"Not only the right, but the duty," responded the padre. He untied the knot and opened the four corners of a square of homespun wool cloth that he had carried into the jacal. He dug through underclothing and brought out the next book he wanted us to read.

I still found myself conflicted. The padre had not answered my question. Were we really supposed to kill people who threatened or even condemned our religious beliefs?

Chapter 9
Tom Tobin

The next time Charley returned to St. Louis, I was fourteen. Because of the money he sent home over the years, our one-room house now had a plank wood floor and more furniture. My mother and Catherine each had their own beds along two of the walls. There was a cast-iron stove for heat and cooking and three chairs for the table. I slept in the loft on a cotton mattress.

The day after Charley arrived, he told us he had contacted several fur buyers and negotiated a good price for his cargo. His timing was good because it soon became clear there was an economic crisis looming. Rumors spread that the British, who were the major credit suppliers, were getting wary. Prices for the merchandise Turley had sent Charley to purchase were starting to fall.

Charley heard the rumors and waited another week to take advantage of lower prices.

I wasn't interested in the talk about selling and buying or what the economy was or wasn't going to do. "Tell us more about the mountains, Charley," I pleaded.

Again, he told us stories about his love of the mountains, exactly what I was hoping for.

"Well, first you got to get there. After you leave Independence, you get to grass far as you can see. Be like the ocean I reckon, least ways that's what them that seen the ocean say. Grass in the spring be all different colors of green and be moving in the wind like waves. It's flat as far as you can see and buffalo every which way you look. Then it gets hilly, and you be following the rivers so there are lots of places Injuns can hide. You have to keep a sharp eye out for them murdering savages or lose your scalp."

Charley stretched his legs and thought for a moment. Then he told us, "Eventually, you can see the mountains way off in the distance, blues and purples rising to the sky, white snow on their tops even in mid-summer."

"That's the Rockies," he said, "but you're still a long ways away. You have to travel weeks before you get there. Once in the mountains, there is white water rushing down over rocks. It falls fast, and spray comes off, and it's clear, clear as anything you've ever seen, and cold, so cold you put in a hand, and it be frozen in a minute or two. You can catch trout with a bug on a hook and get some fine eating. Sometimes you just climb up to the top of a peak and sit and look about. You won't see another man anywhere, but plenty of deer, elk, rabbits, bears, and eagles flying, and hawks too, and beaver. Used to be a lot more beaver than you can find now, but there's some beaver still. At first, you think there is nothing to hear but the wind, but if you sit still and listen, you hear birds and bugs and the elk calling and all the sounds of the wilderness, and you feel you are at home."

Charley stopped and sat, silent. I looked hard at him, trying to see what he was seeing. I desperately wanted to see it and experience it all myself. Charley told me he would take me with him when he returned to New Mexico, and Mama had agreed. He was certain Mr. Turley would find work for me.

After two weeks with us, it was time for Charley and me to say goodbye. All four of us were on the dock, the steamboat had steam up, and its whistle was blowing a warning. Charley lifted Catherine up to give her a hug. He put her down and hugged Mama, while Catherine held on to the back of her long skirt.

"Don't worry, Mama. I have my deal with Mr. Turley, and his word is good. We'll be back next year. You and Catherine will be taken care of," said Charley.

"I know, Charley, you're a good son. You take good care of us. I love you. You be good, Thomas Tate, and you do whatever Charley tells you. He knows how to make it in the wilds. You listen to him, hear?"

"Yes'm."

Charley was now twenty-four and mature beyond his years. At fourteen, I was bursting with the enthusiasm for freedom. I was on the verge of living all those adventures I had thus far only experienced through Charley's stories. I would see the mountains, I would be his partner in the whiskey business, and I would travel the frontier. Maybe I would be a mountain man.

We arrived in Independence, and I saw a brother I had never known. My big brother was all business, in charge, efficient, and commanding. Because of his hard-nosed trading, he was bringing back several thousand dollars in Mexican silver as well as all the goods Turley needed. The coins were carefully hidden in the new flat containers he had purchased for himself that would soon be used to transport whiskey. I soon learned how to pack what we were taking and how to load and unload the mules quickly and efficiently. I was determined for Charley to know that I would be a help to him and able to carry my own weight.

Two of the Mexicans Charley left in Independence had tired of the city life after spending all the money Charley left with them. They had joined a wagon train headed for Santa Fe.

The third morning in Independence Charley gathered the six horses he and his hired help had ridden from Taos. He saddled one and told me and the three Mexicans who had stayed to saddle the others. We mounted and left the camp leading the extra horse.

"Where we going?" I asked.

"I'm going to trade these riding horses for mules. Gonna use my own money to buy me a riding mule and one for you. You gonna need your own mule."

"Mules? Why you gonna trade horses for mules? This one I've been riding seems fine. Mules are too slow to run from Injuns, don't you think?"

"Mr. Turley told me I could trade for mules. I've been wanting one for myself for a spell. Lots of trappers ride mules. They're smarter than horses and can smell Injuns a long ways off. They're also stronger and keep going longer on less feed. Don't need to feed them grain. Some might kick you if you get them pissed, but they don't try to buck you off on a cold morning. They're calm and sensible, just a better mount all around, and the pack mules would rather follow a man on a mule than one on a horse."

I wasn't convinced. "But a mule can't outrun an Injun pony—you told me that."

"Usually that be true, but it's best not to get in that situation in the first place. If you get a head start on Injuns, the mule will keep going at a fast pace a lot longer, and you will outrun them."

After selecting, examining, and dickering all morning long, Charley traded Turley's six horses for six riding mules, straight up. The going rate for both horses of good quality and mules old enough to behave was fifty to seventy dollars, depending upon the age and fitness of the animal. After the trade, Charley started negotiations for two more high-quality riding mules. The one he chose for himself was a jack, a male, gray in color. It was big, fifteen and a half hands high at the withers. Charley carefully examined the mule's teeth and determined he was three years old. He instructed me to lead the mule directly away and then back to him, first at a walk, then at a trot. Next, he observed the mule from the side as he walked and trotted. Finally, Charley saddled the mule and rode him through all of his gaits, reining up in front of me. The mule cost him sixty dollars after some hard bargaining.

I picked out three mules I thought I liked. After putting each of them through the same careful examination and watching them move, Charley rejected two of them. "This one is good. Get up and ride about for a while, see if you like the way she feels."

The mule was a female, a jenny. She was significantly smaller than the gray, but I was barely over five feet tall and weighed not more than a hundred pounds. The jenny was the color Charley said was dun, a light tan, with a dark brown mane and tail and a brown stripe the length of her back. I was still not convinced the mule was a better choice than a fast horse, but Mama had told me to do what he told me, and it sure looked like he knew what he was doing. My mule cost him sixty-five dollars.

We rode side by side back to camp, leading the six new mules.

Charley reached out and grabbed my arm to get my attention. "Listen up, Tom, I've got something important to tell you. Once a man is out away from civilization, not many folks care about who your ma or pa be. But at the forts and pueblos, that's what the Mesicans call towns, some folks will not be fair with you. No need to say anything about Ma being a freed slave, understand?"

I had no problem understanding what he meant. "I understand. I won't say anything."

The next morning, Charley arranged for us to accompany a large group of traders headed for Santa Fe with wagons full of goods. The pack mules laid back their ears as they were loaded, braying their indignation. But with minimal stubbornness, they soon followed us on the trail, taking their place in the line of wagons and other mule trains.

The trip to Bent's Fort was uneventful. I quickly learned the basic skills necessary for comfortable living on the trail. Charley took me along when he hunted meat for our camp, and I brought down my first buffalo using Charley's flintlock rifle.

Charley rested the mules for two days at Bent's Fort, and we separated from the traders that were going to Santa Fe. We led the mules west along the Arkansas River, retracing Charley's route back to Arroyo Hondo. On the way, he pointed out the bald, treeless mountain on the western horizon. "That's called Pike's Peak." That same day, he pointed with his left arm out straight. "Do you see the two peaks off to the south? They're the Spanish Peaks. Injuns call them Wah-to-yah, meaning breasts of the world. We're heading there, but they are about seventy miles off."

Early on the second day out of Bent's, we arrived at the Huerfano River, near where an isolated hill, not quite a mountain but shaped like a pyramid, rose from the surrounding plains.

"The Mesicans call that Huerfano Butte. Huerfano means orphan," Charley explained. "The river's the same name. West of the hill is the Taos Trail. The river runs around the north side of the butte."

We followed the Huerfano River then up a small stream that Charley called Oak Creek. Next we followed Oak Creek toward the mountains and worked our way up and over Sangre de Cristo Pass. Charley continued to point out important landmarks. I concentrated hard, memorizing landmarks, surroundings, and the names given to them. Charley insisted I needed to observe and remember everything. Only then would I be able to find my own way. He said I needed to be able to close my eyes and draw a map in my head of where I'd been and how to get to any place I'd been before.

Once over the pass, we descended into a broad, almost flat valley. We passed several springs where bubbling clear, cold water ran into small streams that merged into creeks meandering lazily through the valley downhill. There were also small springs of bubbling hot water and mud. Scattered bands of buffalo and elk were grazing in the distance, keeping us in sight but moving away when we got within a quarter mile or so.

Charley turned in his saddle to face me. "This is the San Luis Valley. There's good hunting and some good farmland, I think."

I took it all in, doing my best to add each bit of information to the map I was building in my head. There was no need for me to answer.

When we arrived at Turley's store in Arroyo Hondo, still seven miles north of Taos, we found a crowd of people outside chanting and waving their fists.

Charley ignored them, and we went inside the store, where he introduced me to Simeon Turley.

"Simeon, this is my brother, Tom. He needs work."

Turley, a slight man the same height as me, looked at me long and hard, and said nothing. I couldn't imagine what he was thinking but told myself not to speak until he said something first. Finally, he asked, "How old are you, Tom?"

"I'm fourteen."

"What can you do?"

"Most anything you need, I reckon."

"You're small, Tom. Are you strong enough to lift heavy loads and move them around? If so, I can use you in the store."

"I reckon I can."

Charley chimed in. "He's plenty strong enough, Simeon. He's a good worker, and he can be a big help to me on my trips."

Simeon chuckled. "All right, if you work half as hard as your brother, I suppose you'll earn your keep. I'll pay you twenty-five dollars a month plus five a month to cover your food. We'll find out soon enough if you're worth it."

"What are those people outside mad about?" I asked.

"They're on strike, demonstrating against the governor," Mr. Turley answered. "Two years ago, the Spanish government from Mexico City sent a Spaniard, Colonel Albino Perez, to be the governor of New Mexico. For as long as anyone around here can remember, only men native to this country ruled the territory. The New Mexicans are not happy with the change. And even worse than having an outsider govern them, Perez has added new taxes to cover his expenses and his salary. The people understand the tariff system imposed on traders bringing in manufactured goods. They're comfortable paying taxes when they buy those goods, but the new tax is a general tax on all individuals. They don't like that. What you see is a tax revolt."

Turley continued his explanation. "What made it worse is that Perez initiated an arrest warrant for the mayor of Taos, who spoke out against the tax. He is charging him with embezzlement. Perez sent men from Santa Fe to arrest the mayor and cart him off to jail in Santa Cruz de La Canada. The mayor is a native of Taos and very popular here because he is considered fair, honest, and generous to the poor people he governs. A few days after his arrest, a mob attacked the jail in La Canada and freed him."

"They seem very angry about it," Charley said. "Why are they complaining outside your place?"

Turley shrugged his shoulders and ran a hand through his graying air. "I haven't any idea why, or what they expect me to do about it."

Charley and I settled in, sharing a small adobe house located near the store. I found working in the store was not very difficult or complicated, and many of the customers spoke at least some English, so I learned about everything that happened next from them. The story they told was that with the help and leadership of the former mayor, the strikers wrote out a detailed plan with their idea of how to organize the government of New Mexico. Part of the plan said no new taxes would be allowed.

Perez called out the militia and marched a hundred and fifty armed men from Santa Fe to La Canada. Outside La Canada, a mob of about five hundred angry and defiant men confronted Perez. All but twenty-five of Perez's men quickly changed their allegiance. Perez galloped back to Santa Fe, leaving his twenty-five loyal stalwarts to follow on foot as best and as fast as they could manage. Then he slipped out of Santa Fe, heading for Albuquerque. But the mob, led by the former mayor, was ready for him. They stationed men on the road to Albuquerque and captured Perez and those with him.

A friend of Charley's was hiding on the roof of a house not more than a hundred yards from the one in which Perez and his companions had been jailed. A few days later, he told us that by mid-morning, the mob had grown large enough to fill the plaza. The crowd was angry, shouting, egging each other on. They dragged Perez out of the house by his hair, killed him, cut off his head, and played a game of football with it. Then, Charley's friend told us the Secretary of State, Jesus Maria Alarid, who was known as El Chico, was hustled out of the house, along with two other men. All three were hacked to pieces with machetes. Finally, the crowd murdered Don Santiago Abreu, the governor prior to Perez's arrival. Charley's friend said he did not have any idea why Abreu was on their list, but three men covered head to foot with blood from their previous victims attacked him. One gouged out his eyes, the second cut off his hands, and the third grabbed the tongue from his screaming mouth and cut it off. Mercifully, a shot rang out, putting a ball into his forehead, and stopping his tortured screaming.

A few days later, a customer at the store told me there were nearly two thousand rebels in Santa Fe. They elected and installed Jose Gonzales of Taos as governor. The customer said Jose was supposed to be a good buffalo hunter but was well below average in smarts.

A wealthy man with political ambitions lived in Albuquerque. His name, Don Manuel Armijo. His response to the insurrection was to organize a large number of men with previous military experience into an effective army and take them to Santa Fe. It took him a month to get ready. During this time, the mob got tired and had mostly gone back to their lives. The once furious men had families to care for and neglected work to do at home. Since the rebel government was not collecting any taxes, it had no funds to pay them. The upstart Jose Gonzales and his few remaining followers abandoned Santa Fe and fled to La Canada as soon as Armijo and his army entered and occupied Santa Fe. To celebrate his bloodless victory, Armijo immediately dispatched a messenger to Mexico City to describe the revolt, the murderous atrocities committed by the insurgents, and how he had crushed this rebellion. He also informed the central government that as a matter of expediency, he, with their indulgence, would assume the governorship.

Since reclaiming their territory cost them nothing, the central government responded with gratitude, confirming Armijo as governor with all attendant honors and titles. They also sent Armijo four hundred well-trained troops led by a Colonel Justinani to make certain the will of the central government was not again threatened. On 11 January 1838, Governor Armijo and Colonel Justiniani marched to La Canada, routed the few remaining insurgents who had answered the call to defend their revolution, and captured the buffalo hunter. Armijo immediately put Gonzales in front of a firing squad.

Charley and I kept our heads down and didn't take part in any of the political talk. We did our work and collected our pay. Everyone assumed I was Charley's full brother, and I went by the name Tom Autobees. There was no need to confuse anyone.

During the winter of 1837 and 1838, Charley returned to his whiskey-selling enterprise, taking me along as his partner. We added a supply of wheat and corn flour to our loads of Taos Lightning. For the next four years, we made fall and early winter sales trips, expanding our territory and the size of our mule trains as new trading posts opened along the eastern slope of the Rockies. Each spring we took Turley's accumulated pelts east, although the number and price for them continued to fall. Charley continued to teach me what I needed to know as a mountain man. We even stopped to trap a few streams where the beaver had made a comeback.

My brother had many mountain man friends and was a welcome sight in the wilderness since he kept a few jugs of the private stock he had aged for two years in a charred oak barrel. He doled out this booze to his friends around the campfire. All who tasted it agreed it was 'fine stuff', and its fame spread throughout the mountains. It wasn't long until all the trappers kept a sharp eye out for us every winter.

During our 1840 spring sales trip, I was seventeen years old and had my first encounter with hostiles. We were packing with ten of Charley's mules. Each carried twenty-five gallons of liquor and fifty pounds of flour on the trip out, and two-hundred-fifty-pound packs of pelts on the return. Charley was on his mule, Ol' Gray, and I was riding Jen. Each of us led five loaded pack mules. We were two days out of Fort Lupton heading north when we stopped early to camp in a well-protected canyon. We staked out the mules to graze a batch of grass blown free of snow, where green sprouts pushed up from the spring sun.

Before the sunset, Charley's old mentor Jim Beckwourth helloed the camp and rode in. He gave Charley a hug and me a nod, not knowing who I was. He was much taller than Charley, and I could see he was mighty strong. He was dark, his face wrinkled from being in all kinds of weather for so long. He explained that he was on his way to Fort Lupton to sell his pelts from the spring hunt. He told us he and his Crow wife had been living with a band of Crows, and the band had recently elected him one of their chiefs. They bestowed this honor on him because he was able to find and trade for liquor, while the traders the Crows routinely traded with, the American Fur Company, didn't have much to share.

That same afternoon, I shot a young buffalo cow from over two hundred yards with my recently purchased flintlock. The three of us feasted on buffalo steak and boudins, a mountain man delicacy and the closest thing to a green vegetable in the trappers' diet. Following Charley's instructions, I cut foot-long sections from the first part of the intestine where it connected to the last of the animal's four stomachs. Then I roasted them over the fire until the outside was brown and crisp and the grass inside was sizzling.

"Well, Charley, these be about the best boudins I been eating for a time. How have you been doing? Who's this pilgrim with you?" Until that very minute, Beckwourth had not said anything about me being with Charley. He did seem to even know I was there.

"He's my brother, Tom. We're good. How did you find us?"

"I've been looking for you. Heard tell you're peddling Taos Lightning. Got any samples?"

Charley took out one of his special jugs from the ten packs lying on the ground in a protective circle around our camp and handed it to Jim.

"This is my special jug, just for a taste for my friends. I have to make it last the whole trip. I've plenty of the regular for sale. It's the same strength, but no taste, at least them that say they know their liquor tell me."

Jim took a big swig and smacked his lips in appreciation. "Yes, sir, that's about as good as it can be, at least out here in the wilderness." He held out the jug to Charley, who took it and replaced the cork.

"You still don't partake?"

"Nope. You want some of the regular?"

"I could take a mouthful or two. What about you, Tom? You have a taste for it?"

I shook my head.

"That boy able to talk, Charley?"

"Oh yeah, he talks if he has something to say. He listens real good and learns fast."

"That be so, boy?"

"Yes, sir," I said, still overwhelmed by meeting the man Charley had talked about so much.

"Can the boy hit anything with his rifle?"

"He shot the dinner from about two hundred yards."

"Well, that's good because I've been followed for two or three days. Blackfeet trying to work up their courage. They'll be watching us close about now. Your mules eat their fill yet?"

"Probably. Should I bring them in?"

"Good idea."

Charley nodded to me. Taking our rifles, we went to where we had staked out the mules to graze, beyond the light of the fire. I looked about nervously until Charley grabbed my arm and shook his head. We kicked the stakes loose and brought all twelve mules inside the barricade of packs, tying them along with Beckwourth's horses to the same strong rope I strung between two saplings. Jen, aware that something unusual was happening, raised her nose to the stars and sniffed, then sniffed again. After a third sniff, she brayed, and the other mules added their voices.

"She's got a whiff of them," murmured Jim. "Those mules gonna keep that up? They do make a tolerable noise. I don't reckon them Injuns will try anything until after we're bedded down and snoring."

I went over to one of the packs and scooped five handfuls of dried corn into a small bag. I went first to Jen, then to Ol' Gray, and fed each mule a small measure of the corn from my hand. After the last of the mules and Jim's horse and packhorse had received their treat, all the animals calmed down and started dozing, heads lowered.

"Will they come in the way you came, Jim?" Charley asked.

"Probably circle round. Best we spread out our bedrolls up close to a pack and cover every direction."

I couldn't keep my heart from beating faster and faster. I felt as though I was going to pee my pants at any moment. I watched Charley carefully and tried to do everything he did to prepare, but I wondered, for what? I had no idea what to expect or how the three of us would fight off an unknown number of Blackfeet. Charley said they were the most dangerous of all the hostile Injuns. We all checked the loads in our rifles and made certain the firing pans were charged with powder. Then we laid down on our blankets, resting our heads on our saddles. We pulled our buffalo robes over us but kept our loaded and primed rifles next to us on the side of the robe that opened. I was especially careful not to spill out any of the prime. We were soon snoring, not in unison, faking sleep.

A half hour after we started faking sleep, all the mules suddenly jerked their heads up, ears twitching, eyes searching the darkness. Each of us slowly cocked our rifles. With ear-shattering shrieks, four Indians jumped over the barricaded packs, arrows notched, bows pulled back to their ears, searching to find targets. All three of us rolled out of our bedrolls onto one knee and fired, each putting a fifty-four-caliber hole in the chest of a different Indian. The fourth Indian let his arrow fly, striking Charley in the left arm. He was notching another arrow when Beckwourth swung his rifle, clubbing him to the ground. Beckwourth immediately straddled his back, pulled his head up by the hair, and slit his throat down to the bone, almost decapitating him.

The mules were braying, the two horses rearing and neighing with fear, and all were pulling at their halter ropes. The rope they were all tied to broke, and they went thundering out of the camp.

"Hope those critters calm down and stop before they get too far," Jim murmured. "Let's make certain the three we shot are dead, then we'll have a look at your arm, Charley."

The arrow had pierced Charley's upper arm but missed the bone. Beckwourth pushed it through while Charley gritted his teeth. He snapped off the arrowhead, then pulled the shaft out backward. The wound bled dark blood. Beckwourth ripped off a strip of cloth from Charley's shirttail with the same knife he'd used to cut the throat of the fourth Blackfoot, but he wiped off the warrior's blood on his pant leg first.

The large caliber slugs from our rifles fired at close range, left large holes in the front of the chests of the three dead Indians, and huge holes where they exited.

I leaned over one of the packs, retching. "What's that stink?" I croaked. I couldn't stop my hands from shaking or get the buffalo meat I ate from leaving my churning stomach. Then I noticed my pants were wet.

"That's blood and shit and pee, with the stink of a dead Injun," Jim answered. "You live long enough out here you get used to it. You did good, boy, it's all right to heave up your dinner. Let's see if we can find the ponies of the savages, my ponies, and your mules."

As the sun came up over the edge of the hills, it revealed the four scalped corpses Jim had dragged about a hundred yards away. We had managed to round up all of the animals in the dark, including the four ponies of the Injuns. I built up our campfire until it provided some warmth. Charley brewed a pot of coffee and roasted strips of buffalo meat skewered onto green willow branches.

After eating his fill, Beckwourth, sitting on his bedroll, leaned back on his saddle. "You up for a little trading, Charley?"

"Reckon. How's your furs grade out?"

"'Bout average for spring plew, some prime, mostly ones and twos."

Charley nodded his understanding. "Well, I'm selling Taos Lightning four dollars a gallon. How many pounds of plew do you figure you got?"

"Don't know for certain, probably fifty or sixty pounds, give or take."

Charley hefted one of Jim's packs and thumbed through about a third of the pelts while he calculated. "That looks to be about right. I'll give you thirty-five gallons of whiskey for all of it."

Beckwourth stroked his beard several times. "That the best you can do?"

Charley rubbed his forehead. "Lupton won't give you more than a hundred dollars for those packs. We both know that's true. I'm selling whiskey for four dollars a gallon. Lupton or Vazquez will charge you eight or more a gallon, and it'll be cut with plenty of water, especially if they get you drunk first. Your pack will only be worth fifteen or sixteen gallons of cut whiskey from them. You take my deal, you'll be a popular Injun when you get back to the tribe with thirty-five gallons of uncut, even more, if you cut it."

"I'm already the most popular black Injun this part of the world." Beckwourth spat in his hand and offered it to Charley. Charley spat in his hand, and they shook, the deal done.

Beckwourth departed, pleased with himself and his deal. I watched, trying to imagine if I would ever be able to match the business skills of my brother. I hoped so. Charley and I loaded the mules and continued to our next stop.

That evening, I borrowed Charley's file and proudly put a notch in the barrel of my rifle.

Chapter 10
Tom

After Charley and I returned to Turley's from our 1840 trip to St. Louis, he met Serafina Avila, a widow three years older than him. She and her three small children lived in the village of Santa Dolores only a short distance from the Turley establishments. Serafina was desperate for a man to provide for her and her children. After they started living together, I had the house we shared to myself, and although I missed his company, I felt like I was finally a grown-up. Ten months after Charley moved in with Serafina, she gave birth to a boy they named Mariano.

Before we left for our trip to St. Louis in 1842, Charley and I both became naturalized Mexican citizens. This made our coming and going easier, especially when dealing with the Mexican authorities. On our return from the 1842 trip, Charley converted and joined the Catholic Church and Padre Antonio Jose Martinez married him and Serafina on November 28, 1842. The good padre registered Charley's name in the church archives as Carlos Ortibi, his understanding of Charley's pronunciation of Autobees.

Serafina was a good friend of Señora Maria Candelaria de Herrera, the wife of Felipe Bernal. Bernal and his family lived in Santa Dolores with their fourteen-year-old daughter, Maria Pascuala Bernal, and their other children. Serafina introduced Maria to me after my return from St. Louis in the late summer of 1843. Always shy and uncomfortable speaking to strangers, I was struck speechless by the tiny, beautiful girl who stood in front of me. I had reached my full height of five feet four inches and was almost a head taller than her. Her black hair hung below her waist, and her dark brown eyes were shielded by long black lashes. This added to her allure, as did her pink lips parted in a smile that showed white teeth. She was pleasingly plump. High breasts showed as soft mounds above her low-cut blouse. I could only imagine how soft she would be in my arms.

I was so taken with her I wondered how I could possibly make this vision my wife.

Her voice was soft, and the Spanish she spoke was musical. "You have nothing to say to me, Señor?"

My command of Spanish was still rudimentary. "Si, Señorita. I, uh, uh…" I couldn't find any more words.

She lowered her eyes and giggled, then hooked her left arm inside my right elbow. "Come. We take a stroll, no?"

We walked slowly past the church on the northern side of the Plaza de Dolores three times, followed discreetly by Maria's eldest married cousin. Maria chattered, filling my awkward silence.

The following Sunday afternoon, I knocked on the door of the Bernal household. Señora Bernal answered the door.

My carefully rehearsed Spanish was still halting. "Uh, may I…visit with Señorita Maria Pascuala, please?"

That afternoon, Maria started teaching me Spanish. As we walked around and around the square, her cousin still following, she pointed at things and gave their name. I repeated them, and she would say a short sentence using that word, and I repeated. She corrected the way I said it until I got it right. In this way, I learned verbs and tenses, but it took some time before I could actually tell her how I felt about her.

On one of our Sunday afternoon walks, Maria said, "My mother told me you will be a good husband for me."

"I'm sorry, I don't understand."

She pointed to the ring finger of her left hand, made a circle around it, then said, "Mama," and pointed at herself, then at me.

"Your mother said we should get married?" I was in shock.

"Si," she said, "no ahora, mas temprano."

Since Maria's mother was a close friend of Charley's wife, she knew my brother was a man of substance and a good provider, who also took care of his mother in far-off St. Louis. Serafina learned I also contributed money to our mother on a regular basis.

Until Charley and I left on our annual whiskey-selling trip in the late spring of 1842, I visited the Bernal family as often as I could. As my command of

Spanish improved, because of the patient tutoring of Charley, I began to tell stories of my adventures on the trails when Charley and I traveled in the wilderness. With time, I felt myself an accepted member of the Bernal family and my impossible dream of making Maria my wife seemed possible.

We were sitting in the Bernal's' garden the evening before Charley, and I left.

"Es possible nuestros casados?" I asked, hoping I had proposed correctly.

Her face lit up with her smile, and she gave me a hug.

"Seguro, mi Corazon, I will be your wife, but you must ask my father."

I did so that same evening, and we were engaged.

While Charley and I were out selling Taos Lightning in 1843, Turley invested in several wagons for us to use to transport pelts and buffalo robes to Missouri and bring the goods he needed west in the summer of 1844. The wagons carried much more than pack mules could, and they didn't require unloading and reloading. We trained several of Turley's mules to serve dual purpose, pulling wagons as well as packing.

During that trip east, I added a second notch to my flintlock rifle. Charley and I, with four employees, joined a group of Santa Fe traders at Bent's Fort headed toward Independence. The group, as always, elected a captain, but the man was unwilling or unable to keep discipline. During the day, the train spread out with as much as a mile between separate groups of wagons. We did congregate in the evenings to form a circle of wagons for protection.

Charley and I were careful to keep all six of our wagons close together; Charley leading the way and me bringing up the rear, so we were a tight group within the spread-out convoy. We were traveling east, with the Arkansas River flowing no more than five hundred yards to our right, when a large band of well-mounted warriors charged from their hiding place toward us, screaming. Charley led us into a defensive circle. We were well trained and frequently rehearsed, and soon formed a tight circle of wagons with the mules milling and braying, some still in their traces, inside the circle.

The Comanches—Charley identified them by their arrows—split off and rode in a large circle around our makeshift fort, about a hundred yards away from us. They filled the air with earsplitting noise meant to scare us. Occasionally, they fired their muskets, but I knew it was difficult for them to reload while riding a galloping pony bareback. Most of their arrows, shot from short bows, missed us.

Charley made certain all of us were ready, shouting over the screaming Comanches and braying mules. "Aim carefully, but fire one at a time," he instructed. "That'll give the rest time to get ready to fire while the others reload. Understand?" He had drilled us for this, and we were prepared.

"I'll take the first shot, then Bill, Jacob, Samson, Will, and Tom last. Aim carefully and look for the ones that seem to be directing them. If they are riding on the offside of their pony, go for a heart shot of the pony. They've got to be close to hitting us with their muskets or arrows. We need to keep them far off."

He took a shot, knocking an Indian off his pony. The pony immediately broke rank and wandered back toward the river. Each of us took our turn, in order, and two of the circling ponies fell. Their heads hit the ground first, then they collapsed on their side, and both trapped their riders beneath them. I rested my rifle on the edge of the foot box of my wagon and set the front hair-trigger by pulling the rear trigger back partway. I then switched my finger to the front trigger and took careful aim at the head of a Comanche who had turned away to ride out of range. Using the hair-trigger kept the rifle on target. The Injun I was aiming at was over two hundred yards away, obviously feeling safe, when his head exploded.

Charley set his hair-trigger to fire again, but the Comanches suddenly retreated to the safety of the riverbank, out of range of our deadly rifles. They were no match for an enemy that was well-prepared and disciplined.

"Hold up," Charley ordered. "They've given up for the time being. Let's get the mules unhitched and calm them down a bit. Good shooting, boys. Tom, you kerplunked that Injun's head right off." I nodded, proud that my brother had noticed.

We unhitched the mules and pushed the wagons into a tighter circle. Charley sat on the ground, his back resting on the front wheel of his wagon, and lit his pipe. I squatted in front of him. "You reckon they'll give up, Charley?"

"Can't know for certain, Tom. Best wait a bit. I reckon the rest of the caravan will be coming to see what all the shooting was about."

Twenty minutes later, the wagons behind us—and those that had pushed ahead—came rushing up, too late to be of help. Charley and I took a small group of men to reconnoiter and found that the Comanches had departed with their dead and wounded comrades. The two who had been trapped under their horses also escaped. That evening, I sat crossed-legged in front of our campfire and filed a second notch in the side of my rifle barrel.

For the rest of the journey, all the wagons stayed within shouting distance of each other. The remainder of the trip was uneventful, except for the common problems of thunderstorms, heat, dust, and mud. One day, the whole caravan stopped to watch as a tornado spun erratically off to the north of the trail. I was thankful it stayed away from us. There were also the usual problems involved in driving teams of mules that were not always inclined to work together.

In 1844, when Charley and I arrived in St. Louis, we called at the gun shop of Jacob and Samuel Hawken. During the past year, many of the mountain men we ran into or who found us on our Taos Lightening sales trip showed us their new percussion cap rifles, developed by the Hawken brothers. They were fast replacing the flintlock. The flintlock required the shooter to fill its small pan with gunpowder. When the shooter pulled the trigger, the hammer struck a flint, creating a spark that lit the powder in the pan and resulted in an explosion that then ignited the powder in the barrel, ejecting the bullet. The powder in the pan had to be dry and the rifle held level so the powder did not spill out. During a fight, especially if it was raining, these requirements were a problem. The flintlock also needed frequent flint replacement.

The new system used a copper cap that held a special priming mixture. A thin coat of shellac protected the priming mixture and made the cap waterproof. A hole was drilled and threaded into the breach of the barrel. A nipple screwed into the hole punctured the cap, setting it off when the hammer hit. It was still necessary to charge the barrel with powder and ramrod the ball, usually wrapped in a patch of cloth or thin animal skin, into place. But the new rifle needed only to have a new cap inserted, and once powder and ball were loaded, it was ready to fire. It was faster to reload and fire, and there was no longer the delay between setting off the powder and firing the rifle which made it a lot easier to hold the rifle steady on the target.

It wasn't a perfect system. Keeping the percussion caps ready to load into the rifle was difficult with fingers stiff from cold weather. The major disadvantage of the percussion cap was that when they were all gone, the rifle was useless, while flints for our flintlock rifles could easily be found.

Charley and I bought identical new Hawken rifles. They had the same double set triggers as our flintlocks, and both were fifty-five inches in length, with a thirty-eight-and three-quarter-inch octagon-shaped barrel. Our old forty-two-inch-long Hawken flintlocks had a barrel length of only twenty-six inches. The new rifles added twelve inches of rifling that provided accuracy to three hundred yards—in the hands of an expert, even farther. The new rifle took a fifty-four-caliber ball, the same as our flintlocks. We bought two fifty-four caliber flintlock pistols so we could use the same sized ball for all of our weapons, as well as a large supply of caps, linen patching, nipple picks, nipple wrenches, new wire picks, and the stiff-bristle brushes needed to clean the touchholes. There was no need for new bullet molds or powder horns. Ramrods came attached to each new rifle. We kept our flintlocks as backup weapons.

That evening, I filed two notches into the barrel of my new rifle and scratched a crude 'T' into the metal butt plate where it extended under the stock.

After Charley and I purchased our new Hawkens, I scoured the shops of St. Louis for gifts for my novia and her family. I bought a hand mirror in an ornate ivory frame, several yards of lace, both black and white, and a necklace made of silver with shiny purple stones. My last purchase was a gold wedding band.

Before leaving for St. Louis, I had been instructed by Padre Martinez, the same padre who married Charley and Serafina. I had converted to the Catholic religion. As a wedding present, Maria's mother gave us a small adobe house that stood on a large lot on the east side of the Plaza de Dolores across from the church.

On our wedding night, Maria, now shy, stood with me in the flickering light emanating from the adobe chimenea in the corner of our bedroom. I slipped her skirt down, and she stepped out of it. I tried to gently pull her blouse over her head, but it got caught in her long hair.

"You are clumsy, my love. Here, let me help you." She stood barefoot in front of me in her underclothes, more beautiful than I'd ever seen her. She slowly removed her underclothing as I ripped off my clothes. Naked, we embraced and kissed, only the second time we had done so, the first being at the end of the wedding ceremony. Still entwined, I walked us to the bed and fell on it, twisting to land first so as not to crush her. She was softer than I imagined in the dreams that had tormented me for months. We explored and enjoyed each other until the light of dawn slowly crept into the room.

I was completely happy. I looked forward to each day, comfortable with my work and thrilled by Maria and our life together. She was the love of my life and the reason I was so content.

The summer of 1845 found Charley and I again on the trail to Missouri. We visited our mother and sister, leaving them well taken care of for the coming year. The day after we left for the return to Taos, it started raining and continued nonstop. The trail was slippery with slimy mud, but whenever we tried to leave the beaten path, our heavily loaded wagons sank until the axles were covered. Then we had to unhitch a team and use two teams to drag the stuck wagon out, with all the men pushing. We often encountered bogs on the trail that required exceptional effort to pass through. Our route back to New Mexico took us through Council Grove. It normally took ten to twelve days to get there, but that year, it took thirty. Mules and men were exhausted and covered with caked mud when we finally arrived. We found several other traders waiting to make up a train. The rain finally stopped, and during the following week, enough men, wagons, mules, and draft horses arrived to get underway. The traders elected Charley as captain of the train, and we were off, in good weather at last.

After the trail crossed the Arkansas River, four hundred miles from Independence, it forked into two branches. The mountain branch followed the Arkansas River to Bent's Fort. The other trail was the longer Cimarron branch, but it avoided the difficulties of Raton Pass. After crossing the Arkansas River, we camped to dry off. That evening, one of the traders, James Webb, approached our campfire.

"Evening, Charley. Tom. Can I join you for a chat?"

"Help yourself," I answered. "Want some coffee?"

"Yes, thank you."

I rapped a tin cup upside down on a rock, poured a cup of steaming boiled coffee, including some grounds, into the cup, and handed it to Webb.

"I've been thinking of riding ahead to Santa Fe so I can arrange with the Mexican authorities to pay the customs duties in advance. By doing that, I can get my goods released sooner and maybe make a few extra dollars. Do you boys think that's possible?"

"Sure, if you know the way and are brave enough to go it alone," Charley observed.

"Well, that's why I'm talking to you. Would one of you be willing to guide me and a couple of my men who are handy with their rifles as far as Arroyo Hondo?"

Charley laughed. "Well, hoss, you've come to the right place. My brother is anxious to get back to his new bride. Ain't you, Thomas?"

I looked up from the oily surface of the cup of coffee I was contemplating. "What are you offering?" I asked.

"I'll pay fifty dollars in Mexican silver."

Charley looked at me and smiled. I shrugged. "Make it seventy and I'll do it."

"How about sixty?"

"All right, sixty then."

I spat on my right palm and extended it. Webb did the same.

As Webb walked away, Charley chuckled. "Well, Tom, I reckon you learned a bit since we've been together. Fifty was good, sixty better."

The next day, Charley started on the northeast trail to Bent's Fort heading for Taos with his wagons, those of James Webb, and another trader, Alexander Barclay. All the other traders followed the Santa Fe Trail to get to that city directly. I led Webb and his two men ahead of Charley and his wagons. The four of us pushed hard, covering forty to fifty miles a day, and soon arrived at Bent's Fort, where we learned the Ute Indians had been feuding about something with the governor of New Mexico. The men who gave us this news didn't know what the fight was about, but the Utes had declared war against both the Mexicans and the Americans.

After leaving Bent's Fort, I took my charges forward with more caution. Jen and I were only a dozen or so yards ahead. We rode over the Sangre de Cristo Pass without incident and were only a half-day out from the new pueblo of Rio Colorado when we passed through a grove of pinions onto an open plain. I was leading them toward a line of cottonwoods on the banks of the Rio Culebra about a half mile away. I spotted some movement in a line of trees ahead. I stood in my stirrups and raised my left arm, signaling for everyone to halt. I stared hard at the tree line, then turned Jen and hurried back to Webb and the others.

"People are hiding in that line of trees ahead," I said. "Get your guns ready and follow me back to those pinons we just came through. Now!" I spurred Jen into a lope.

A volley of shots rang out behind us. I had my Hawken in my right hand and used my left to pull my old flintlock from its scabbard slung on the left side of my saddle. In the grove, we dismounted and found shelter behind some fallen logs.

"Don't shoot at anything unless you can clearly see who it is," I said.

We watched the movement of several people in the cottonwoods. Finally, a group of men emerged, yelling, shouting, and shooting muskets and rifles into the air.

I looked carefully and started laughing. "They're Mexicans. They're having a good laugh at us running like we did."

Much relieved, we led our animals out and met the group of twelve men coming toward us. I greeted my brother-in-law Jesus Bernal with an abrazo. Speaking Spanish, Jesus introduced me to the men with him.

He put his arm around one man's shoulders. "This is my cousin Felipe Espinosa. He is a very good tracker and hunter. Some Utes stole sheep and cattle from Rio Colorado while Felipe was visiting, so we asked him to help us track them. We have been following through the night, but they had too long a start."

"So," I said, "if he is your cousin, does that make him my cousin as well?"

"I think it is probably more complicated than that, Señor Tomas," Felipe said, "but I think everyone who has lived in this part of the world is related in some way. I am very pleased to meet you."

"And I, you," I said, and we shook hands.

I translated the conversation for Webb, then turned to Jesus and continued in Spanish. "I have to take these men to Arroyo Hondo, or I would come with you to find the thieves."

"I understand, but we are ready to turn back," answered Jesus. We again embraced, and they all watched as my charges and I rode on.

After we arrived at Arroyo Hondo, I sent Webb on the trail to Taos. "It's only seven miles, and the road to Santa Fe is safe and easy after that," I told him.

Webb paid me the silver, and I told Simeon Turley that Charley was only about a week or so behind and had all the goods he had ordered. Then I made haste to rejoin my bride.

I was satisfied with my life. Charley and I were accepted and welcomed as full members of the Santa Dolores community. I worked a normal ten-hour day, then rode Jen home to good meals and quiet evenings while Maria Pascuala chattered nonstop about her day. Occasionally, she would coax stories of my travels out of me. We participated in local celebrations, even dances, where I was known to be enthusiastic but clumsy. On Sundays, we attended Mass in the church a few steps away from our little house. Life was good.

Chapter 11
Felipe

Seven years passed, and our pueblo flourished. Children grew up, and my nephew, Jose, became more like a brother with each passing week. I still went hunting with Ignacio, but now Vivian went with us. Then our lives took a turn for the worst. It was 1846 when Colonel Sterling Price and his Missouri Volunteers, the advance party for General Kearney, took Santa Fe without a fight. New Mexico appeared quiet, but many of us, especially me, were seething. The barbaric American invaders were loud, uncouth, rowdy, and drunk when not on duty, sometimes when they were. The soldiers seemed incapable of putting more than three words together without blaspheming. They considered those of us who had lived here for generations to be stupid and inferior—even though a majority of the gringos were illiterate and a high percentage of us could read and write. Most egregious, the invaders were clearly prejudiced against the Holy Catholic Church. They made fun of the wooden statues of saints that we adored. Although most of us were poor, we were proud of being courteous, of speaking politely, especially to strangers, and of having a deep and abiding love for family, God, and the Catholic Church. Feelings of disgust and hatred toward the barbaric Americans festered and grew.

On the day Padre Martinez came to visit the Brotherhood, it was mid-winter, a time of stark brilliance, clear air, and crisp cold. The silhouettes of barren rock appeared to be surreal edifices poking into a watery blue sky. Foothills and mountainsides below the tree line contained irregular patches of dark evergreens and somnambulant brush. The rocky peaks were dusted with dry, crystalline snow and dominated the horizon. The cold permeated anything motionless. Padre Martinez told us that after General Kearny arrived, he appointed a group of civilians to govern the new United States Territory.

Kearny chose Charles Bent as governor. Bent was a successful trader, one of the brothers involved in the operations at Bent's Fort. He was a citizen of Taos, and his wife was from a respected New Mexican family. Donaciano Vigil was appointed Secretary of the Territory; Richard Dallam, the Marshal; and Charles Blummer, the Treasurer. Joab Houghton, Antonio Jose Otero, and Charles Beaubien were appointed Superior Court Judges. Kearny filled lesser offices with citizens of the United States and some trusted Mexican supporters. The padre told us the first items of business for these men were the institution and enforcement of American laws. He said the gringos assured the new citizens of New Mexico that their government would honor and protect the titles to our property, provided we supplied the necessary documentation. However, they were already claiming huge tracts of land not settled or already deeded by land grants for future development.

The occupiers went loudly about their business, and their obnoxious behavior continued to stimulate discontent. More and more of us, even the pueblo-dwelling native populations, were disturbed and angry.

Only three weeks after that visit, Padre Martinez arrived in El Rito late on a Wednesday afternoon, an unusual time for him to visit us. However, we welcomed him, and he ate dinner with our family. He asked Papa to call a meeting of the Brotherhood. After eating, we all went to the Morado. Papa entered first, then the padre, then me and the rest of the men of the pueblo, each of us following the proscribed procedure for entering.

Soon the little building was crowded with the ten original brothers plus all the initiated sons, including myself and Jose Vivian. We stood leaning against the wall or sat cross-legged on the dirt floor, waiting to find out why the padre from Santa Dolores was in our pueblo on a weekday.

Padre Martinez offered a prayer, blessed the assembled men, and then removed the ceremonial robes he had put on just before entering the Morado. He spoke softly; those farthest away strained to hear his words. "Brothers and men of El Rito, I come to you with a heart heavy with sadness and burdened with anger. As you know, the gringos have invaded our beloved land. It is not enough that they insult all of us as men. They also insult the church and our saints. They are drunks, foul-mouthed, and rude beyond belief. They say they will honor our property and our laws, but they rush to institute their own laws. They will soon start taxing us, even the mother church, and when we cannot pay those taxes, they will take our property. They took Santa Fe without our brave soldiers being allowed to fire a shot at them because of the treachery and greed of our former Governor Armijo, the same man who crushed the rebellion led by our brave comrades a few short years ago."

He went on to describe how the leaders of that short-lived revolution, all men known to us, were already out recruiting fighters. Then he said, "I am here to enlist your support. We, with your help and God's, are going to rid this land of the invaders. When I send word, I ask that you join us in Taos, and we will expel these noxious gringos from our lands. You must bring any weapons and all the ammunition you possess and be ready to obey our leaders and fight for our freedom. I know not all of you can leave your families. Some must remain here in El Rito to care for the women and children, and the livestock."

He looked directly at me. "Felipe, we have discussed all these issues. Can we depend on you?"

I was sitting on the floor and jumped to my feet. "Si, Padre, I will answer the call."

Jose Vivian got up from the floor and stepped forward. "I will be with my brother."

The padre enlisted the promise of several others to join the revolution. Three of the older men, including our father, did not volunteer, as they had a greater obligation to take care of their families, the livestock, and the welfare of the pueblo. Early the next morning, Padre Martinez departed to continue his mission.

A week later, Vivian and I were in a group of revolutionaries led by Tafoya, who took us southwest to La Canada. When we reached La Canada, our leader stood on a bench in the main plaza and harangued the pueblo's population.

"The dog Kearny has taken his cavalry and gone to California to conquer our people there," he told them. "Most of the rest of his army is on its way to Chihuahua to conquer the motherland. The gringos that remain here are a rabble—crude, ignorant, untrained, and poorly led. We will not find them this weak again for a long time. We must strike now while they will not know what has happened to them. As good Catholics, we must kill these gringo brutes, restore the flag of Mexico, and protect the church."

The people of La Canada shouted their approval and support. Vivian and I helped him sign up many recruits. The next day, he took us all back to Taos. I was filled with zeal and pride to be doing something concrete to protect the church.

Four days later, Vivian and I were among the armed men who beat on the door of Charles Bent's home. Others climbed onto the roof of the house and began to tear through. Several men in both groups were Indians from the Taos Pueblo, who were also disgusted by the actions of the Americans. We broke through the front door and crowded into a small entry room, but it opened only to the courtyard. Bent and his family were nowhere to be seen. We were milling about in the courtyard trying to decide what to do next when Bent appeared in a doorway across from us.

"Why do you break into my home? What is it that you want?" Bent shouted.

We fell silent.

Then, a man from the back of the mob shouted. "We want your head, gringo! We do not want any of you gringos governing us. We have come to kill you!"

Bent shouted back. "What have I done to wrong you? Have I not cured those you brought to me who were ill without charging you anything? When you have come to me for help, have I ever failed to help you?"

Another voice sputtered with rage. "That may be true, but no gringo will govern us. The gringo soldiers made you governor, but we will not have it. You must die!"

There was a roar of agreement, and in an instant, the courtyard filled with the smoke of gunpowder and the whistle of arrows. Bent staggered, arrows sticking in his head, arms, and torso. There was a huge hole in his right shoulder from a musket ball and another ugly wound in his abdomen. Dark blood oozed from his wounds. Bent's wife pulled him back into the room and slammed the door shut but failed to lock it. I rushed through it to see her helping him to the other bedroom. She pulled the door shut behind her and slammed the bolt. Vivian and I were in front of the crowd that pushed into the barred door. My heart was racing; my brain trying to justify the brutality of what we were doing.

Chapter 12
Tom

On a cold early winter night in 1846, I was asleep in my house in Santa Dolores, Maria Pascuala by my side. I woke to the sound of someone pounding on our door. It was a friend of ours, Charles Towne, who lived in Taos. He had raced his horse to Santa Dolores to warn me and Charley.

"A mob of Injuns and Mesicans killed Governor Bent and are on the way here to kill all the Americans they can find. They are not harming any Mesicans, though, so your family is safe."

I was standing at the door in my long johns.

"Que paso, Corazon?" Maria said, sitting up in our bed and pulling the blanket up to her chin.

"There's trouble. I must go to Turley's as fast as possible. It's a revolution, and they want to kill every American they can find."

"But you are a Mexican citizen."

"They won't be looking to see my papers. They are not bothering Mexicans, so you will be safe." I turned to Charles. "Hell's bells! I just remembered Charley is in Santa Fe delivering White Lightning to all the bars where the drunken American soldiers go. Turley and his American employees, and maybe some American traders, are at Arroyo Hondo. Ride there and warn them. I'll follow as soon as I can."

I got dressed and grabbed my weapons and ammunition. I ran to the backyard, saddled my fastest horse, and pushed as fast as the horse would go to Arroyo Hondo. There, I helped fortify the distillery building. I watched Turley collect his money and documents and ask his brother, Jesse Turley, to act as his agent in the event of his death. Turley sent his wife, his brother, and the children to her family to keep them safe.

His wife clung to him, crying, as did all of his children. He pushed her away and shushed the children. "You must go so I know you and the children are safe."

Then he took me aside and showed me where he had secured his valuables, some documents, and his will in a hiding place in his house.

"If I'm killed, Thomas, and you survive, tell my wife about this. If we are both killed, I hope she will remember this place."

As the sun rose slowly over the eastern mountains, I situated myself as a lookout on the upper floor. Nothing happened all morning long, but then I saw the silhouettes of men along all the ridges nearby as they surrounded the distillery. I called down to those below. Turley rushed up to see for himself as a lone man approached, waving a white flag.

"We do not wish to kill you, Señor Turley," the man shouted, "but you and your men must surrender to us. We are taking back our land."

Turley shouted back. "I heard what happened to Governor Bent and the others in Taos. If you want us, you will have to come and take us. Otherwise, just go away—we will not interfere with you. We'll leave you to the American soldiers."

The man returned to his comrades. Moments later, the mob started howling and shouting. That noise was replaced by the steady beating of drums and chanting. On the ridges, heads bobbed up and down.

"The Injuns with them are working themselves up," I declared. "They'll be coming before long."

One Injun, feeling especially brave or maybe bulletproof, danced out into the open. I took careful aim and shot him in the chest. Another warrior, screaming and shaking his fist at the building, ran out and started dragging the dead man back to safety. Another of Turley's men killed that man as I reloaded. A third man ran out to help those already down, and I put a bullet into him. The mob fired in return, and in a few minutes, every glass windowpane in the building was shattered. Bullets bounced off the rock walls and thudded into the adobe bricks. For the rest of that day, a cloud of smoke from the black powder rifles of both sides hung low in the canyon.

With darkness, the mob seemed to gain courage. I didn't see anyone sneaking up to the building, but I smelled wood smoke. The doors to the place, and the vigas where they projected from the wall, had been set ablaze by oil-soaked rags set afire. Once the fires started to spread, the attackers used ladders and broke through the adobe walls on the second floor, then set more fires. Some of the defenders, trapped on the second floor as the flames spread, were able to chop through the wood floor and drop down to join our comrades. They retreated to a corner where they stacked sacks of milled flour as a barricade. I still had caps, powder, and balls but started to worry about running out. I managed to barricade myself on the second floor of the building after retreating from the spreading fire. My heart was racing, but my hands were steady, and I forced myself to remain calm. I had a good vantage point where I carefully picked off every target that presented itself, but I was separated from the rest of the men in the building. That worried me some. As the fire spread toward me, I managed to dig a hole in the adobe wall, slip through, and drop to the ground. I escaped into the darkness and ran all the way back to Santa Dolores.

When I arrived, Maria hugged me close, her face pressed against my chest. "You smell like gun smoke, but I am so happy you are safe," she said. "I was so worried about you. Some of those men from Taos were here, but they said they only want to kill Americans. The men that came here were all Mexicans and said they would protect us from any Indians who wanted to harm us. You need to go to Santa Fe to be safe, Tomas."

I saddled Jen and embarked on the seventy-mile ride on the icy night. I circled Taos undetected, then bypassed La Canada, and continued to Santa Fe. I rode without stopping, found the garrison, and told the commander what I knew.

I was angry. My livelihood was at risk and I couldn't understand why the mob attacked Turley's. When I found Charley, he was swapping stories with a bunch of our hunter and trapper friends.

"Don't know if you all know it, but the Mexicans have started a revolution," I told them. "They killed Bent in Taos and attacked Turley's place. I was there and managed to escape. The building was on fire when I left. I have no idea if Turley and those with him got away."

There were a lot of questions I couldn't answer. Then Ceran St. Vrain, a partner in Bent's Fort and an experienced mountain man, joined us. He was a man of average height but thick in the shoulders and chest, dark hair, and a beard but no mustache. His eyes were dark and deep set, and his eyebrows sloped down from the top of his nose. St. Vrain told us he was commissioned by Colonel Price to organize a company of volunteers to scout for the army. Those who enlisted would be paid the standard rate for army scouts. He was looking for men with experience fighting Indians and living in the wilderness. Charley and I were first in line to place our marks on the enlistment papers. We and our friends were itching to avenge the deaths of the Americans killed in Taos. Another survivor of the Taos revolt, Dick Green, Charles Bent's Negro slave, managed to slip out of Taos on one of Bent's horses as the mob ran amok. He made it safely to Santa Fe and reported what had happened. Green was given a rifle and accompanied us, but his name wasn't on the official roster of St. Vrain's volunteers.

We left Santa Fe on January 23, 1847; us scouts and Colonel Price's officers were the only ones mounted. The rest of his troops were infantry and artillery, all marching behind four twelve-pound howitzers pulled by mules. The supply wagons brought up the rear. The colonel sent us scouts ahead. The next day, about one-thirty in the afternoon, close to La Canada, we found the Mexicans waiting for us. St. Vrain sent word back to Price, who hurried to join us. I watched some of the rebels run into the town and hide in some houses. Others found places to fight us in the hills surrounding the village. Price left his supply wagons behind and rushed to place his troops in a battle line along a small creek that flowed past the village, only a few hundred yards from the walls of the town. The banks of the creek protected his troops from the rebels' rifles. At about the same time, he ordered his artillery to fire on the town. The rebels learned his supply wagons were still a mile away. With his scope, St. Vrain watched them prepare to attack the supply train and rushed us back to protect it.

I rode into the fray, my pistol in one hand, my Hawken in the other. The inexperienced rebels who had reached the wagons were not ready for the furious attack and deadly force of Indian fighters. The few that survived fled for their lives. We escorted the supply wagons to rejoin the army. Price then ordered his troops to charge the rebels after ordering St. Vrain to circle us around the pueblo and block any attempts to escape.

The attacking American infantry maintained good discipline, and the battle was soon over. The rebels broke and ran in every direction. The ground was so rough and broken that it was tough to chase them down while mounted. Most of those who got out of the town escaped, despite our efforts. St. Vrain told us Price counted thirty-six enemy killed and many more wounded. Price said he lost only two men, with six wounded. All of us scouts escaped injury.

The next day, we moved up the Rio Grande del Norte, seven miles to the pueblo of Los Luceros. The following day, Captain Burgwin and his company of dragoons arrived, along with Lieutenant Wilson and the six-pound cannon Price had ordered him to bring. I reckoned that Price's forces now numbered close to five hundred men. The day after that, we rested, and then marched to La Joya.

St. Vrain told us the pueblo of El Embudo was Price's next objective, but before he could reach it, his army had to pass through the Embudo defile, a narrow road through high rock walls, barely wide enough to allow three men to walk side by side. St. Vrain dispatched me and Charley and two others to investigate. We managed to sneak up on the rebels guarding the canyon without them seeing us and counted about seventy-five rebels waiting in ambush. Price ordered Burgwin's dragoons and St. Vrain's scout to attack, remove the rebels, and go on to subdue El Embudo. He turned the rest of his men around, telling us he intended to take them back to La Canada and from there, to Taos.

All told, our forces were about a hundred and eighty men. Charley and I led the way, and we rode toward the objective. Suddenly, Charley threw up his hand. "Hold on, Tom, I just saw a bunch of them running to new spots. We didn't see that group before."

St. Vrain and the rest of the scouts were not far behind. When they joined us, Charley explained that we must have missed some rebels who saw us and hid. Seven of us, including me and Charley, were sent out to sneak up and do another count. There were actually several hundred rebels waiting.

I tied Jen to a nearby shrub, looked around for Charley, and spotted him standing ten yards away, looking up into the hills to the left of the defile. I walked over. "You reckon we can get them out of those rocks, Charley?"

"I reckon so, Tom. It appears most of them are peons. The Injuns with them are probably from the pueblos. They are not likely to be as tough as those tribes we've fought."

"Reckon we should stay together?"

"Yeah, we'll take turns firing and loading. When St. Vrain gives the word, you and I should go up over that hill yonder. We'll use the rocks for cover as we head up. Put some shot in your mouth and keep low. Got plenty caps?"

"Yeah."

We heard St. Vrain shout and looked around to find him. He circled his right arm holding his rifle over his head and yelled, "Men, with me. Let's roust 'em."

He charged uphill to the left side of the defile. Burgwin followed his lead and charged up the right side, his men yelling, close behind.

We were experienced Indian fighters, accustomed to stopping, aiming, and firing our rifles and then reloading while running, without bothering to use wadding for the bullet. Charley and I took the path he had identified. We and St. Vrain were leading the attack; the rest of the Indian fighters close behind. I found the fighting frustrating. We were firing in the general direction of the enemy but were not able to aim at a specific target. I didn't know if I was hitting anyone or not. But we continued to advance. The disciplined soldiers advanced more carefully. Under the direction of their sergeants, each squad advanced a few yards, stopped, fired a devastating volley, and then the next squad advanced through them, stopped, and fired a volley while the previous squad reloaded. The rebels were unprepared for this kind of disciplined fighting from the soldiers and the ferocity of the scouts. Within minutes, they were fleeing toward El Embudo, many leaving their weapons behind. They also left nearly eighty dead and wounded.

We arrived in El Embudo to find it empty of all but a few rebels who surrendered without a fight. I talked to one of the prisoners who told me that when they got to El Embudo, many men had left their weapons. The leaders fled, and most of their followers did the same, scattering in all directions.

St. Vrain's volunteers had taken a few casualties. A longtime trapper known to me only as Papin died of a chest wound. Dick Green, Bent's slave, was seriously wounded. A few others had minor wounds that did not prevent them from continuing. St. Vrain and Burgwin decided we would spend the night in El Embudo. The next morning, we moved up the valley six miles through sleet and snow to Las Trampas. We made camp, and the officers decided to wait for Colonel Price, who arrived early the next morning. We stayed in camp resting, but it was bitter cold. The following day we struggled through deep snow, those of us with mounts taking turns breaking through. The infantry followed us, the artillery and supply wagons moving forward over the trampled snow and ice. We reached the small pueblo of Rio Chiquito late in the afternoon on 2 February, exhausted and cold. Many of the men suffered from frostbite. We were just six miles from Taos.

We reached Taos at about ten the next morning and discovered that the rebels had retreated to the Taos Indian pueblo three miles north of town. The Taos Pueblo had two large adobe buildings that ran north and south, facing each other on either side of a small stream. Part of the rooms, stacked on each other, were seven stories high, a few eight. There were about a hundred and fifty yards of open space on either side of the stream. Twenty-five yards west of the most western building was the San Geronimo de Taos church. Surrounding all three of the buildings was a six-foot adobe wall with picket posts and narrow rifle ports. There were also rifle ports in the walls of the buildings.

The colonel decided to concentrate his attack on the western flank of the church. It was too cold to rest comfortably, although many of us built fires to stand around. It was about two in the afternoon when the colonel finally gave the order for the artillery to fire at will. Charley and I stood as close as we could to our fire, watching as the soldiers fired the twelve-pound howitzers and the six-pound cannon as fast as they could reload them. I had never seen how much damage those big guns could cause. The bombardment continued for two and a half hours. The artillery turned the adobe wall to rubble, but the thirty-inch-thick adobe walls of the church seemed to absorb the punishment with little effect on the building except for the large lead balls stuck in deep depressions. Return fire from the pueblo did no damage. We were all cold, wet, and exhausted. St. Vrain called all of us scouts together and told us Price had decided to go back to Taos, let everyone get a hot meal, and billet us in houses so we could build fires and get warm. As we marched away, the Mexican and Indian rebels must have thought we had given up, they started cheering.

Two days later, as the predawn light made deep shadows in the nooks and crannies of the multistoried buildings, we were back. Price put the dragoons to the west of the church. St. Vrain and his scouts were first told to join Captain Slack, who had a small contingent of cavalry, on the east side of the pueblo. We were to intercept any rebels attempting to escape toward the mountains to the east. Price positioned the rest of his forces about three hundred yards north of the church with the artillery arranged to fire on the rear and western walls of the church. Before the sun burned through the clouds, the valley was smothered in black smoke. The artillery fire was once again ineffective, so Price ordered Burgwin and his men to charge the western wall while we scouts charged the northern wall.

Most of us Indian fighters had our tomahawks, and Burgwin had armed several of his men with axes. We were ordered to chop our way into the church. Some of us fashioned ladders, and Charley and I ran to the church wall to set our ladder and scrambled to the roof. We managed to chop through and set some vigas on fire. While Charley and I were on the roof, three defenders, obscured by dense smoke, managed to escape through a side door and run to the closest building. I saw them and fired at the one in the middle. He started to fall, but the man on either side grabbed him, pulling him to safety. I hadn't killed him—he was just wounded. No notch in my barrel.

Some of Burgwin's men chopped at the western wall of the church with axes while Burgwin took a small party around to the front and tried to break down the door. One of the defenders fired a rifle through a slit and seriously wounded Burgwin. His men dragged him back to the relative safety of the rubble from the western wall. By this time, his soldiers had succeeded in chopping a hole through the thick wall of the church.

Our fires on the roof had burned through enough so Charley and I could pick out targets below and fire at them. After we had hit two, the rest found places to hide from us. While all this was happening, other soldiers brought the six-pound cannon to bear. They began firing heavy concentrations of grapeshot at the small opening Burgwin's men made. At mid-afternoon, they advanced the cannon to within sixty yards of the church and concentrated fire on the hole. When the hole was enlarged, they brought the cannon to within a few yards of the wall. Charley and I jumped to the ground as they fired three explosive shells followed by three rounds of grapeshot through the hole. I peered through the hole and saw only fragments of wood from the pews and other furnishings mixed with body parts of the defenders. The explosions inside the tightly closed church had been horrific. As I watched, a squad burst through the front door, but all the defenders inside were dead.

After the church was under our control, Price ordered us to attack the building on the west side of the stream. The troops methodically advanced while us scouts aimed at the rifle slits in the large complex to prevent any effective fire at the advancing troops. Once the troops gained access to the building, many of the enemy fled. Some escaped to the eastern building, but most headed for the mountains to the east. We remounted and rushed to intercept them. It was a slaughter. We ran down and killed fifty-one men. Only a handful of rebels managed to escape. We had one man badly wounded and another who received a minor wound.

That night, we were in the same apartments the enemy had just abandoned. I built a cooking fire, and we had both hot food and coffee for the first time in days. After eating, Charley and I stretched out on the floor, exhausted.

Early the next morning, the remaining rebels surrendered. Over a hundred and fifty Mexicans and Indians were killed in the battle, and a large number were wounded and taken prisoner. Only seven Americans were killed and forty-five wounded, but some of the wounded died in the days following. None of those killed or wounded were friends of mine.

We learned the leaders of the revolution were either killed or captured. Jesus Tafoya died in the fighting at La Canada and Pablo Chaves at Taos. Pablo Montoya and the Indian Tomas were among those who surrendered at Taos. Manuel Cortez was not present at Taos. I heard later that he escaped capture and became a bandit. He recruited some Apache Indians, and they terrorized New Mexicans in isolated mountain villages for a time before he disappeared.

Early in the morning of 5 February, Charley and I sought out Captain St. Vrain, finding him with several scouts in one of the apartments in the east building of the pueblo.

"Charley and I need to find out if our families are all right," I told him. "We want to go to Santa Dolores and Arroyo Hondo. Maybe Turley and some of those with him got away."

"Sure, Tom, I understand. You and Charley go ahead but take at least a half dozen of the boys with you in case you run across more rebels. Don't take anyone who is not willing to volunteer, understand? Report back when you're done."

"Yes, sir," Charley and I replied in unison.

We were both anxious to find out if our families were safe. We were tired of being soldiers, tired of fighting, and really tired of killing. The rumor going around was that Turley had been killed. If his operation was destroyed, we needed to find some way to take care of our families, as well as Mama and Catherine.

Much later, I learned what happened to Turley and the others from Johnnie Albert, the only other survivor from the massacre. He told me while fighting was hand-to-hand inside the burning building, Turley got them all to retreat to a still intact and barred door to the outside, where they again barricaded themselves. The fires made it unbearably hot. After they shed their hats and coats, they were attacked by the rebels. They removed the bar, shoved the door open, fired a volley into the crowd outside, and tried to fight their way through. Most of them, including Turley, never made it through the door.

"I managed to fight my way through," said Johnnie, "swinging my two-pound Bowie knife with one hand, my rifle with the other. Once I broke free, I ran into the dark until I fell to my knees and crawled to some shrubs on a hill close by. I managed to keep away from the light of the flames but pressed into the ground every time there was an explosion from the stored alcohol. Eventually, I managed to circle around the mob, find the Taos Trail, and follow it north."

Johnnie managed to keep his knife, rifle, and ammunition. He struggled to keep moving, exposed to rain, sleet, snow, and ice for eight days. On the second day, he killed a deer, made a fire, and ate seared but mostly raw venison. What kept him alive was the skin of the deer. He wrapped around himself, with the hair next to his body. He made it to pueblo on 27 January. The news of the murders of Bent, Turley, and the others angered and saddened those in that little community, he said, but all they could do was send the news to Bent's Fort and from there back to Missouri.

Chapter 13
Tom

Charley and I and six of our friends from the company of scouts pushed our mounts hard to return to our families in Santa Dolores. The eight of us charged into Santa Dolores but found the town calm. When I dismounted in front of my house, Maria Pascuala opened the door, screamed, and ran to me, her arms stretched out. I threw my coat open and wrapped it around her, holding her close.

Maria Pascuala murmured into my buckskin shirt. "I was so worried about you, my love."

"I know, my love. I worried about you as well. So, all your family is safe, your mother and father, brothers, and sisters, aunts and uncles, cousins, all of Charley's family?"

"Yes, yes, everyone is safe. The Mexicans who rebelled did not allow the Indians to harm any Mexicans or their children."

"Good. That is good. Listen, my love. Our friends are waiting for us. As soon as he hugs his family, Charley and I must ride with them to determine the fate of Mr. Turley and the others. I will return to you as soon as I can, but we have to go to Taos to report what we find."

She held me close for many moments, her arms around my neck until I took them away and put them on her hips. She looked up at me, wiped away her tears with the back of one hand, and smiled. "I understand, my love. I will be here, waiting."

When we reached Turley's mill and distillery, we could only gaze with despair at the burnt-out ruin. Only the stone walls of the ground floor remained. The roof had collapsed. When it fell, it burned through the floor, and that collapsed. Explosions from the liquor had demolished most of the adobe walls. We scraped and dug through the ruins, looking for the bodies of our friends.

We eventually found five charred bodies frozen stiff by the February cold. We were able to identify the bodies of Turley and Billy Austen, but we were not certain of the identities of the other three. We spread out and searched the entire area but found no more bodies. The rebels had taken away their killed and wounded. We hitched up one of Turley's wagons, loaded it with the dead, and took them to Taos.

As we rode to Taos, I moved Jen next to Charley and his mule. "Have you thought about how you are going to be able to support your family with Turley gone and the whiskey business with him?"

"Yes, I've been worrying about that. Do you have any ideas?"

"Not a single one," I said. "But we have to figure out something. We've both got families to take care of as well as supporting Mama."

"I know, I know. I'll keep thinking about it. There's got to be something we can do."

As our sad group entered Taos, we were joined by a detachment of soldiers returning from Rio Colorado, where other rebels had killed two Americans. Tied to the backs of mules were the frozen bodies of those two men. Despite the frozen ground, we set to work digging a mass grave. Into this grave, we placed the remains of those killed at Turley's and the American soldiers killed in the battle of the Rio Colorado.

Captain St. Vrain told all of us scouts that we could return to our homes. Almost seven months later, a messenger from Colonel Price came to my house. He informed me that since I had never been officially discharged from St. Vrain's company, and since that company was commissioned by the army, I was still a soldier. The colonel ordered me to report to him within two days. I asked the messenger if my brother Charley was getting the same message. He said no, only me. I could not imagine why the army wanted me after all that time and not Charley as well.

When I arrived at the colonel's headquarters in Santa Fe, his sergeant told me to go directly into his office. "He's been waiting for you to arrive."

As I walked into the office, the colonel looked up and smiled at me, the first time he had ever done so. I was surprised he even knew who I was. "Ah, Tobin, I was hoping you would arrive today." I had decided to take back my real name when I joined St. Vrain's volunteers. "I need you to do something for me. I need you to ride to Fort Leavenworth as fast as possible with this packet of official reports. They contain critical information the army requires.

Because you are the smallest and lightest man with wilderness experience, you will be able to get there soonest. I'll give you two of our fastest horses, but you'll need to do what you can along the way to replace them. Do you understand what I need you to do?"

I understood, but I wasn't happy about it. My mind raced to find an excuse. Finally, I blurted out, "Yes, sir, but my Maria Pascuala is about to give birth. I need to be with her. Besides, it will be a dangerous trip. A man traveling by himself will be easy pickings for hostiles. If I get killed, my wife will be a widow, and our babe, an orphan. What happens then?"

"I realize I am asking a great deal of you, Tom, but my head scout, Fitzpatrick, tells me you are the only man he knows who can do this. This is an extremely important mission. Your country needs you to do this. All of us have left family to serve our country. Now I'm asking you to do the same."

"Will I get paid for doing this?" I asked.

"Yes, of course, you will continue to draw the wages you had as a member of St. Vrain's volunteers. I believe that is thirty dollars a month. Is that correct?"

"Yes, but if this mission is so important and dangerous, shouldn't it be worth more?"

The colonel grunted and shook his head. He stared at me, but I didn't let him scare me, and I stared right back. Neither of us said anything for what seemed like a long time. "All right. I can authorize two dollars a day. Will that make you happy?"

"It will allow me to take care of my family. Can you pay the wages directly to my wife in Santa Dolores? Also, what happens if I get myself killed?"

I could see Price was getting irritated with me. "Then your wife will receive widow's benefits, assuming you are legally married."

I decided to shut up.

He wrote something on a piece of paper on his desk. "This is a note to remind me to send your wife your wages. I will start by sending her the wages owed you thus far for your service with St. Vrain's scouts."

"Thank you, Colonel." I gave him a half-hearted imitation of the salute he was accustomed to receiving from his soldiers.

I returned home that same day to explain everything to Maria and say goodbye again. The following day, carrying only a single blanket rolled up in my buffalo robe, a lariat, my knife, my Hawken, my percussion cap pistol, two hundred caps, a hundred bullets, gun powder, and a small amount of salt, I started the journey of over eight hundred miles. The pistol was only accurate up to fifty feet or so, and I needed both hands to hold it steady, but it could come in handy if needed. I was very aware of the dangers I faced.

I weighed only about a hundred and thirty pounds at that time. I could and did push the horses hard, but I was well-acclimated to the hardships of travel and living off the land. I switched horses every ten miles or so until I reached Fort Mora, a trading post about eighty miles north of Santa Fe. The owner of Fort Mora was a longtime acquaintance and former liquor customer. One of the army horses had gone lame, so I left it at the fort in exchange for a tough Indian pony. I rode the pony and remaining army horse hard for two days, sleeping only four hours the first night. The second night, I quietly approached a sleeping camp of buffalo-hunting Utes. I circled the camp and found their untended herd of hobbled ponies grazing. Both horses were exhausted so I moved quietly into the herd, and roped a likely-looking mount. I led it out of the herd, put my saddle on it, mounted it, and departed.

Even though I was tired, I managed to keep both my wits and eyes sharp. At times, I had to hunker down in a draw or ride miles off the trail to avoid hunting parties scouring the country for meat. I shot small game and one deer but was only able to build small, well-concealed fires to cook the meat, and then only at night. The Indians would see smoke from a fire during daylight. Two more times I was able to sneak into hobbled herds of horses and exchange my spent horse for a fresh one. While I slept, I tied my hobbled horse to my leg so it wouldn't stray during the night. I followed the Santa Fe Trail and the Arkansas River as far as Big Bend and then rode cross-country to Council Grove. On that portion of the trip, I twice encountered government supply trains and, after explaining my mission, obtained a fresh horse. From Council Grove, I traveled northeast to Fort Leavenworth. I reached my destination and delivered the colonel's dispatches without comment. I figured I had averaged about fifty miles a day. Pretty good for the circumstances.

I rested for a few days and joined a company of troops going to Santa Fe as replacements. It took us more than three weeks to reach Bent's Fort, but I didn't have to worry about being caught by Injuns. At Bent's, I left the troops and traveled the now familiar trail over the Sangre de Cristo Pass. The entire journey had taken about two months.

Three days after I arrived home, Maria Pascuala delivered us a son, born on 15 October. Padre Martinez christened the infant Juan de Jesus Tobin. But tragedy struck on 17 December when my two-month-old son died. Neither I nor her family were able to console Maria, and she filled our little house with tears. I stayed close, trying to comfort her, but I also grieved, silently, for little Juanito. It seemed to me that everything in our lives was as destroyed as Turley's enterprise.

Chapter 14
Tom

Late that same fall, one of our old friends, John Albert, rode into Santa Dolores to reunite with Charley and me. Charley's wife, Serafina, prepared a large afternoon meal, and we sat around the table. While eating, we discussed how we were going to make a living and support our families.

"I believe what we can do is farm. More folks are coming out here all the time, and they will be needing food," Charley said.

"Where you gonna find irrigated land to farm?" Albert asked. "All the farmland around here is spoken for."

"The St. Charles River valley, near Pueblo," Charley answered. "There's plenty of land, and it's good farm country. What do you two think?"

Albert frowned. "Who owns the land you're talking about?"

Charley was chewing but swallowed and replied, "We can probably find someone in Pueblo who can help us figure it out."

I spoke up. "Well, if we have to pay somebody something for the land, I don't have much to pay with. I guess both of you are in the same fix."

"Maybe we can just pay a small amount and get credit for the rest until we make a crop," said Albert.

"It is worth pondering. I'll think on it," I said.

Late that March there was an early break in the weather. We tracked down Albert, and the three of us traveled to Pueblo. We identified some land in the St. Charles River valley, contacted a lawyer who found out the land was owned by the government, and arranged with the authorities for us to purchase what we needed for a dollar an acre. We returned to Santa Dolores and hired two local men, Salvador Avila, and Antonio Chaves, to help with the new farm. On the first day of April, Albert and I left for the St. Charles valley with the two hired hands, but Charley had a claim against Turley's estate and hoped to get that settled before he joined us.

We arrived in a small valley of the St. Charles River and staked out our farm ten miles south of the town of Pueblo, just west of where the Taos Trail crossed the river. We walked the length of the valley on both sides of the river and decided where to build our irrigation dam. With the help of our two hired men, we built a jacal for shelter. Then we put the hired men to work making a supply of adobe bricks while we rode into Pueblo to purchase additional supplies. While we were in Pueblo, Albert told me he thought building a farm from nothing was going to be too difficult. He decided to get out of the partnership. I managed to find three men who had been in St. Vrain's scouts with us and who had a few dollars and needed employment. When I described what Charley and I had in mind, Pascual 'Blackhawk' Riviere, 'Colorado' Mitchell, and LaBonte agreed to join our venture.

Our three new partners and I started building our diversion dam and irrigation ditches. Avila and Chavez continued making adobe bricks.

Meanwhile, Jesse Turley, Simeon's brother, and a court-appointed administrator settled Charley's claim against the Turley estate. Charley received $475.50, and ten days later, at a public auction to dispose of some of Turley's remaining goods; he spent $458.75 to purchase the supplies and tools we needed for the new farm. A week later, he left his wife and children in Santa Dolores to join me on the farm.

Because of the flat terrain of the valley, a minimal amount of leveling was necessary. Before long, we plotted, plowed, and planted fields. Three adobe houses were finished. I shared one of them with Charley. We recruited another hired hand, Old Trujillo when he wandered by on his way to Pueblo. Avila, Colorado, and Old Trujillo shared the second house, and LaBonte, Chavez, and Blackhawk lived in the third.

Our first growing season was exceptionally good. The previous severe winter had deposited deep snow on the plains and in the mountains. Our fields were still moist from the snow, and the April rains were kind. The fields didn't require irrigation until late in July. That fall we harvested a bumper crop of corn, pumpkins, squash, beans, and several different varieties of chili peppers. Mitchell, Blackhawk, and LaBonte took their share of the harvest to Pueblo to sell. Charley and I stored a significant portion of our share at the farm but also loaded pack mules with some of the harvests and set off for home, planning to market what we had in Taos. By the end of October, we were both on the road back to our families in Santa Dolores.

I burst through the door to my house. Maria Pascuala screamed, then recognized me and ran to me, arms outstretched. "Oh! Tomas! I am so happy; you are safe and have returned to me."

"Where else would I go?"

She held me close and spoke into my chest. "I don't know. We heard nothing from you or your brother for over six months! No word. No letters. Nothing."

"Well, we were very busy, and we did very well. We made good crops, and I brought you plenty of corn and beans for next winter. We also brought along extra to sell in Taos. We still have a lot of everything stored back at the farm. I hear there will be some American soldiers at Bent's Fort for the winter, and they will need provisions. Charley and I will do some hunting this fall to supply us with meat."

"Still, you should send me some words when you are gone so long. You must learn to write or at least send some word back to us. I worry about you when you are gone from me."

"Guess I'm too old to learn to read and write, but I'll try to do better. If it goes this well next year, maybe Charley and I can trade off and come home for a week or so each month. Would you like that?"

"Yes, that would be wonderful."

I dropped my arms, but Maria Pascuala still hung from me, her arms around my neck. "Well, woman, I haven't had anything to eat since this morning. Are you going to feed me or just hang on me?"

"I am hugging you. That should be food enough."

I patted her buttocks, then grabbed a handful in each hand. "If you don't stop and feed me, I'll just carry you off to bed right now."

"Ah, my husband, you give so many promises, so little action." Her words were muffled, her face pressed tightly into my neck.

I didn't get anything to eat until it had been dark for several hours. There is no need for me to say anything else—life was good again, but different.

Chapter 15
Felipe

After our disastrous experience as revolutionaries, everything changed for me and Vivian. Life in our pueblo went on as before, but we felt disconnected from it. We considered ourselves grown men, but the people didn't treat us any differently than they had while we were growing up. In the fall of 1850, we went on an extended hunting and exploring trip and wandered west into the lands of the Navajo. We intended to avoid contact with any natives on the trip but brought along a small store of knives and iron pots to trade or give as gifts if any were encountered. After filling our water bags from a sparkling spring at the base of a mesa, we took a rugged, partially overgrown, and apparently seldom-used switchback path to the top of the mesa where we set up camp. The night was clear; the moon and stars seemed close enough to reach up and touch.

In the morning, as the sun was peeking over the horizon, we awakened to the barking of dogs and the bleating of sheep. We sauntered to the edge of the mesa and stood, transfixed, stunned by a broad vista of stark purple monuments rising from what seemed an almost level expanse of semidesert below. As the sun rose behind us, in the shaded portions of the vista, purple shadows changed to red and orange. Sunlit rock monuments thrust into a cloudless sky. At the base of the mesa, a boy and three dogs herded a large flock of sheep toward the spring. We watched, fascinated, as the dogs gently coaxed the sheep where they wanted them to go.

"Those dogs control the sheep perfectly, Vivian. So many sheep for only one boy and three dogs. I have read about sheepdogs but have never seen one working. Have you?"

"Never, but I have read about them too. I wonder where that boy got those dogs."

"Are you thinking what I am? Perhaps we could trade for some dogs like that. With dogs that can herd sheep like that, the two of us could put together a large flock. We would be independent from the pueblo, grown men making our own future. There is plenty of land to wander over to keep the sheep fed all year. We could make a small house, put it on a wagon, and pull it with two mules. We could look for good pasture all year long. We would be safe now that so many of the savage tribes have died from illness. If some savages found us, we would give them some of the lambs for food, and they would be our friends. What do you think?"

"I think this is a very good idea, Felipe. Let's go down and talk to that boy and see if he knows where we can trade for dogs such as those."

We purposely made a lot of noise working our way down to the spring where the young Navajo, perhaps twelve or thirteen years old, waited to see who we were and what we were doing on top of the mesa.

"Hello, young man," I said. "We come in peace." We both held our arms out, showing empty hands. "Do you speak Spanish?"

"Yes, a little bit, but you must speak very slowly, please."

"Ah, good, we are interested in your dogs."

"The dogs? Oh yes, they are very intelligent. They keep the sheep together and protect them. They are very good with the sheep."

"Did you train them?"

The boy seemed puzzled. "Train them? I do not understand."

I searched for a word he might understand. "Teach them. Did you teach them to work the sheep?"

His face lit up with understanding. "Ah. Yes. I teach them with my father, but they learn mostly from each other."

Without being directed to do so, as far as I could tell, the three dogs spaced themselves in a semicircle, holding the sheep close to the spring. Each of them was resting, their muzzles extended, touching the ground, watching the sheep carefully. The boy called out a guttural Navajo name, and one of the dogs got up and came to him, looking over his shoulder at the sheep to make certain none of them strayed.

"This is the papa of those other two. He taught them both. The black and white male over there and the other, the female, are his son and daughter."

"Do you have more of these dogs? Would your father be willing to trade with us for at least one of these dogs, as many as three, perhaps?"

The boy smiled. "Perhaps. With what would you trade?" He looked meaningfully at our rifles.

"I think we can be very generous," I replied. "But we will have to spend some time with you to learn how to control the dogs. How long do you think it will take for us to learn what to do with them?"

"Who knows? How smart are you? The dogs are very smart, but you must be smarter." He laughed at his own joke.

The young Navajo explained that if we all went on horseback, his home was only about an hour away. The dogs would take care of the sheep while we were gone.

I took my left foot out of the stirrup and held out my hand. "Come up. We will go to your house." I swung the boy up onto my horse behind the saddle, kicked my horse into a lope, and we were off, our two packhorses following.

On the way, Vivian said, "You speak Spanish quite well. How did you learn? Does anyone else in your family speak our tongue?"

In halting Spanish, the boy answered, "My uncle was captured by the Apache when he was ten years old. They sold him to Mexicans in Santa Fe. He was a slave for four long years but took a horse from the man who owned him and escaped. That was when I was very small. He returned to the tribe, and he taught me your tongue. Mexican traders come here sometimes to trade for our blankets and sheep. It is useful to be able to talk to them."

The boy's family was welcoming, more so after the boy told his father what we wanted.

Four yearling dogs and six recently weaned pups surrounded and sniffed at us. I presumed we emitted a wonderful mélange of new smells. One of the yearlings, a female with black hair, four white feet, and a white star marking on her head, sat on my right foot and pushed her nose into my hand. I laughed and petted her head.

"She likes you," said the boy. "She is good with the sheep and learns very fast."

Vivian knelt in the dust, and a slightly larger female, close to forty-five pounds, white with large brown splotches on her back and chest, came over to sniff his face. Vivian held her head with both hands and blew gently into her muzzle. She licked at his face, wagging her tail.

"That one is also good with the sheep, not as good as her sister, but she is very brave. The last time I took her with the sheep, she attacked a whole pack of coyotes that were trying to kill one of the lambs."

We squatted in the fine dust in front of the hogan, a structure similar to our jacal, and began serious negotiations.

"So, what do you want for these two females?" I asked and waited for the boy to translate.

"My father says he will take a rifle for each, with powder, the lead balls, and extra lead and the mold to make more balls."

"That is impossible," I said. "We might be able to give you one of our rifles and some powder and bullets, but not both and not all the powder. We have only one mold to make more bullets and must keep it. We are on a hunting trip and must be able to kill for food. We have a cougar hide and three elk hides in our pack. Would you be interested in them?"

The boy consulted with his father.

"My father says one rifle and the skins are not enough. What else have you to trade?"

I consulted in rapid Spanish with Vivian.

Vivian pulled a knife, still in its sheath, from one of the packs and extended it to the boy. "We will add this very fine knife."

The boy said nothing but handed the knife to his father, who took it from the sheath and tested the blade with his thumb. There was another exchange in Navajo.

"My father says to me this is almost enough, but not quite enough for two fine dogs. What else have you got?"

I stood up, walked to one of the packhorses, and untied one of the large canvas bags hanging from the side of the packsaddle. I rummaged inside and withdrew a cast-iron cooking pot.

"This is a very good cooking pot. It will last your family for many generations. This is all we are willing to trade for the dogs. If this is not enough, we will take you back to your sheep and look for dogs elsewhere."

There was another short but rapid exchange in Navajo.

"My father says to me you have made a very good trade. The dogs are worth much more, but he will take what you offer."

"Good." I turned to Vivian. "We will give them your flintlock, and we'll get you a percussion cap like mine in Taos when we return. Is that good with you?"

He nodded in agreement. "Yes, of course. I think it is a fair trade."

Negotiations concluded we joined the family for a meal of mutton stew and thick flatbread, very unlike the thin tortillas made by our mother, but tasting similar. When we finished eating, I was eager to start bonding with the dogs and learning how to control them.

I stood up and put a hand on the boy's shoulder. "We should get you back to your flock, and we must start to learn how to work the dogs. Will the dogs follow us, or do we have to carry them?"

"They will come with us when I call to them," the boy answered, with a wide grin.

He mounted behind me again and called to the two dogs. They trotted alongside the horses, tongues lolling out of the side of their mouths. The rest of the dogs sat and watched, along with the boy's father, mother, and small sister. Fine dust obscured them as we put distance between us and the hogan.

Vivian and I spent the rest of that day bonding with our dogs and learning to control them. I named my dog Estrella because of the star-shaped patch on her head. That night I fed her by hand while petting and talking to her. The next day, she never lost sight of where I was. Even while working the sheep, she kept track of me.

Vivian asked the boy what he called the white dog with the brown splashes. The boy told him they just called her the Navajo name for sister, so that became her Spanish name, Hermana.

The following day, the boy directed all five dogs in cutting out about a hundred head of sheep from the flock. He then drove the rest of the flock away. He told Vivian and me to work Estrella and Hermana with the hundred, moving them where we wanted them to go and learning how to direct the dogs. By mid-afternoon, the two dogs seemed to anticipate what we wanted them to do. Estrella made most of the decisions. Hermana carefully watched and followed her lead.

That evening the boy told us he was leaving the vicinity of their spring the next morning. I told him we would be heading home, and he agreed that we had learned well enough how to direct the dogs.

The trip back to El Rito took us six days of easy travel. I shot two more deer along the way, and we stopped early each evening to roast the meat, rest our horses, and allow them to graze. We played with the dogs and fed each of them by hand, bonding closer each day. By the time we reached home, the two dogs were never more than ten feet away from us and slept curled up next to us at night. Sitting at our campfire each night, we concocted the details of our plan.

We were camped the night before getting back to El Rito. Vivian asked what had been on my mind since we first discussed our plan. "Do you think Papa will object to our plan, Felipe? What if he says he needs us to stay with the family?"

"I have also been wondering about this. If he objects, we have to come up with some arguments about why we need to do this. We should both be thinking of what we can say to him."

Once home, we explained our plan to our father, and he responded. "You are both old enough, past old enough, to start your own lives. Felipe, you have twenty-three years and Vivian almost twenty. You are men now and should have lives of your own. This is what I propose. There is a good market for lumber in Taos. You should go to the forest for the next five months. I will work with you when I can. We will set up a place to saw the logs into planks and make as many planks as we can. We will sell the planks in Taos so you can purchase sheep. The pueblo now has how many sheep?"

"We have almost two hundred ewes and twenty rams," Vivian answered.

"Good. I will ask the brothers to sell you half of them. I will ask the Bernal brothers to build your house on one of our wagons. You may also take two of my mules, and you already have your own horses. What else do you need?"

Vivian and I looked at each other and smiled with relief.

"You are very generous, Papa," I said. "We have everything else. We will work very hard the rest of this fall and winter and saw lots of planks. This is a good plan, and we are appreciative." I turned to Vivian. "Do you agree with me, brother?"

"Yes, yes. We will work very hard, Papa," Vivian answered.

We spent the fall and winter felling large trees, and the team of mules dragged the logs to our camp. We dug a trench and built a scaffold over it and used the mules to drag each log onto the scaffold. Our father had purchased a new two-man saw. We took turns, one of us standing in the trench below the log, the other on the log, as we sawed off thick planks. We sold six wagonloads of lumber for good prices. We cut twice as many planks as the Bernal brothers said they needed for our little house on wheels. The extra planks were payment for the work done to build the casita. It was furnished with two bunks and an iron stove. We slid it onto the bed of one of the family's wagons. With all the money we had left, we purchased fifty pregnant ewes from the pueblo and a hundred and fifty ewes and twenty fine-looking rams in Taos. The following year, our flock more than doubled, many of the ewes giving birth to twins. Three ewes had triplets. We sheared all the sheep when the weather warmed and bought more sheep with the wool. After castrating all the male lambs early in April, we headed north with our flock to the San Luis Valley. Estrella and Hermana were now in charge of their own sheep. Vivian and I relished our independence.

I had first gone to the San Luis Valley with Ignacio while learning to hunt. Since then, Vivian and I had hunted there many times. The valley straddled the high plateau of the Rio Grande Rift. It stretched over two hundred thousand varas long and over one hundred thousand varas at its widest part. The valley floor was flat in many areas and had numerous cold, clear springs as well as a few hot springs. The Rio Grande flowed from the San Juan Mountains south through the valley. Many small spring-fed streams and creeks flowed into the valley from the mountains on both sides. Those that did not feed the Rio Grande soon disappeared into the valley floor or formed numerous small lakes west of the Sangre de Cristo Mountains. It was an ideal place to graze our sheep on the abundant grass shared only with buffalo and elk.

Once we were in the valley the sheep grew fatter daily on the succulent grasses pushing up. The greasewood bushes, just beginning to show their buds of rose-colored flowers, filled the air with their smell. The sheep frequently grabbed a mouthful of the succulent bright green leaves from this bush, relishing its salt content. We skirted the huge sand dunes just west of the Sangre de Cristo Range, then meandered around the many small lakes west of the dunes. Small hunting parties of Ute Indians visited our camp from time to time. The gift of a castrated lamb or two provided a welcome change of diet for the Utes, and we were not molested. The Indians watched Estrella and Hermana manage the flock with fascination, and whenever a group visited, they would ask for a demonstration. The casita on wheels also attracted much attention. Those who had seen it described it to others, and all who came to our camp insisted on peering into the strange dwelling on wheels.

Three years passed, and our flock expanded. We castrated the male lambs for meat and kept the females for breeding. We sold the wool we harvested each spring for dollars or traded for other valuables. We exchanged intact rams with other herders to prevent inbreeding. Each year more settlers, both Mexican and American, started settlements and farms in the valley, but there was still plenty of open range.

I was twenty-six years old when I left Vivian with the main flock while Estrella and I drove fifty wethers south, selling some of the meat animals at each small village we passed through. At the Santa Ana pueblo, I was fascinated by a young woman who came to draw water from the well in the central plaza. She was my height and very well endowed both above and below her narrow waist. Her black hair was in a single braid that traveled back and forth across her back as she worked the winch with both hands to bring up the bucket of water. She had a slight smile on her lips, probably thinking about something other than her task. Her arms were bare, and I noticed that her left arm was noticeably shorter than her right.

She had beautiful hair and a face like the Virgin Mary. She would bear many healthy children. The arm was nothing. I determined to sell the rest of the sheep and come back for her. That same afternoon I sold all the remaining wethers and returned to the central plaza to wait by the well.

At dusk she returned, carrying her water jug on her right shoulder.

"Estrella, bring that girl to me," I ordered, gesturing with my right arm.

My dog ran to where the girl was bringing up another bucket of water from the well. She circled the well and nudged the girl with her nose. The girl looked down at the dog and took a step back. Estrella nipped at her ankle but did not touch her. The girl let the handle of the winch go and the bucket splashed down into the water. Moving away from the dog, she was gently herded until she stood with her back toward me.

I praised the dog. "Good girl." I then took the girl by the shoulders and turned her around to face me. "My dog's name is Estrella. I told her to bring you to me. She did well, no?"

The girl nodded, and tears rolled down her cheeks.

I felt bad that I had frightened her—it was not my intent. "Do not be afraid. I am not going to hurt you. I am sorry if Estrella and I scared you." I started to wipe her tears away with a finger, but she flinched, pulling her head back. I felt even worse. "I just wanted to meet you. To talk to you. You are very beautiful. Do you know this?"

The girl held up her withered arm as though that would change my mind about her.

"That is of no concern to me. You can use it, no? Can you also speak?"

"Si, Señor."

She studied me. Much later, she would tell me she thought the dark Indian-looking man was quite good-looking, although I smelled of sheep.

"You came through earlier today with sheep. I saw you and your dog then."

"That is true. I sold all the sheep, and now I have money to buy you something pretty. Would you like a pretty scarf?"

"Why would you buy me a scarf?"

"Because I am smitten with you, and I want to make you my novia."

"Novia? You do not know me, and I do not know you. Why would you say such a thing?"

"Because I am a man who knows what he wants. When I first saw you, I knew immediately that you would bear my children."

"How is that possible? How can you say such things? My papa would not give me to such as you." She turned and started to walk away.

I took hold of her arm, gently. "No? Well, let's ask him."

She retrieved her water jug. I filled it for her and then walked next to her, leading my saddle horse and packhorse, Estrella at my heels.

The negotiations didn't take long. Jose Salvador Hurtado was a poor man, and Maria Secundina was the oldest of four brothers and three sisters. Beautiful as she was to me, I didn't think there had been many suitors for her because of her withered arm. I looked around the one-room adobe shack where at night ten people slept on the floor.

I squatted to be eye to eye with Señor Hurtado, who sat on the only stool in the room. "Listen, Señor, I am prepared to give your daughter a better life. My brother and I have a large flock of sheep, and we make a good living from them. We have four horses, two mules, and now close to eight hundred sheep. Next year we will have more." I reached into a coin purse tucked into the top of my homespun pants and took out a twenty-dollar gold piece. "I am giving you this gift to help feed your large family. I am not buying your daughter, but if she agrees to go with me, I will take very good care of her and will marry her. It is the custom of my people to be responsible for the welfare of a wife's family. If I marry your daughter, you and your family will be my obligation. If she does not agree to leave with me, you can keep the gold coin, and I will go away. You will not see me again."

Señor Hurtado stared at me, pondering the offer for only a few seconds. "Maria Secundina, you should go with this man. He is a very good man, very generous, and he will treat you well. I would like him to be my son-in-law."

The next morning, I watched as Maria Secundina tied her only other dress and some tattered but clean underclothes into a small bundle, said goodbye to her mother and siblings, and climbed up behind me on my horse. We stopped in Taos, where, after she gave me quick glances for my approval, Maria selected enough fabric to make at least two new dresses and some decent underclothing. We then traveled to Santa Dolores, where Padre Martinez married us. A year later, on May 29, 1854, the padre christened our first daughter Maria Vincenta.

Chapter 16
Tom

The farm prospered. Charley and I were able to go home to our families in the winter and took turns going home for a week each month for the rest of the year. Six years went by with nothing of significance happening. In mid-November of 1854, I traveled again to Bent's Fort to negotiate with Lt. Colonel William Gilpin to sell Charley's and my share of the year's harvest. While we were negotiating, Gilpin informed me that the army needed my services again.

"Last summer, Apache and Comanche Indians killed forty-seven Americans while attacking government trains going to and from Santa Fe," he said. "They captured and destroyed over three hundred wagons and took over eighteen hundred horses, mules, and some cattle. My scouts inform me that the hostiles are now moving into winter camps somewhere in the Canadian and Washita River canyons. However, we can expect them to resume their attacks on the wagon trains in the spring. My orders are to find as many of their winter camps as possible and attack them before they make their spring migration to the plains. If any hostiles are not destroyed and they manage to make their way to the Arkansas Valley, I am to sweep them from the valley during the summer. Because you know the country so well, I need you to scout for me."

The pay he promised was more than I was able to earn for six months of hard labor farming, and it would only require me to be away from home for about three months. I accepted the job and returned home to be with Maria until the army called for me.

In early December of 1854, I received a messenger from Colonel Gilpin to meet him in Mora, New Mexico. Maria Pascuala was about two months pregnant and just starting to show. I gave her a last hug and kissed her and then the baby in her belly, believing I would be back long before the baby came. Then I mounted Jen.

"Take care of yourself and the baby. I'll be back before you know it. I won't be more than three months at the most. This is good money, and I won't have to be away from home for such a long time." Since she got pregnant again, Maria seemed to be happier than she had been for some time.

She took my hand and squeezed it, forcing a smile. "Yes, yes, I know, Tomas. I have my family to look after me. Be safe and come home as soon as you can. I miss you already."

It was cold, with patches of snow on the ground, when we rode out of Mora into the plains. The mountains were heavy with snow. The army went southeast along the Mora River for sixty miles to where it emptied into the Canadian. We followed the Canadian south, then east. Most mornings, accompanied by at least two Apache scouts, I went ahead of the troops searching every canyon, gully, ravine, and draw of the Canadian River tributaries for any sign of the hostile tribes. The searching continued for nine weeks, but no camps of Injuns were found. I learned sometime later that, fortunately for me and Colonel Gilpin's troops, the expedition didn't travel all the way to the Washita River where thousands of hostile Injuns had camped all winter. If we had collided with them, we would have been overwhelmed.

Gilpin hired me because he needed someone who was not afraid to be on his own on the plains, knew the country, was a crack shot, and could ride great distances without having to rest. On several occasions, he sent me to ride cross-country to Bent's Fort carrying messages and to guide a small detachment with additional supplies back to his troops. I managed to avoid observation by hunting parties of Indians because of Jen. She was now in her prime and knew her job. She could smell or hear Injuns from a long way off and warned me far enough in advance so I could find a place to hide or change my route to avoid discovery.

After deciding to give up the search, Gilpin ordered us north, heading for Fort Mann, eight miles west of what became Dodge City. I had completed the task he needed me for, so he discharged me. I headed home. Maria Pascuala and I had a joyous reunion, but her now significantly protruding belly made close hugging difficult. Jose Narciso Tobin was born on July 4, 1855, strong and healthy. When he was two weeks old, Padre Martinez baptized him. Gilpin spent the summer searching but never found any hostile Indians along the Santa Fe Trail.

At the end of October, I made a devastating discovery. "Maria Pascuala," I said quietly across the front room of our three-room house. "Come here, please. Look, Jose Narciso does not follow with his eyes. He looks straight ahead. When I move silently, he continues to look straight ahead. When I make some noise, he moves his head to find the sound but doesn't try to look at me. I think the boy is blind."

"No, no, Tomas. It can't be true." She scooped the baby up and held him close, murmuring into the soft wool blanket she had woven for him.

I put my arms around my wife and baby. "There is a new American doctor in Taos. We will take him there. Perhaps there is something he can do."

The American doctor was abrupt and took only a few minutes to examine our son. He decided that little Narciso was indeed blind. "I'm afraid you'll just have to take care of the little bugger, Tom. He's blind as a bat, and there's nothing I can do to change that."

Maria was devastated. "How could this happen to us, Tomas? Our first baby died while still an infant. Did I not pray many times to the Virgin for a healthy child this time? What did I do wrong? Why is God punishing us? Have you done something contrary to the teachings of the church?"

"Calm yourself, Maria. Neither of us has done anything wrong. Our son is not blind because of anything we have done or not done. Doesn't the church teach that God has a reason for everything? We just don't understand or know the reason. We must accept this child as a blessing, not a curse. We will take care of him as best we can, and the brothers and sisters we will make for him will help take care of him. Think of how much joy this baby brings. He does not know he is afflicted, and so he is happy. He rarely cries, and then only for good reason. We must take joy from his happiness."

Maria carried the baby with her constantly, never letting him out of her sight. She was convinced little Jose Narciso's affliction was somehow her fault. I was unable to convince her otherwise. I seldom spoke to her and then only if I had something important to say. It was a relief when, late in January of 1856, Charley and I received a message from Kit Carson, one of Charley's companions from his trapping days. All the Americans living in the Taos area were friendly with each other, but Carson had a special friendship with both Charley and me, respecting our sobriety and reliability. Carson asked that we come to Taos for a meeting.

Two days later, we were in Carson's house in Taos. "Charley, Tom, sit down. Got some good stogies here. Have yourselves a smoke. I know you don't drink, so there's no sense in me offering."

Charley and I each took one of the proffered cigars, and we all lit up.

"You both know that Old Tom Fitzpatrick is now the Indian agent at Bent's?"

We nodded; neither of us felt the need to answer.

Carson smiled. "Well, Old Tom sent a letter to Colonel Washington, who's in command of the ninth Military Department in Santa Fe. You know the Treaty of Guadalupe Hidalgo formally ended the war with Mexico?"

Again, we nodded.

"Well, in that treaty, both the United States and Mexico agreed that they would gain the release of either country's citizens held captive by Injuns. Old Tom told the colonel that there was a band of Kiowa camped near Bent's Fort with a bunch of Mexican slaves. You all heard anything about that?"

"Not surprised," Charley answered.

"Anyhow, Major Beall here in Taos got orders from Colonel Washington to gather some scouts and take his men up to Bent's and find that camp of Injuns. He wants the Mexicans cut loose. Major Beall asked me to find four good men. I thought about you boys first. I plan to talk to Asa Estes and Dick Owens too. You boys in?"

"Asa and Dick are good hands. Steady. I reckon we'll be proud to ride with you, Kit," I answered.

"Well, that's good. I'm glad you feel that way. The pay's only regular army scout wages, but that's a lot better than what a man can make trapping or farming these days. Beall will give us an advance to keep the wolf from the door this winter. The major says he'll be ready to move out by the first of February. Can you be ready to go by then?"

"Sure. No problem, Kit," Charley said.

"How about you, Tom? I was sorry to hear about your boy being blind. Is Maria Pascuala doing all right?"

"Not so good. Lots of female crying at home. Be good to get away for a while. The boy seems to be a happy child. Maybe Maria Pascuala can get used to it better if I'm gone."

Carson leaned in closer to us. "You boys heard about Fremont's disaster?" He whispered.

This time Charley and I looked at each other, then at Carson, and shook our heads no.

"No? I thought everyone knew by now. Well, he took thirty-three soldiers and a hundred and twenty odd mules west from Pueblo to explore and survey the country, thinking of finding a quicker way to California. Bill Williams signed on as his guide. Old Bill took them to the Huerfano then west across the Sangre de Christos over Mosca Pass. They went down into the San Luis Valley and crossed over west to the San Juans and traveled north and west along the base of the mountains 'till they got to Carnero Creek."

Both Charley and I knew that country well. We nodded our understanding of the path taken.

"Well, Fremont claims that Old Bill told him they could save a couple of days by going up the Carnero and joining up with the Saguache Creek Trail near Cochetopa Pass."

"Old Bill never told him that, not in winter, unless he's gone plumb loco," I exclaimed, and Charley agreed.

"I'm thinking the same," Carson said. "But that's the way they tried to go. They made it through that narrow rock canyon that the Carnero comes through about three miles up when a blizzard hit them. Fremont claims Old Bill got them plumb lost, and they were snowed in and couldn't get up or down. The mules started dying from lack of food, and the men ate them and near everything else, they could stomach."

Charley snorted. "Old Bill's never been lost in his life. Blizzard or not, that's a poor story."

Carson nodded. "Can't say I think different. Anyhow, the day after Christmas, Fremont sent some men to walk back here to Taos for supplies, mules, and horses. The rest of them just sat there in the snow because Fremont wanted to continue his mission once they got more supplies and mounts. The men he sent floundered around, and it took them three weeks to get here. I gathered food and supplies and set off to find Fremont. Fremont and what was left of his men just sat up there starving the whole time. We found them and brought them here." Carson leaned back in his chair. Charley and I just waited for him to continue. "Before we got there, some of his men decided to try and get back here on their own. They're still scattered out there. Nobody knows where. I have men out looking for them but don't know if they can be found after all this time. I'd go out myself, but we've got this job with Major Beall starting next week."

Then Carson leaned forward. "Before you go home, do you two want to meet Fremont? He's in one of the back bedrooms, still recuperating. He's been eating me out of house and home."

"Sure," I said. "I'd like to take the measure of a man like that."

Charley nodded his agreement. We walked out into the courtyard, and Carson knocked on a closed door.

"Enter."

We crowded into the small bedroom. It was too hot because of the too-big fire going in the corner fireplace.

"Major Fremont, I would like to introduce you to two of the best Indian fighters and guides in these parts. This is Charles Autobees and his brother Tom Tobin."

Fremont got up from the bed and shook our hands. "Happy to meet you, Charles, and Tom, is it? How is it that brothers don't have the same last name?"

"Same ma, different pa," Charley answered. "You look to be mostly fit for being out so long, Major."

"Well, thank you, Charles. I'm feeling much better than a few days ago. Mrs. Carson's a great cook, and I'm afraid I've been eating more than my share."

"Not so, sir. We just want you to get back to full strength as soon as possible." Carson reassured him but gave us a knowing glance.

Fremont reached out his hand again. "Well, it's been nice to meet you boys. If I ever need some handy scouts and guides and Mr. Carson is not available, I'll know where to look." We were dismissed.

On the ride home, I looked over at Charley. "You be willing to scout for that cocky bastard?"

"Not damn likely. You?"

"No way in hell."

Nothing else was said all the way home. We were completely comfortable with each other without having to talk, and it was common for us to be together all day long without saying a word.

A few days later, Charley and I returned to Taos, and at dawn on 1 February, we joined Kit Carson and reported to Major Beall. He introduced us to his junior officers, one was in charge of a company of dragoons, and the other a detachment of infantry from Company G. They had two disassembled mountain howitzers loaded onto mules. Lt. Pleasanton joined us at Raton Pass with another company of dragoons. The total force, including Charley, me, Carson, and all the soldiers, numbered about a hundred men.

We made a seventeen-day journey over Raton Pass, down the Purgatory River, and from there to Bent's Fort. The major hoped to disguise the true purpose of the mission by taking this leisurely course. I doubted the Kiowa would be fooled but said nothing. The longer Beall took, the more I would be paid. Before we got to Bent's, Charley's old friend Tom Fitzpatrick rode out to greet Beall. It was the first time I had met Fitzpatrick. He was thick in the body, slightly taller than me. His dark hair covered his ears, and his dark mustache was trimmed neatly. He had a narrow nose and eyes close together, but he seemed to be looking beyond the person he was talking to, searching the horizon for danger. Beall and he spoke while both were still mounted. Carson, Charley, and I were close enough to overhear them.

"Hello, Major, I'm glad to see you made it here safely." Fitzpatrick leaned out to shake the major's hand and nodded at Carson and Charley.

"Thank you, Mr. Fitzpatrick," said Beall. "As you probably know, Colonel Washington received your letter and commanded me to come here and free the Mexicans held by the Kiowa."

"Yes, sir, I am aware of your orders," Fitzpatrick said. "However, you should know that there are somewhere between two and three thousand warriors in and around Bent's. The Kiowa got wind of you coming and figured out the reason for your visit. There are big bands of Arapaho, Cheyenne, Comanche, and Apache all camped in the vicinity, and the Kiowa have managed to recruit all of them as allies. It is my considered opinion that if you try to take their Mexican slaves by force, your command will be wiped out. I strongly recommend you give me the time to negotiate a treaty with these tribes. We need to give them something in exchange for the release of the Mexicans they hold. They trust me. Let's not get them on the war path."

I looked first at Charley, then at Carson. "That's one hell of a lot of Injuns."

Carson put a finger to his lips, telling us to keep quiet.

I had been right in my thinking that the Kiowa would not be fooled by the major's attempt to disguise what he was doing. Carson, Charley, and I moved our mounts closer to make sure we heard everything Fitzpatrick had to say.

"Are you joshing me, Mr. Fitzpatrick? You want me to ignore my orders and retreat from the field without even an attempt to accomplish my mission?"

"No, sir. I'm asking you to give diplomacy a chance to work. My goal is to save you from a course of action that will, most assuredly, result in the death of most of your men and the death of enough Injuns to put the survivors and all their kin that ain't here now on the war path for a long time. That will cost the lives of a lot of folks."

"I'm not happy giving in to these heathens, Mr. Fitzpatrick. However, I will seriously consider your suggestion. We'll make camp here. I suggest you go back and bring all the traders at Bent's out here. I'll gather all my officers, and you can make your arguments again to all of us. I'll abide by the majority decision. Is that fair?"

"Sounds good to me. I see Kit Carson, Autobees, and Tom Tobin are all with you. Who else with Injun fighting experience you got?"

"Mr. Estes and Mr. Owens are the other scouts."

"Yes, sir, I know all of them. They're good men. I suggest you include them in the powwow. They know the Injun way of thinking. I'll go get the men from Bent's and be back here in a few hours."

"We'll be here."

We made camp nearby, where a creek supplied water and there was grass enough, although brown and shriveled, for the animals to graze. The soldiers put up their tents and started fires to make coffee and cook food. The major's tent was put up in the middle of the campground. Although it was February, the sun was out, and there was no snow on the ground. Fitzpatrick arrived in mid-afternoon with several traders from the fort. He made an even more impassioned plea for restraint and the opportunity to negotiate with the Kiowa. All of us scouts voiced our agreement with him. Fitzpatrick's argument and our support convinced Major Beall's officers, and they added their votes for Fitzpatrick's plan.

Major Beall conducted the meeting while sitting in his camp chair in front of his tent. All the other participants were either seated on the ground or standing in a semicircle in front of him. He allowed everyone to speak but said very little himself. After everyone had his chance to voice an opinion, Beall got up from his chair and paced back and forth in front of us, hands clasped behind his back. After almost five minutes of pacing, he stopped and faced us.

"Gentlemen, this galls me. I have never before failed to carry out my orders, and my orders are quite clear. I am to retrieve those Mexican citizens held by the Kiowa. Mr. Fitzpatrick, I will give you the opportunity to negotiate the release of those captives, but you must make it clear that if it is not accomplished, I will return with more troops and take them by force of arms. That is a promise you need to make to these savages. I'll give you a month."

"That may not be time enough, Major. I'll have to communicate with St. Louis to guarantee the promises I make to them. That could take at least three months."

"I will allow three months, no longer. Mr. Carson, we will decamp first thing in the morning. I will rely on you and your men to get us back to Taos by the most direct route. Gentlemen, I have to think about how I'm going to report this capitulation to my superiors. Dismissed."

We were back in Taos in three days. I thought we were done working for the army for a while, but the major was told that a Ute chief by the name of Montoya and some warriors had stolen some cattle from a place near the Rio Colorado. He assigned Lt. Whittlesey, with sixty-seven dragoons, a mountain howitzer, and me, Charley, Antonne Leroux, and Asa Estes, all of us still officially employed as scouts by the army, to capture the cattle thieves. Carson convinced the major he wasn't needed. The whole company rode army horses while two army mules carried the disassembled howitzer. Because of a late start, we stopped for the first night at the ruins of Turley's mill. Charley and I went home to spend the night with our wives and children.

The next morning as Charley and I rejoined the soldiers, a courier arrived from Taos. We heard him tell Lt. Whittlesey that Montoya was in Rio Colorado. The lieutenant detached Leroux, Estes, and seven troopers to ride ahead and capture Montoya. The scouts and the troopers arrested him and brought him back to where we were camped. Whittlesey sent Leroux and Estes back to Taos with the prisoner. When they arrived in Taos, Major Beall ordered Montoya thrown into jail.

Sometime later I learned Montoya didn't know the army was after him. He claimed that a different band of Utes, not the one to which he belonged, were hunting buffalo on the plains of Eastern Colorado. Those Utes had run into a large band of Arapaho, their historic enemies, and the Arapaho had beaten them badly. They escaped but lost most of their belongings and all the meat they had acquired on the hunt. They were starving, so they sneaked into a herd near Rio Colorado, slaughtered a few cattle for food, and ran off with a few head. Montoya tried to explain that he had nothing to do with the theft and promised that his people would pay for the cattle.

I think Major Beall was still smarting from his failure to chastise the Kiowa. He was in no mood to listen to anything the captured Injun had to say. A few days later, Montoya escaped but was recaptured by Captain Valdez of the Mexican Volunteers stationed in Taos. The Mexican Volunteers oversaw the jail, and Montoya's escape embarrassed the captain. The Ute chief tried to escape again two days later, but according to the captain's report, he was 'riddled with bullets and killed.'

Charley and I were still in Rio Colorado. While there, we circulated among the people, trying to learn from where the cattle were taken and if anyone knew which direction they had gone. One day, late in the afternoon, I happened to see Felipe Espinosa coming out of a store with another man. I hailed him, and we shared an abrazo.

"Felipe, you have not aged a bit since I last saw you. How long has it been?"

"Tomas, I can't say. A long time, and much has happened since. Let me introduce you to my brother—this is Vivian. We are on our way home after a successful winter hunt. We just stopped here to buy some sugar for our mother."

There was no doubt he and Vivian were related; they looked so much alike. We spent a few moments talking about our families and laughed that we had both married women named Maria.

"What are you doing here, Tomas?" Felipe asked.

"Apparently, some Utes stole some cattle. The owner wants them back and has enough pull with those in charge of things to make something happen. I think they were just hungry, but my brother and I got roped into helping to look for them."

Felipe said, "We saw a small group, probably Utes, herding maybe six head. I think they were going to go around the butte to the south and into the San Luis. This time of year, there is usually an encampment of Utes west of El Cerro de Olla."

"They didn't seem to be in a rush," added Vivian.

"Yes, I know the place. Thank you. This is helpful information," I said.

Felipe cleared his throat, then seemed to be trying to make up his mind about saying something. He thought about what he wanted to say for some minutes. I waited.

"I know you, Tomas. I know that you and your brother are good men and have made yourselves a part of our Mexican way of living. However, most of the gringos we come in contact with are crude and disrespectful of us and especially of the Catholic Church. The rebellion was put down with overwhelming force, and we have very few rights now."

"I know this, Felipe, but you must be careful about who hears you say these things."

I watched as they mounted their horses and rode off, leading their pack horse. Felipe turned in his saddle and gave me a wave. I waved back, thinking that he sounded very bitter about what was happening between all the Americans who were crowding into the country and their attitude and treatment of the Mexicans who had lived there for generations.

Early the next morning, Charley and I led the troopers up into the spruce and pine forests covering the slopes of Ute Butte. We left them resting in the forest and climbed on foot to the high, snow-covered top of the mountain. From the summit, we could see the Rio Grande flowing through a deep canyon along the western flank of the mountain.

"There," I said pointing to the southwest. "Still plenty of deer and elk here. I wonder why them Injuns had to steal them cattle."

"I see 'em," said Charley. "They're headed toward Kettle Mountain."

We returned to the troops and led them into the Rio Grande canyon.

"We're gonna have to travel about two, maybe three miles upstream," Charley explained to Whittlesey. "There's an animal trail and a place we can get across."

Charley and I rode ahead, found the trail, and led the troops down to the river. It was running high and fast with early melt. We crossed one at a time, first me, then Charley, then the lieutenant, and finally his men through cold water that reached above the bellies of the horses. The first mule carrying parts of the howitzer balked. The soldiers finally induced him to cross, but the animal still had to swim a short distance with his heavy load. The second mule absolutely refused to get into the water, repeatedly rearing back when forced to the edge of the roaring river.

"Smart mule," I remarked. "Load's too heavy for him to swim."

"Reckon," Charley muttered.

Whittlesey, standing nearby, overheard the exchange between us. "Sergeant Johnson, take two men and unload that first mule. Go back across with it and unload the second mule. Then distribute the load between the two of them. If that doesn't work, let the first mule take it across in a couple of trips. Get that weapon across."

"Yes, sir. We'll catch up quick as we can, sir."

"Let's move out then," Whittlesey ordered. "The rest of you with me."

He pointed for Charley and me to go ahead, then spurred his horse and set off at a fast trot with twenty-three troopers following. We rode hard for ten miles across the country still covered with melting snow and mud. It was hard going for the horses.

Near the base of Kettle Mountain, we pulled up and waited for the troopers to catch up. I pointed to a grove of pinion trees about a half mile away.

"That's their camp, and they've seen us. Looks like five of them are coming to powwow, Lieutenant."

"All right, Tobin." The lieutenant squinted hard. "I see them now. We'll wait here and see what they want."

Five Injuns—at least three of them looked like they knew how to fight— rode up. The oldest looked over the small party of troopers with a sneer on his face. He spoke in Spanish.

"Why are you here?"

"Wants to know why we're here," I interpreted.

"Tell him we are here to fight."

"My chief says to tell you he is here to fight."

"Good," the warrior growled, looking hard at Whittlesey. He uttered a few words to the four with him. They turned and pounded on their horses' sides with their heels, and the animals ran back toward the camp.

"Give them a fair head start," Whittlesey ordered. "Tobin, you're supposed to be a crack shot. Can you get one of them before they get too far?"

"If that's what you want."

"Do it. Troopers, deploy as skirmishers and charge after Mr. Tobin fires!" Whittlesey shouted. "Use your carbines when within range, then continue with pistols and sabers. Mr. Akerman, you sound the charge on my signal."

I dismounted, handed my reins to Charley, checked my Hawken, aimed, and fired. One of the Utes jerked to his left, almost knocked from his horse. The man riding next to him pushed him back upright, then grabbed his horse's rein to lead him into the trees.

Lt. Whittlesey waved his sword over his head, spurring his mount. The bugler sounded the charge, and the spread-out troops followed their leader. I jumped back on my horse. I reloaded my Hawken while my horse was at full gallop, holding my reins with my teeth. As ordered, the soldiers fired their carbines when they saw a target in range. Charley held his fire.

"Tom!" he shouted. "The trees in back of the Injuns!"

I saw what he had seen. Many more warriors were hiding in the trees. "Lieutenant!" I shouted. "Warriors in the trees! Maybe fifty or more!"

Whittlesey looked around wildly, finally realizing he was leading his men into a trap. "Bugler!" he shouted.

The bugler's horse reared up, came down hard, bucked, and ran straight into the waiting Utes. The soldier was hit with several arrows and musket balls. He was dead before he hit the ground.

Whittlesey swung his horse to the right, stood in his stirrups, and screamed at his men, pointing with his sword. "Right flank! Right flank!"

The troopers urged their mounts up the steep slope, but it was covered in deep snow. The exhausted horses lunged and jumped but were soon bogged down.

"Dismount. Dismount," Whittlesey croaked. "Take cover in the trees."

Charley and I were already looking for cover from which to make a stand. I thought the whole thing was one hell of a mess. The Utes knew we were following them and were ready for us. It was stupid not to think of that earlier.

"Follow the scouts! Follow—" Whittlesey's voice gave out. His mouth was open, his lips moving, but there was no sound.

Charley and I took refuge behind the trunks of three fallen trees. One trooper probably didn't hear the order for the flanking movement. He didn't follow until he noticed his mates heading away from him. He turned to follow, but it was too late. Six Injuns on horseback surrounded him. He swung his saber but was dragged off his horse and killed with knives and tomahawks.

The lieutenant and eight troopers joined me and Charley in our little fort. Other troopers found whatever shelter the trees provided. Charley and I took turns firing our rifles and reloading. We couldn't tell if we wounded or killed anyone.

Lt. Whittlesey took a handful of snow in his mouth to soothe his throat and found his voice again. During a lull, he shouted instructions to his troops.

"Follow the lead of the scouts. Pair up. One fires while the other reloads. Don't fire without a good target."

I wondered if he wasn't quite as stupid as I thought him to be. It seemed he was relying on us to know what to do. If we killed enough of these warriors maybe the rest would decide we weren't important enough to die for and leave.

The Utes were outgunned; we were outmanned. We could see that most of the warriors were armed with bows and arrows. Only a few had inaccurate smooth-bore muskets. Our soldiers all had rifled carbines, muzzle-loading pistols for close work, and sabers. I could see at least five Utes down and not moving. There were, no doubt, several wounded. Two more of our soldiers were killed. The two forces held each other at bay for about twenty minutes before the Utes withdrew, riding off to the southwest. They took their wounded with them, along with two of their dead. They did not risk trying to get the dead warriors who were within the range of Charley's and my rifles.

Whittlesey realized our horses were too exhausted to give chase, so he ordered the men to set up camp. Sgt. Johnson and his two men, the mules, and the howitzer finally arrived while the troopers were rummaging through the Ute camp for anything that might be useful. They hadn't unsaddled their horses. The troopers filled in the newcomers about the fight while Charley and I scouted the surrounding forest, making certain we were alone.

Suddenly Charley stopped, crouched, and raised his hand. I immediately crouched and scuttled close. Charley stretched his arm to the north.

"See there?" Charley pointed to a bit of dust rising from the ground. "Dozen or more of 'em headed this away. I reckon they were planning to join up with those we run off," he whispered. "We best get back and tell the lieutenant."

We hustled to where our soldiers were waiting and told Whittlesey about the group of Injuns headed toward us.

"Do they know we're here?" He asked.

"Don't think so," I said. "But they might. Can't tell."

Whittlesey ordered his men to mount up and follow single file as we led them along the edge of the trees, doing our best to get close to the Injuns before being discovered. The Utes were on guard. They spotted us, turned their horses, and hurried back the way they had come. The ground was level and well-drained. It provided good footing for the horses, so the lieutenant gave the order to charge. A running fight took place until the already tired army horses gave out. My horse started to weave, then to stumble, and I quickly pulled him up and dismounted. Whittlesey ordered a halt, and we all watched as the Utes disappeared north.

The exhausted horses and men slowly returned to the abandoned Ute camp. The horses were finally unsaddled, groomed, and fed a ration of grain. My horse was slightly lame, so I led him over to the small stream than ran along the side of the camp and stood him in the cold water.

Charley came over and squatted on the bank. "You hurt?"

"Naw."

"You kill any, do you reckon?"

"Don't know. Maybe winged some. You?"

"Think I killed one for certain. That animal gonna be all right come morning?"

I slowly walked around the horse, squeezing to find any painful places on its legs under the water. "I reckon. Nothing seems too swelled up or sore."

The following morning, we broke camp and moved toward home. We traveled slowly, resting the horses often. That evening, the troops set up camp at Arroyo Hondo. Charley and I slept in our own beds.

A few days later, Charley and I were sitting at the table in my house talking about what to plant at our Pueblo farm in the coming full spring when he changed the subject. "I heard that Whittlesey told Beall that they'd killed ten of the enemy; and from the blood on the snow, he reckoned many more must have been wounded, but their comrades carried them off. He also said he captured two women and the son of one of their chiefs but let them go."

"That so?" I asked. "You see any captured women, any prisoners? I sure didn't."

"Nope, me neither. Maybe we're just not observant enough."

"Maybe so." I smiled. "Do you think all soldiers lie like that?"

"Just the ones I've been around," mumbled Charley.

"You suppose he was after a medal for that mess we were caught in?"

"Don't know, but I'll bet anything he never said shit about what you and I did. And neither he nor the major have any idea they managed to piss off the entire Ute nation."

"I'm sure that's true," I said. "Good thing neither you nor I give a shit about medals."

Chapter 17
Felipe

In the summer of 1855, we were camped in the San Luis Valley near the Rio Grande, about eighty miles north of El Rito. Papa sent Jesus, the fourteen-year-old son of Diego de Arguello, one of the original settlers of El Rito, to Vivian and me with a written message.

"My sons," the note read, "come as fast as you can to El Rito with all your animals. We have big trouble, and we need you here."

We questioned Jesus, but he did not know what the emergency was. We left that same day and four days later arrived in El Rito, where our father explained the problem.

"Two weeks ago," he said, "we had a visit from Federal Marshal Richard Dallam from Taos. He told us that we may no longer harvest the trees or use our pueblo's common lands for any purpose. He says the United States Government owns our lands, except for the irrigated fields here in the valley. The United States Government does not recognize our title to the common lands."

"How is that possible, Papa? We have the testimonio. Did you show it to him?" I was incredulous.

"Yes, of course, he does not understand more than a few words of Spanish. He accepted the testimonio with one finger and his thumb as though it was filth from the outhouse. Then he said, 'This paper is worthless; the writing is smeared, and it is torn. The court will not recognize this as a legal document'."

"What do we do?" I asked. "The testimonio has always been our document of proof that the pueblo has title to our common lands. That is the way it has always been. What did he say when you told him that, Papa?"

Papa looked dejected, his shoulders slumped, a frown on his face. "He said there is nothing he can do. That we should hire a lawyer, and then we can go to court and maybe establish our claim. The courts of the United States are fair, he said, and we will get an honest hearing."

"Did you find a lawyer?" Vivian asked.

"Ignacio de Leon and I went to Abiquiu, but there is no lawyer there with experience in these matters. Then we went to Taos and found a lawyer who has experience with the gringo courts, but he has so many cases he would not take ours unless we gave him five hundred dollars first."

As he told us this, Papa's shoulders slumped even more, his face slackened, and I saw tears in his eyes. He wiped them with the back of his hand.

I felt my face flush with anger, and a sour taste filled my mouth. "Five hundred dollars just to take the case? What was he going to do for five hundred dollars?" I asked. I was becoming more and more angry with every minute.

"That was for only his word that he would investigate our case to see if he would accept it. If he agreed to represent us, that would be an additional cost, depending on how much time he would work on the case. I am old before my time, Felipe. I have not the energy to make this fight. That is why I sent for you and Vivian." Tears rolled down both cheeks, but he ignored them.

I believe that was the first and only time I ever saw Papa cry. Even when our sister was raped, he did not cry; he got angry and resolute. "I understand, Papa. Vivian and I will take care of it. This fight will cost much money, it seems. I will leave Maria Secundina and the baby here with you. Vivian and I will take all the sheep to Santa Fe. The market is bigger there, and we will get a better price for them. We will also sell the mules and the casita on wheels. We will leave tomorrow, but tonight we will ride to Santa Dolores and talk to Padre Martinez. Perhaps he will have an idea."

That same evening, Vivian and I sat at the table in the padre's house, drinking coffee. I explained the problem.

"Yes, I have heard of these happenings," the padre told us. "The gringos do not understand the concept of communal lands. They are taking all such lands away from the people. There are many gringo land speculators. They bribe the officials, who then sell the land to the speculators for practically nothing. Many are getting rich from this thievery. A favorite trick is to make some excuse that the testimonio is not legal. They say it is too dirty, too torn, too unclear, too smudged because too many people have handled it."

"That's exactly what they told Papa," said Vivian.

The padre continued. "They make any excuse. The first thing you must do is take the testimonio to the governor's office in Santa Fe. We will pray that someone there can find the original expediente. Then you must pay the clerk to make a certified copy of it. Take both the testimonio and the certified copy with you to the lawyer named Licenciado Ramon Vigil in Taos. This man has studied the laws of the gringos, and he is one of us. Tell him I sent you to him. Getting a clear title to your lands will be difficult, but I think he will help you."

"There is only the forest and the pasture, Padre. Why should our lands be so valuable to the gringos?" Vivian asked.

"Who knows? Perhaps they think there is gold or silver, or more likely they just want it because they are able to take it. This is exactly what I warned you about years ago. These men do not believe in God, or his laws, or the church as God's instrument. This is why we fought them, but they were too strong for us. They are Godless and evil, but we are now under their rule, and more and more of them arrive all the time. They invaded our country to expand their own. They are everywhere, and they have the army to force their laws on us."

Until that moment, Vivian had asked all the questions I had in my mind. Now I could no longer remain quiet. "Is it impossible to fight so many, Padre? Maybe there should be another revolution."

"I am afraid the time for fighting with guns has passed, my son. You must try to fight them in their courts, with their own laws. You know of the Treaty of Guadalupe Hidalgo?"

"Yes, of course. It says that all the property belonging to Mexicans should be respected and that we own the lands we were given and worked so hard to develop. How can they ignore the agreement they made with us when the war ended?"

"Indeed, but they do. You must ask these questions of Licenciado Vigil."

That same night, Vivian and I rode back to El Rito. My head was swirling with angry thoughts. I could not believe we were so helpless and such victims of the gringos and their greed.

The next morning, Vivian and I moved our flock toward Santa Fe. Once there, we sold everything except our saddle horses and the dogs. Then we learned it would take two days for the clerk to make a copy of the expediente. We paid him the twenty dollars he said it would cost and two days later went in search of Licenciado Vigil. The lawyer's office was in the front room of a large house that stood at the northeast corner of the main plaza. The man who greeted us when we knocked on the door was short, rotund, with a small round head and a welcoming smile. He was dressed in a black frock, dark wool pants, clean white shirt, and polished boots. He smoothed his sparse hair over his bald pate with his hand. "Sit, sit yourselves, Señores. Our friend Padre Martinez sent me a message that you would come to see me. How is the padre?"

"He is well, Señor," I replied, handing the lawyer a packet of documents including the notice from the marshal, the worn testimonio, and the new copy of the expediente.

The lawyer took a pair of round spectacles from the breast pocket of his coat, adjusted them over each ear, and perused the documents. Vivian and I sat patiently, waiting.

The lawyer finally looked up. "If we were still part of Mexico, there would be no problem. These papers give your pueblo clear title to your farmlands in the valley, as well as the common lands under both Spanish and Mexican law. However, we are now part of the United States of America and must obey their laws. A law passed in California gave Mexican landowners until 1853 to file a claim with a land board or lose the rights to their grant. Here in New Mexico, we have managed to extend this deadline until the end of this year. You have come to me just in time. I will make all the necessary arrangements. I will need these documents you brought me. I also need to gather testimony from all those men who were present when the lands were first marked out if they are still alive. We will have to hire official surveyors and have the land properly surveyed. That will cost a substantial amount of money. The lack of a legal survey is going to be a problem for us. I can file immediately with the land board and deliver to them all the necessary documents as they are completed."

"You do not sound very optimistic," I observed.

"I am not." The lawyer looked at us over his spectacles. "This process is going to be very expensive, and you may lose everything, even if we have all the proper documents. These gringos seem to be able to twist the laws to their own purpose. You have to expect this. I am being very honest with you. Do you understand?"

I looked directly into Vivian's eyes, and he said, "Yes, Señor, we do."

Then I said, "We have sold almost everything our family has of value to begin this fight for what is already ours. The other compadres of our pueblo have very little, but they are also willing to sell everything to keep our lands. How much will this cost?"

"I will need two hundred dollars to put together all the necessary documents and application to the land board. The survey will probably cost between one hundred and three hundred dollars. It will depend upon how difficult the country is and how long it takes. The surveyors will not start until they are paid half of the estimated cost and will not give us the required documents until they are paid in full."

"We need to give you how much today?" Vivian asked.

"If you give me three hundred dollars today, I will get started immediately. Do you have that much?"

"Yes, but not much more than that," I answered. "We did not get as much for our sheep as we thought they were worth, and the market for horses and mules is also down. Do you think this fight will cost us more than five hundred dollars? We are poor people. Five hundred dollars is a fortune to us."

"It is possible. The land board rarely rules in favor of those who believe they own their communal lands. The gringo laws do not allow a whole community to hold property unless the community is legally a corporation or business. It is most likely that the land board will rule against us, and then we must appeal that decision to the federal district court. If the district court rules against us, we can still appeal to the U.S. Supreme Court, but that would cost several thousand dollars."

Again, I was flabbergasted at the cruelty of the gringos and their laws. "So it will cost us every centavo we can find, and the gringos will still steal our lands?"

"I will fight as hard as I can for you, but yes, that is the most probable outcome. You have a difficult decision to make. Do you want to talk this over, or go back to El Rito and explain to the entire pueblo what is likely to happen?"

I looked at Vivian. "What do you think?"

"Papa told us to take care of this. I think the pueblo will agree to what we decide. I think we must try to fight. We cannot just give up without a fight. The padre told us this would be difficult, and we discussed that with Papa before we came here. I think we should start today."

"I agree," I said. I carefully counted out three hundred dollars on the lawyer's desk. I looked at the sparse amount of coins remaining and shook my head. Licenciado Vigil stood and extended his hand to each of us.

"You are brave and determined young men. I applaud your courage, and I promise you I will do the very best I can for you. Check back with me in three months. I will know more then, and I will have arranged for the survey."

"Can we still use the land while this legal fight is taking place?" Vivian asked.

"I will not know about anything you might do if you do not tell me about it. If you tell me you are going to do something involving those lands, I have to tell you it is against the law. If you have anything to sell that might have been taken from those lands—firewood, or lumber, or anything of that nature—I suggest you do not sell it in Taos where the marshal of the district court is. La Canada or Santa Fe would be better. You understand what I'm saying?"

I looked at Vivian. His smile was as big as the one on my face.

"Yes, Señor, we do," I answered. "Thank you for helping us. We will return in three months to find out the progress."

Once we were outside, Vivian questioned me. "Did he just tell us we should get busy and harvest as much lumber as we can as fast as we can?"

"Yes, that is what he told us, but he told us not to get caught doing it."

"So we become thieves?"

"How is it possible to steal something that belongs to us? I do not accept that we will become thieves. The forest is ours."

Vivian and I worked hard and fast, felling trees and sawing up as much lumber as possible. We transported the planks to La Canada and sold them. Our hard labor during the three months after meeting with the lawyer netted less than four hundred dollars. Since we couldn't use our common lands for pasture, all our compadres agreed to sell most of our livestock. Those funds were earmarked for the court battle. Vivian and I went to the lawyer and gave him another three hundred dollars. He made the necessary arrangements with the surveyors, and they completed their work in three weeks. Papa and I accompanied them to show the property lines and corner markers we had paced off originally. I also kept them away from where Vivian and I were harvesting more lumber. Because of the rough terrain, the survey cost us an additional hundred dollars. It took another year, and as Licenciado Vigil predicted, the land board ruled against us. Our lawyer sent a copy of the written ruling to El Rito suggesting Vivian and I come to Taos, meet with him, and decide if we wanted to proceed. We made the trip to Taos.

"Has anything changed?" I asked when we arrived at Licenciado Vigil's office. "When we met with you the first time, you told us an appeal to the court was not likely to change anything."

"That is still true. However, recently the courts decided a case in California in favor of previous Mexican landowners, and I can cite that case in our argument. It will probably be at least a year before we get our day in court, and you may be able to profit from that. I have not heard anything about you or anyone else from El Rito being accused of taking anything from those lands illegally."

"That is true. Nobody has been arrested for stealing from us," Vivian replied.

"Good. I do not want to have to defend anyone for criminal activity."

"How much more will it cost to make this appeal?" I asked.

"I know this is very difficult for you, and I understand the financial burden, but it will cost at least another three hundred dollars. That's half what I would normally charge, and I will pay all the court costs from that amount."

I sighed, then counted out three hundred dollars onto the desk.

The Espinosa family as well as the El Rito pueblo was financially destitute. Papa helped Vivian and me cut down more trees and saw them into lumber to sell. Most of it went to La Canada. We hunted to supply meat for the pueblo, sometimes with Ignacio, but most of the time, the three of us went separately to cover more ground and find more animals to kill. The sons of our compadres hunted rabbits, squirrels, and other small animals. Almost every family kept chickens for eggs and food, but we had to tend our crops carefully to insure we had enough food to last through winter. Thankfully, our debt to Abiquiu had been paid off, so we no longer had to find that money each year.

In the early summer of 1858, all the men from El Rito went to the courthouse in Taos. We entered the single-room adobe house, ducking through the low door while removing our sombreros. Vivian and I walked in front of our father, with Estrella and Hermana at our heels. Spiderwebs hung from the low ceiling. As we entered the room, the men from El Rito swiped the webs from their faces. The room was forty feet long and fifteen feet wide. The bare earth floor was damp and cool. On the south wall were two small window spaces, each no more than two feet square. There was no glass. Frayed and dirty cotton cloth, held in place with nails into the window frames, covered the openings. At the far end of the room, there was a small nook reserved for the judge. There were planks covering the dirt floor in the judge's alcove. A rough wood table, one leg partially broken off and supported by some adobe bricks, separated the nook from the rest of the room. A straight-backed chair stood in the nook behind the table.

"These gringos don't seem to care about the impression their courtroom and laws make to their people. This is one sad-looking example of their power," I whispered to Vivian.

Arrayed across the width of the room were three rows of wood benches, their seats worn smooth. In front of the first bench, two beer barrels supported a thick wood plank that served as a desk for the official clerk of the court, the lawyers with their clerks, and an interpreter. The plank sagged under the weight of stacks of books and papers. Two crude chairs were set at either end of the plank. The district attorney, who represented the interests of the United States, leaned back in one of those chairs, his legs extended. Papa whispered that the man in the chair on the other end was Marsha Dallam. There were not enough seats for all the men and boys from El Rito. Those who pushed into the room too late to secure a seat leaned against the dirt wall or sat cross-legged on the floor.

Marshal Dallam turned in his chair to observe us. "No dogs in the courtroom. Take them mutts outside," he ordered.

Vivian and I stood up and walked to the door. The dogs followed us outside. I pointed to a spot away from the door. "Down, stay," I ordered.

Licenciado Vigil was at his place on the bench behind the plank. He stood when Vivian and I reentered and came around to stand in front of our father.

"Licenciado Vigil, this is our father, Pedro Espinosa." I shook the lawyer's hand as I introduced the two of them. "He is the leader of our pueblo."

The lawyer extended his hand to Papa. "I am very sorry to meet you under these circumstances, Señor Espinosa." He then leaned in to speak to us in a whisper. "Our case will be decided in our favor only if the court accepts the boundaries of your lands as originally established and then re-established by the survey we commissioned. I will call each of the men who were present when you established the boundaries and renewed them each year to testify. The judge and other officials do not understand Spanish, so everything will be conducted in English. That man there," he pointed at a man standing nearby, "is an interpreter. He understands both English and Spanish and will interpret everything that is said. However, when the men of your pueblo testify, they must speak slowly, distinctly, and pause frequently to give the interpreter time to translate. Will you explain this to all of them, Felipe?"

"Yes, of course."

My English was rudimentary, and I was thankful everything said in this room would be translated so all could follow what was happening.

A tall, gray-haired man in a black suit strode into the room. Marshal Dallam jumped to his feet and shouted, "All rise. The Federal District Court of Northern New Mexico is in session, the honorable Judge Beaubien presiding."

The interpreter translated in a loud voice, "The marshal says for everyone to stand up, the court is in session and his Excellency Judge Beaubien is in charge."

The judge told the clerk to read the petition. When he finished, the judge told Vigil to proceed with his arguments. Vigil called each of the remaining nine original settlers of El Rito to the stand, one at a time. When Papa took the stand, Vigil asked him about the tenth member of the original pueblo. Papa explained that Vincente Romero had abandoned his family, and his whereabouts were unknown. Vigil led each of the men through a description, in their own words, of how they came to be part of the original settlement, what their understanding of the agreement was, and how the original parceling of the land and marking of the property lines had come about. Each man carefully paused after each sentence as the interpreter translated. The whole process took slightly more than four hours, during which time, the attorney for the United States waved away all opportunities to question the witnesses. Licenciado Vigil rested his case after pointing out the completeness of all the Mexican records and read aloud the wording of the Treaty of Guadalupe Hidalgo that explicitly verified the rights of all Mexican landowners to retain their property under the new laws of the United States. The interpreter translated his English arguments for the benefit of the petitioners.

At four in the afternoon, the district attorney unfolded slowly and got to his feet.

"Your Honor, this case is very simple. The original survey of this so-called communal land was nothing but a stroll around the acres the petitioners wanted. It does not meet any definition of a survey, nor does it meet the standard of Mexican land grants, even those few that were initiated by the mayor of a different community. The new survey simply followed the imaginary lines pointed out by the petitioners to those conducting the survey.

They could have taken the surveyors anywhere. Since there is no real survey, there can be no grant of land, communal or otherwise." He sat down.

"Mr. Vigil, do you have a rebuttal for that argument?" The judge asked.

"Certainly, Your Honor. I have included that argument in the petition and would like to reiterate. The Treaty of Guadalupe Hidalgo says—"

The judge interrupted. "Yes, yes, I am quite familiar with what the treaty says, Mr. Vigil, and I have read the arguments in your petition. Do you have any other, more compelling arguments to present?"

"I do not know what could be more compelling than the words dictated to Mexico by her conquerors, sir. The treaty clearly states that land owned by former citizens of Mexico will continue to be owned by those same people, now citizens of the United States."

The translator was unable to keep up with this and gave up trying. I turned to Papa. "I don't know what they are saying, Papa." At the same time, the men from our pueblo started asking each other what was happening.

The judge slammed his table with his gavel several times and shouted, "Quiet!" The translator had caught up.

"Enough, Mr. Vigil. You and your petitioners may not like it, but there is still a burden of proof that the land grant was legal, and previous use of the lands does not make it so. The laws governing title to land are reasonably clear, and our laws prevail. The petition is denied. The lands in question are part of the Public Domain of the United States of America and this court so rules."

With that, he banged his gavel, got up from his seat, and walked out of the room. The marshal quickly got to his feet and shouted, "All rise."

Vigil turned and motioned for us to stand up. We crowded around him to find out what happened. He shook his head, frowned, and continued stuffing papers into his carpetbag. "I am very sorry, amigos. The judge says we lose. The land is owned by the government."

"So, we have lost our land?" Vivian asked.

Vigil put a hand on Vivian's shoulder and squeezed lightly. His expression conveyed his sadness. "I am afraid so. I warned you this would be the likely outcome. I am so sorry, my friends. We can make an appeal to the higher courts, but they are in Washington, D.C. That would cost thousands of dollars, and we would most likely still lose."

I took a deep breath and sighed. "We understand. That's it then. Come, Papa. We lost our land. It is time to go home and decide what we can do."

Marshal Dallam walked up to our little group.

"Mr. Vigil, I don't talk Mexican—I just understand a few words. Will you translate something for your clients?"

"Of course, Marshal, what is it?"

"I have learned that your clients have been harvesting lumber from those forests and selling it in La Canada. I have ignored these transgressions, although I have ridden out myself and observed the sites from which they conducted this activity. I ignored the problem until now, but it cannot continue. Your clients can apply for a permit to cut timber, but there are fees for that. Tell them if they continue to harvest from those forests, they will be arrested and prosecuted," said Dallam.

Vigil translated.

Vivian grabbed the lawyer's arm. "What about the few animals we have left? Can we use the land for pasture?"

Now it was Vigil's turn to sigh. He turned his back to the marshal and spoke through clenched teeth. "If you get a permit to graze or cut wood you will be able to, but it will take time for the government to grant those permits and they will charge fees for each use you make of the land. I can ask the marshal about obtaining the necessary permits if you want. All the paperwork will be in English and probably difficult for you to understand, but I can help you with it."

"Never mind. We will not pay to use our own lands," I muttered, my own teeth clenched tightly. "Come, Papa, Vivian, we are done here."

As we walked out of the adobe hut, I heard Vigil and the marshal talking. Had he been in league with the gringos all along? I started adding in my head all the money we had given him.

In the street, I climbed up onto the driver's bench of the last unsold wagon belonging to the pueblo. The bed of the wagon was full of men from El Rito asking unanswerable questions of each other. I reached a hand down to help Papa up. He suddenly clutched at his chest and fell backward into the arms of Vivian. All of the men jumped to their feet.

I jumped down. "What is it, Papa? What is the matter?"

His voice was barely a whisper, and I leaned in close to hear. "I do not know. I have terrible pain in my chest, and my whole left side is numb."

Papa gasped as he slid through Vivian's arms to the ground. He jerked and stiffened.

Vivian bent over Papa. "He is not breathing, Felipe, do something! What is happening? Papa, Papa, can you hear me? Here, hold my hand."

I leaned over and put my ear to Papa's chest. "There is no heartbeat, Vivian. Papa is dead. This business was too much for him. The gringos have killed him the same as if they put a bullet in his heart. Come. Help me put him in the wagon. We must take him home and bury him. You ride to Santa Dolores and bring Padre Martinez."

I kept my voice calm but could not stop the tears streaming down my face. "Compadres," I told the men in the wagon, "our leader is dead. The gringos have stolen everything but the small plots of land we grow our crops on. It is not fair, but it is true. We have fought them in their court, but we lost, and there is nothing left for us to do. It is possible we can obtain permits from them to use our land as we did before, but they will charge us for that. I don't know how much, but it will probably be more than we can afford to pay. I am so sorry."

They all sat down heavily, overcome by the events of the day, and paralyzed by Papa's death.

It was impossible to support our extended family from the small plot of irrigated land in El Rito. We needed more farmland and to get back into the business of raising sheep that could be pastured on lands that were free for that use. We no longer had our little house on wheels, but both Vivian and I were accustomed to living rough. Perhaps with time, we could accumulate enough money to get another casita. In the fall of 1858, Vivian and I sold the property in El Rito to a dry land farmer from El Canada who had cash and wanted an irrigated property. He paid us five hundred dollars. After buying two wagons and additional tools for farming, we still had a few dollars from selling the El Rito property. We used those funds to purchase twenty ewes and one ram. Estrella and Hermana seemed embarrassed to oversee such a small flock.

We moved our mother, two sisters, our nephew Jose Vincente, and our youngest brother, Juan Antonio, to a property we purchased with a large mortgage, near San Rafael. San Rafael was a new settlement fifty-five miles northwest of Taos on the western side of the San Luis Valley along the Conejos River. The developers were selling larger tracts of farmland than the small plots of El Rito and offered long-term mortgages. We gave them two hundred dollars as a down payment and agreed to pay them two hundred a year for ten years for a hundred and fifty acres, professionally surveyed and staked off.

There was an earthen diversion dam in place, but we had to dig our own irrigation canals. Maria Secundina's parents, siblings, and several other relatives moved to San Rafael at the same time. Three other families from El Rito sold their lands to the same farmer and purchased property near us.

Chapter 18
Tom

Many settlers moved into the San Luis Valley in the 1850s. Juan de Jesus Bernal, my brother-in-law, moved his family thirty-eight miles north of Arroyo Hondo into the fertile valley formed by Costilla Creek flowing west from the Sangre de Cristo Mountains. The creek provides a dependable year-round supply of water for irrigation and household use. A year after Juan moved there, the town of La Costilla developed, and two Americans opened a general store so the people in that area no longer needed to make the long trip to Taos for supplies.

That same year of 1851, the Culebra Settlement was started nineteen miles north of La Costilla. Two years later, the village of San Acacio was started about four miles west of Culebra, and in 1854, thirty miles west of Culebra, the villages of Guadalupe, San Rafael, and Conejos were settled along the Conejos River.

Before all that settlement, only buffalo, elk, deer, Injuns, occasional trappers, hunters, and sheep herders roamed the valley. The farmers changed the landscape and made a problem for the Utes who considered the valley theirs. Young braves, anxious to prove something, made raids into the settlements, stealing livestock and occasionally fighting with settlers who tried to defend their property. As more and more people crowded in, staking their claims to a new land and a new future, the attacks came more often and got more deadly. The Taos Trail became a dangerous road unless the traveler was part of a large group.

In May of 1852, Major George Blake and his soldiers started constructing a fort to protect U.S. citizens. The site the army chose for Fort Massachusetts was just off the Taos Trail on the west side of Ute Creek, at the base of Blanca Peak.

Fort Massachusetts used the same picket construction common to forts in the frontier. Twelve-foot-high logs with pointed tips were buried vertically, two feet deep, next to each other. The logs were chinked with mud on the inside. The fort was two hundred seventy by three hundred twenty feet with two bastions across from each other that allowed a line of fire along each of the four walls. About thirty-five yards southwest of the fort was a corral with ten-foot-high pickets. It was almost as large as the fort itself and included horse stalls, feed storage, and tack rooms.

A long time before St. Vrain joined the Bent brothers in the construction of Bent's Fort, St. Vrain, and his partner applied for and obtained a huge Spanish land grant near the junction of the Arkansas and Huerfano rivers. The partners paid for a professional survey and made certain all the paperwork was legal and carefully done. After the Mexican-American War, the St. Vrain grant was one of the first to be recognized.

One evening in early January of 1857, Charley and I were sitting on the inside patio of Charley's Santa Dolores home catching the last bit of winter sunlight.

"Captain St. Vrain's after me to move to the Huerfano to farm," Charley announced. "Fort Massachusetts is mostly finished, and the Injuns will be gone soon enough. Reckon the country will be safe for families."

"He's been pestering me too. If he gets some folks there to farm and build a settlement it will make his claim more legal and further increase the value of the land. But since we sold the Puebla farm to our partners, our trading with the Arapaho and others in the spring and summer has given me enough to get by. My house here in Santa Dolores is comfortable, and Maria Pascuala's happy to be close to family. She's got the church across the plaza, and there is the new school for the children. Little Jose Narciso is older now, but he needs a lot of care. The twins are still babies. I don't reckon it's a good time for me to move. It's still dangerous for a young family even with the fort."

Charley nodded his understanding and changed the subject. "Will you still be able to send Mama money this year?"

"Yes. I put two hundred to her account with Magoffin's. You?"

"Yeah, I done a might better last year, put three hundred. Reckon she'll be all right?"

I chuckled. "Reckon she has more than me."

Charley decided to go ahead on his own. He hired six Mexican men from the village of Rio Colorado and traveled to the site he purchased on credit from St. Vrain, about two miles upstream of the junction of the Huerfano River with the Arkansas. It was rich, level land on both sides of the Huerfano. He planned to grow corn, wheat, and vegetables and use the abundant pasture to raise horses and mules. He told me that he expected a new stream of immigrants who would need replacement animals and food.

Charley and his men started making adobe bricks and building houses, forming a settlement that became known as Autobees Plaza. As soon as they had shelter, they built a diversion dam and dug irrigation ditches. They cleared, leveled, and plowed several hundred acres of land in time for spring planting. They planted most of the land with corn but used some acreage for beans, pumpkins, and chili peppers. They completed most of the hard work by late June, and their crops were growing fast.

The men took turns, two at a time, returning to Rio Colorado to bring back their families. Serafina and their children stayed in Rio Colorado while Charley worked at this new venture, but he lived in his new house with an Arapaho woman named Siccamo. When I learned he did this, I was surprised and a little disappointed with him, but I understood that he would feel unsettled without a woman. While the other settlers were bringing their families to Autobees Plaza, Charley built a small house not far from his larger house and installed Siccamo in the new casita. Only then did he come back to Rio Colorado to get his official family ready for the move.

I was visiting Charley when a man showed up and tried to convince Charley to go with him as a guide. He told us that he was a cousin of Edward F. Beale, the newly appointed Superintendent of Indian Affairs for California and that Beale was leading an exploration party to survey a central route to California. Senator Benton had convinced him to follow the same path that his son-in-law Fremont, the same idiot that Charley and I met at Kit Carson's home, had attempted in 1848–1849.

"Didn't he know Fremont's trip was a disaster?" Charley asked.

The man, whose name was Heap, told us he didn't know about Fremont's trip, but there were political considerations. "Benton probably ignored the result of Fremont's expedition because he wanted the railroad connecting the east coast to California to run through his state of Missouri. Beale was unable to find anyone who knew the entire route to California, so he settled on a man who claimed to know the route to Cochetopa Pass and from there to the Colorado River."

"I still don't know why you came to find me," said Charley. I could tell he was getting irritated.

"Please, Mr. Autobees, let me just tell you why I'm here."

Charley looked at me, and I said, "Might be an interesting story. I'm happy to listen."

Heap continued. "At the junction of the Gunnison and Colorado Rivers, we managed to lose most of our firearms and provisions trying to cross. Beale sent me back to Taos with several men. My instructions are to return with firearms, provisions, and a guide who knows the way to California and can safeguard us. I left my men in Taos and rode hard to look for you, Mr. Autobees. You were highly recommended."

"I'm not interested, Mr. Heap," said Charley. "I'm in the process of moving my family to my farm up north, but this is my brother, Tom Tobin. He knows the country as good as me. In fact, he is more than likely a better hunter, guide, and interpreter of Injun than me. He's the man you want to oversee the camp and keep you out of trouble."

"Well, Mr. Tobin, how long do you think it will take to get us to California?"

"That depends on how anxious Mr. Beale is to get there, and what problems we find along the way. I expect about six months, maybe a little more."

"I'm authorized to offer you eight hundred dollars to get us there."

I was surprised by the amount. It was enough to support my family for over a year. "I can't go with you unless you give me an advance to support my family," I explained. "And I have to tell you, I've never been to California. I don't know the road, but I can find someone in Taos who has made that journey. You willing to pay that person too? He won't come cheap."

"Yes, we will, but we also need your skills to get us there. With your help, we'll find a guide in Taos who knows the way. Would three hundred dollars in advance secure your service?"

We sealed the deal with a handshake and the exchange of dollars. The next morning, Heap and I rode to Taos. While Heap set out to buy the firearms, ammunition, provisions, and mules to pack everything back to the waiting expedition, I made the rounds of the local cantinas looking for Jose Gallegos. Gallegos had traveled the Old Spanish Trail with Kit Carson, and I knew he would be a reliable guide. I found him in a cantina drinking pulque, fermented cactus juice that, to me, looked like cow snot. He stood up as I came up, and we gave each other an abrazo.

"You sober, Jose? Been here drinking long?"

"Ah, Tomas, I've only been here for a few hours. Of course, I'm sober."

"Well, the new Superintendent of Indian Affairs for California was on his way there with several men, but they managed to dump most everything they had with them into the Colorado River, so they're stranded. I've been hired to get them to California, but I've never been there. I know you went with Carson. Do you remember the way?"

"Of course, I remember. It's horrible!"

"Well, if you're interested, I will take you to Señor Heap and introduce you. He pays well and seems to be a man of substance. He's a cousin of the new superintendent."

"What happened that they lost their belongings?"

"Seems they built a canoe from a big cottonwood but managed to turn it over on their last trip across with most of the arms and provisions in that load."

"That's poor planning on top of ignorance."

"Yes. Well, I guess that's why he hired me to prevent mistakes and in case we come upon unfriendly Injuns."

"Well, I would not go with these men if you were not along, Tomas."

We left Taos, and eight days later, we found Beale's camp in a shallow canyon cut through the rock by many years of flowing water. As we rode to the camp, I took in the surroundings. To the north and south were gradual slopes that rose from the river valley to flat, dried-out plains. A little grass and a lot of loose rocks, shaded from brown to gray depending on the angle of the sun, filled the plains. Closer there were big rocks, some big enough to hide an army. Beyond those, formations with sheer sides rose to high mesas. Scattered in the plain was a woody broom-like plant the Injuns used to brew a tea they claimed would cure most anything. I could see juniper and pinyon pines at the base and tops of the mesas. Sandstone walls showed layers of gray, brown, tan, vermilion, and green that changed color as the sun worked its way across the sky.

The men in the camp ran to greet us as we dismounted. There was a lot of hugging and sharing of what had happened while they were separated.

Heap introduced Jose and me to the group, Beale last.

"Pleased to meet you, sir." I shook Beale's hand. Then I squatted, picked up a twig, and put it in my mouth. "Did you know there're Injuns with eyes on your camp?"

Beale looked around quickly.

"Just keep looking at me," I told him.

Beale continued to glance over his shoulder. "Indians? Where?"

"Back on top of the mesa to the southwest a bit. They're probably Utes. Looks like they were about to make a move when we came in sight, so they pulled back. I reckon if we ride toward 'em, they'll be willing to powwow. My advice is we pick out the chiefs and be ready to shoot them first if they want to fight. Mr. Beale, you, Mr. Heap, and Jose should be out front with me. Can you and Mr. Heap kill an Injun ten yards away if you have to?"

"Yes, we can if we have to, Mr. Tobin. If you fire, we will as well," Beale replied, a determined look on his face.

"Good. That's our plan then. I see you both have the new revolving pistols. Seems a good enough weapon for close work. If it comes to a fight, you both fire your rifles and then ride straight at them and use your pistols."

I stood up, tightened the cinch on Jen's saddle, and checked both my Hawken and my single-shot pistol.

Beale told the men the plan. Then he told them to saddle their horses but leave everything except their weapons in the camp. After everyone was mounted, I touched Jen with my heels, and they all followed me; Jose behind and off to the side. I rode straight to where the Injuns were concealed, with my rifle ready, the muzzle pointed up, the butt resting against my right thigh. When we got close, I stopped Jen and called out in Ute.

"We come in peace. Do you speak Spanish?"

I counted twenty Ute Indians who came out to meet us, all riding well-cared-for ponies. I reckoned more of 'em were still hidden behind the hill. One of the Utes separated himself from the party and rode toward us. When he was about sixty feet away, I hollered. "That's far enough."

"I speak some Spanish," the war chief said.

"I think you speak more Spanish than I speak Ute," I answered. "We're not looking for a fight, but you can see we are well-armed. That musket you're carrying is not very accurate at a distance, and we all have rifles. If it comes to it, I will kill you first and my compadre will kill that chief behind you, the one with three eagle feathers and red war stripes on his face and neck. See the man I mean, Jose?"

"Yes, Señor Tomas, I see him."

"Well then, Chief, what do you think? Are you ready to die today?"

"You are the small man called Tomas Otobee. True?"

"I am."

"We have no reason to kill you, Señor Otobee. What are you doing on our lands?"

"We are just passing through, on our way to California. This hidalgo here is Señor Beale, the new Superintendent of Indian Affairs for California. I am here to make certain he arrives in California safely."

"It is good. There is no reason for a fight. Go in peace, Señor."

He turned his horse around and spoke to the other warriors as he passed through them. They all rode off to the southeast, the hidden ones following.

Beale rode up next to me. "That was very impressive, Mr. Tobin. What on earth did you say to him that caused that result?"

"He must have seen me at some time, but I don't remember him. He knew my name and, I guess, my reputation. I told him that he and the chief behind him would be the first to die. I guess he believed me."

Beale smiled and said, "Mr. Heap made a wise choice."

Everyone returned to the camp. Three of the men prepared a good meal using the provisions we had brought and a deer I shot the morning before we found the camp. The next morning, I got everything organized and we crossed the Colorado. Jose and I led the party to the Green River, Jen and I leading the way across the ford. We made camp that night on the opposite bank of the Green. The following day, Jose found the Old Spanish Trail he intended to follow all the way to California. He led us to the meadows of Vegas Santa Clara, where the animals rested, eating grass, and drinking from some of the many springs of clear, sparkling water. The next day, we crossed the Santa Clara River. After two more days of travel, we reached the Muddy River. Jose told me it was at least forty-five miles from this water to the next, with desert between. If we tried to do it in the daytime, we would probably lose some animals, maybe some men.

I found Mr. Beale stretched out in the grass and sat down next to him. "I reckon we should start this afternoon and travel through the night, Mr. Beale," I said.

"Why is that?" He asked.

"Jose says it's forty-five miles across the desert to the next water. We can't do it during the day. Either we start tonight or wait a day and go very early tomorrow night."

"Well then, let's not delay. We'll leave tonight. Will you inform the men, please?"

We left the Muddy around at dusk, and I pushed hard to arrive at Las Vegas mid-morning. We found the ample grass that gave the place its name. There was also a trickling stream of good water. I supplied the camp with fresh venison.

Our next stop was at Cottonwood Spring, where we found more good grass and water.

That evening Jose told me what was ahead of us. The next portion of the trail was the most difficult. There was little water even during the best times of the best year. The mules would be able to browse and sustain themselves, but the horses would have a difficult time. It was the middle of August, and the Mojave would be hotter and drier than anything any of these men had ever experienced.

"What do I tell them to do, Jose?" I asked.

"You tell Mr. Beale we need to leave way before sunrise tomorrow. We will go into the mountains, just past the summit of the pass." He pointed in the direction of the mountains to the west. "There we will find Mountain Spring. There should be some grass for the animals around the spring, and hopefully water as well. We need to leave very early the next morning to go down the mountain and into the desert. Escarbado Spring is only about twenty miles, but it will be the first taste of the desert. It will be very, very hot. Do you know the word escarbado?"

I had to think for a minute. "Means to dig, no?"

"Si, it is always dry this time of year, and we will have to dig down for water. If God wills it, we will find enough water for the animals. There will be no grass, and the horses will go hungry. Your mule and the pack mules will find only bushes."

Escarbado Spring was as Jose said. He showed me a spot in the dry wash that cut through the desert floor.

"This is the place to dig."

I picked four men to dig first. They tired fast, and I joined three other men digging. After we dug down almost six feet, a dusty brown liquid gradually filled the hole. After three or four animals drank, we had to wait about half an hour for the water to rise high enough for the next group of animals to drink. After seeing what the animals were drinking, the men drank sparingly from the canteens they had filled that morning before leaving Mountain Spring.

That evening, Jose told me what to expect next. "Tomorrow, we reach Resting Spring, about thirty miles from here. There will be good water, grass, firewood, and shade trees to rest from the sun. If we leave here early enough and move as fast as possible, we will be able to rest in the shade there during the most difficult time of the day."

The temperature dropped from well over a hundred degrees before the sun set to under seventy degrees before dawn. I pushed ahead hard, frequently having to go back and encourage one or more men who were lagging behind. It wasn't long before the sun heated the desert floor. Once it was hot, we moved more and more slowly until we finally reached the promised shade, water, and grass at Resting Spring.

Jose told me what we were going to face next. "The water of the Armargosa runs shallow and only ten feet across. It is bitter to the taste—that is why it has the name. Only very thirsty animals will drink it, but you must allow them to do so. The next water is about fifty miles southwest of that place, across the worst part of the desert. We must again travel all night and go as far as we can while it is cooler."

We left Resting Spring the next morning with full canteens and rode five miles to the Amargosa River. The water was worse than Jose had described. The mules absolutely refused to drink, and only three horses drank more than a swallow. As soon as the sun started to set, we left the Amargosa, traveling along the southern border of what Jose said was called Death Valley. We rode steadily all that night. Two hours after sunrise, the sun was a hot ball of fire in the sky, cooking man and beast. I was carrying my Hawken across my lap. The metal became hot enough to burn through my coarse canvas pants. The trail before us shimmered in the heat, ghost-like mirages forming and disappearing as we rode. Heat rose from the rocks and sand. A hot breeze formed dust devils that swirled around us until an evil wind from the west blew them away and battered us with fine sand. We covered our faces with pieces of cloth and squinted into the burning sand that engulfed us. Every now and again, Jen would bray to guide horses and pack mules to her as she followed the trail, head down.

It got worse. The dust storm lost force, but the heat got more intense. Three of the pack mules stopped and refused to take another step. I supervised as they were unloaded and distributed only the items I deemed essential to other animals. Even unloaded, and with Jen's encouragement, the three unburdened mules refused to go on.

"Just leave them," I instructed. "Everyone walk, leading your animal. Stay in line and call out if you fall. Whatever you do, keep your head covered. This sun will cook your brain if you don't."

We trudged on, concentrating on putting one foot in front of the other. I stepped over the sun-bleached bones of a man and looked back to see if anyone stumbled over them. They all stepped over them without seeming to recognize what they were.

Twenty hours later, we finally arrived at a place where more nasty water bubbled up from the ground. Jose said this place was called Amargosa Springs. Rather than a river, there was a narrow trickle of barely running water. Along the stream's bank were cattails and tamarisk trees. The trees had spikes instead of leaves and smelled like salt mixed with dust. The trickle of water flowed down the shallow arroyo about three hundred yards and ended in two small ponds. The blazing sun evaporated water from the ponds, and the water remaining in the ponds was even more disgusting than what came out of the spring. Our animals crowded and pushed all along the small stream, but those downstream had to wait for the ones that pushed themselves into a place upstream to drink their fill before the water got to them. After the more aggressive animals drank their fill of the lifesaving but evil-smelling and tasting liquid, there was very little flowing to reach their mates. The men scrambled farther upstream until they found the source, bitter but drinkable, rising painfully slow out of the parched earth.

We rested for only a few hours and started out again as the sun went down. Blessedly there was no wind, but the dust rose up from the feet of our animals, who dragged the tips of their hooves on the desert floor as they shuffled along. The trail was covered with dirt as fine as milled flour. The horses were in terrible condition, having eaten only a few handfuls of corn over the previous three days. The pack mules fared better, even though they carried heavier loads. I shrunk and lost probably twenty pounds from lack of water, the scant rations, and the hard physical activity. Jose guided us steadily to the southwest. After twenty-eight miles of physical and mental torture, Jen picked up her head, brayed, and broke into a trot.

"There's water ahead! Jen can smell it," I called over my shoulder.

Two miles further on, we came to the Mojave River, with fresh, clear water, grass on both banks and blessed shade trees to shelter us from the merciless sun. After resting for thirty-six hours, we set off again, following the Mojave River. We traveled leisurely and comfortably to the Barstow River. We crossed that river and rode fifty miles to the southwest, crossing over Cajon Pass. Then we descended into the valley of San Bernardino. We finally rode into Los Angeles late in August.

As we came over the last pass, we saw the town spread out in front of us. I counted at least a hundred houses and buildings. We were told that about eighteen hundred people lived in the town, the same size as Taos, although I believe a lot more people lived in the countryside around Taos than close to Los Angeles. It was sunny and hot, but folks were going about their business and didn't pay us much heed. Beale asked for directions to the government offices. We found the building and left him there. Jose and I went looking for a hotel and a bath.

We spent a few days exploring. After we collected our promised wages, Jose, and I, along with Juan Cordova, a muleteer hired by Heap in Taos, wandered south, following the coast. The rest of the men in the party elected to stay in Los Angeles and find work there. The three of us couldn't believe the sights and sounds of the Pacific Ocean crashing against the rocks of the coastline. We found San Diego, a small town of about seven hundred folks, and spent a few days there.

The trail we traveled to get home from San Diego was well-marked. Many had used it between Santa Fe and San Diego. We headed east from San Diego to the junction of the Colorado and Gila Rivers. We followed the Gila east to where it exited from its origin in the mountains. From there it was an easy cross-country ride to strike the Rio Grande River and turn north to Taos. I was back in Maria Pascuala's arms in mid-October. I had never seen California or the ocean, so as difficult as it was to cross that desert, I felt I'd been rewarded— while also earning a lot of money.

Two months later, I left home with several men from Santa Dolores for a winter buffalo hunt. Traveling north, we crossed over Sangre de Cristo Pass and followed the Huerfano River to Autobees Plaza, where more than fifty people then lived. Charley and several of his men joined the hunting party, bringing along additional pack animals. We went to an area of well-sheltered canyons along Carrizo Creek. Each winter, the wind, snow, and freezing temperatures drove the herds of buffalo south into those sheltered canyons. For generations, the Injuns had hunted buffalo there. The natives constructed rock walls extending at an angle from the sides of the canyons, leaving small openings where the ends of the rock walls and the canyon walls came together. They drove the buffalo down the canyon into these funnels where hunters hiding behind the rock wall killed the buffalo with arrows or spears as they passed. We made use of those same buffalo traps and were soon heading home, our pack animals loaded with enough meat for the entire winter, and with raw buffalo hides to make into robes and sell for cash.

The following spring, of 1858, I started trading again with the Cheyenne and Arapaho tribes on the plains north and east of Pueblo. My supply of alcohol wasn't as generous or as good as in the days of Turley's distillery, but other producers were doing their best to supply the demand. The tools and flour I was able to acquire in Taos and Santa Fe still brought good prices when carried to the native tribes east of the Rockies. I had the cash from the trip to California, and I did well. By that time, I owned twenty-five acres of land in Santa Dolores. My house was the original one given by my mother-in-law on the east side of the plaza, but it had been expanded to eight rooms around a central patio. The land went out from the back of the house and included an assortment of corrals and barns and two irrigated fields on which we raised vegetables and fruit trees.

After the harvest in 1858, I joined Charley on a long-planned hunting and fishing trip. His harvest had been better than expected, and he loaded a wagon with corn, flour, and beans to trade with the Arapaho. The wagon was so heavy it required three yokes of oxen to pull it. The party included three of his men from Autobees Plaza and the wives and children of two of the men. The third man was not married. Siccamo was also along for the holiday. We were underway for several hours when Charley spotted a small herd of antelope, and he and I rode out to shoot one for dinner.

Siccamo spotted several Ute Indians sitting on their horses on top of a small hill across the river. We were only a few hundred yards away from the wagon when she shouted, "Look across the river, Old Man!" She pointed at the Injuns.

Charley and I hustled back to the wagon. The single man took one look at the Injuns, spurred his horse, and galloped away, leaving the rest of us to our fate. A small horde of warriors, whooping and shrieking, galloped off the hill and splashed across the river. Charley crowded all the women and children into the wagon and hid them behind and between large sacks of corn. Siccamo grabbed a rifle and crowded under the wagon with me, Charley, and the other two men. We kept up a withering fire as the Utes circled the wagon. Charley received a wound high in the left arm, near the shoulder, and was no longer able to load his rifle. Siccamo crawled to him and loaded the rifles while he took aim and fired, resting the rifle on a spoke of a wheel. I was amazed that nobody else was injured except one of the children who was grazed by an arrow when he peeked out from behind his sack of corn. After only a few minutes, the Injuns decided the easy pickings were not so easy. I counted seven of the warriors dead and could see that their chief and several others suffered wounds. They gave up and rode off. Siccamo bandaged Charley's wound while the men and I were able to cut two dead oxen out of their harnesses. We turned the wagon around and headed back.

I turned to Charley, who seemed to be in pain. "Maybe you should be riding in the wagon with that wound."

"Naw, be just as painful. I'll be all right."

"I thought the Utes had moved west of here. What do you suppose caused them to be in this area, and why do you think they attacked us?"

"They're pissed about how many settlers are coming into lands they think is theirs. Just a few months ago they attacked the El Pueblo settlement, killed eleven men, and carried off a woman with her two kids. Other settlements have been attacked as well, but they've stayed away from Autobees Plaza."

I smiled. "No doubt because of your reputation. If any of them that we just drove off recognized you, I reckon they'll continue to leave you alone."

Charley scowled. "Maybe so. We'll see."

I understood how the Injuns felt about all the folks pushing them out, but it wasn't something I could do anything about. We sure couldn't let 'em kill folks or carry off women and children.

After leaving Charley at Autobees Plaza, I visited my brother-in-law in Costilla. I spent enough time there to decide it would be a good place to settle. I found a parcel of land for sale at a reasonable price, purchased the land, hired some men from the settlement, and sketched out plans for an adobe house, some storerooms, corrals, and stables. I marked off where I wanted the structures to be built, started the men at their tasks, and returned to Santa Dolores.

While I was busy with my new farm, Charley was making adobe bricks for Lt. Lloyd Beall, the commanding officer at Fort Massachusetts, who had received orders to start constructing a new fort to be called Fort Garland located on land between the Sangre de Cristo and Ute creeks on the trail leading to Sangre de Cristo Pass. The plan was to build the new fort out of adobe bricks, which were much better suited to the environment. Lt. Beall learned Charley had built Autobees Plaza, where all the buildings were made of adobe, so he contacted him, and they struck a deal.

Charley and his Mexican workers were on site making adobe bricks, but Charley got into an argument with one of his workers. They traded insults, then fists. The worker pulled a knife and jabbed at Charley. The knife went through Charley's left bicep and into his chest. They took Charley to Fort Massachusetts, where the army doctor told him he was unlikely to live more than a few minutes more. Charley reacted by drawing his pistol and threatening the doctor, who ran out of the room. Several men present managed to calm Charley down, and eventually, the doctor returned and bandaged the wound.

While Charley was in the hospital, he sent word asking me to come and finish the contract with the army. I arrived within days, and the construction resumed. During that time, I learned that Congress passed a land bounty act, and veterans of the Mexican War could petition for a hundred and sixty acres of land. Since I had served with St. Vrain, I figured I could get in on that. I knew exactly the property I wanted. It was located only two and a half miles southwest of the new fort and extended on either side of Trinchera Creek. It was level and fertile. Many acres of free range surrounded the place, and it was close enough to sell horses, produce, and cattle to the new fort. It was also close enough to discourage any Injun attacks.

In the middle of August, I went home to visit my family. I took the opportunity to ride to Taos to visit a lawyer, John Martin. I paid him to write a letter to the land grant office in Washington, D.C., explaining that I served with Captain St. Vrain's Volunteers during the revolution of 1847.

Shortly after I returned to the construction at the new fort, Charley, almost fully recovered from his wound, came back and took over. I went back to Costilla, helped finish the buildings there, and returned to Santa Dolores where

I packed up Maria Pascuala, my children, and my mother-in-law and moved to our new home in Costilla.

Although my application for the bounty land grant on the Trinchera was not yet approved, I decided to get started developing the site. I hired some workers and started clearing the land of brush and scrub trees, turning the hundred and sixty acres into pastures. I took a trip to Fort Massachusetts and met with John Francisco, who was the sutler for both that fort and the new one. We agreed on prices, and I had a reliable market for the products of my farms and ranches. I brought livestock to stock the ranch and, in the spring of 1859, workers to plow and plant the river valley of the Trinchera property with potatoes, squash, pumpkins, and hay. The fields of my Costilla property were also producing bumper crops.

That same spring, Maria Pascuala and I experienced another tragedy. Our son was born and christened Juan Nepomuceno Tobin when he was six days old. The infant died a few days after that. I returned to the Trinchera ranch to bury my sadness at work.

The army commissioned Fort Garland that same year. The troops and their new commander, Captain Thomas Duncan, left Fort Massachusetts and marched the six miles to the new fort. I supplied the fort with horses and hay and, in the fall, sold Francisco potatoes and several varieties of squash.

During the next year, I divided my time between the Trinchera ranch and my Costilla farm. In July of 1859, my lawyer sent word that the government had approved my land warrant, and the Trinchera ranch was legally mine. I continued to provide the fort with livestock and farm products. In September of 1860, Pascuala gave birth to a daughter christened Maria Sarafina. I called her Sarah, after my mother.

While the Civil War raged in the east, life in the San Luis Valley and on the plains east of the Sangre de Cristo Mountains was almost idyllic. My agricultural enterprises flourished, as did Charley's. The army was a stable and good-paying market for our livestock and farm produce. Both of us lived comfortable, secure lives and continued to send Mama money at least twice a year. We received word that Catherine had married and now had two children. Her husband owned a dry goods store, and she and their children were well taken care of.

Chapter 19
Felipe

Late in 1862, life was not going well for us. Vivian and I were now responsible for supporting ten immediate family members, plus my wife's family, who were as needy as ever. In 1858, my wife gave birth to a son named Domingo. In the summer of 1862, our Maria Manuela was born. Vivian had also married and started a family. We had made thousands of adobe bricks and expanded the house until it contained five small rooms plus the original jacal. I built a two-room house nearby for my in-laws, but I was now living with our mother, two sisters, my youngest brother Jose Vincente, as well as my wife Secundina, and our three children, all in only five rooms. Vivian and his pregnant wife occupied the original jacal.

For two years, rain was sparse, and despite irrigating the fields, the hot days and nights resulted in poor harvests. Our flock of sheep suffered from a disease we had never dealt with before, and we lost many of them. We had not been able to accumulate enough funds to build a casita or purchase a wagon to put it on. It seemed to require every coin we could earn just to feed our family. The coming year was looking more and more difficult.

On the first night of 1863, Vivian and I were camped next to a small stream where we and the dogs were caring for only a hundred ewes, worth about a dollar each. The cold penetrated into our bones. We were each wrapped in a buffalo robe over worn wool blankets. We huddled on either side of a small fire, where a pot of beans cooked for our dinner. Estrella was dozing while leaning against my back. Vivian absentmindedly petted Hermana.

I broke the silence. "Vivian, I am troubled, worried. If we have another year of drought and poor harvest, our family will starve. All of our neighbors in the settlement are in the same situation. When we were in El Rito, we had our common lands and were able to sustain ourselves. I don't know what to do. Do you have any ideas?"

"No, my brother, I do not, and I share your worries. I will soon have a baby to worry about as well. There must be something we can do. The gringos are to blame for this situation. They stole our common lands and turned us into paupers."

I thought about those common lands…The time when Vivian and I encountered the Apache warriors trying to steal our horses. The joyous meal we shared with the men of the pueblo after they responded to our signal for help. The beauty of sheep and cattle devouring the early spring grass. The sound and smell when Vivian and I were sawing planks from the trees we had cut down. Was Vivian thinking of those things as well?

"Do you remember the smell of the sawdust when we were sawing logs into planks, Vivian?"

He inhaled deeply. "Yes, I still remember that smell. Why do you ask me that?"

"I was just remembering some of the good times we shared on the common lands."

Vivian lifted his hand from Hermana's head and rubbed the back of his neck. "That's odd—I was also thinking about those lands, but not about good things—about the time we lost them, and Papa died." We sat quietly for maybe half an hour, each absorbed in our own thoughts. I could not stop thinking about how the gringos had stolen so much from us. Gradually an idea forced its way into my consciousness.

"Listen, Vivian, we cannot continue like this. There are too many mouths to feed and never enough food. The gringos have stolen from us, and we are now barely able to support our families. I think it is time for us to steal from the gringos."

"I am of accord, my brother. Our thoughts are almost always the same, but how can we do this? Despite what the padres, the church, and even the Brotherhood teach, you want us to become thieves?"

"I am as torn as you," I said. "But I have no other ideas about how to deal with these difficult times. Do you?"

"What is your plan, Felipe?"

"This is my idea. Jose Vincentes has over twenty years now. He can stay with the sheep. Estrella and Hermana know what to do and will take care of them. I think we should ride north and take what we can from the gringos—horses, sheep, cattle, whatever we find that is not guarded. It will be easy."

We again sat silent for several minutes as the flames of the campfire burned lower and lower. Vivian got to his feet, went to the pile of wood we had collected that afternoon, grabbed two long branches, placed the end of each on a stone, and stamped on them, breaking them until he had six lengths of firewood that he placed carefully on the fire. He stood watching until each of them caught fire.

"No, I have no other ideas for what to do. I am with you," he said.

Jose Vincentes took over caring for the sheep, and we embarked on our life of crime. We were able to take fifteen head of sheep that strayed from the main flock of a rancher northwest of Costilla. We drove the stolen sheep back to Jose Vincentes and added them to our flock. We found three horses in an unguarded corral and took them in the middle of the night. These we took to Conejos and sold, but we received less than half of what they were worth. I am certain the man who bought them suspected they were stolen. We continued these endeavors for another three weeks. But taking a horse now and then and selling it for less than it was worth was not helping our financial situation. Each time we returned home, we found our wives with worry creases in their foreheads; their mouths set in silent determination not to blame us for the children crying because there was not enough food. Spring came and went, and our families were still hungry and wearing tattered clothes. Each time we left, I found myself wanting not to return, not to have to deal with all the misery. I had to think of something more radical to do.

In the early summer of 1863, I introduced a new idea. "My brother, we are not doing well taking a few horses and sheep from the gringos. I have a different idea. I think we should go south to the Santa Fe Trail. There are many wagons full of good things going to and from Santa Fe. We will hide next to the road, and when a single wagon comes, we stop it, tie up the teamster, and take what we want. It will be easier than taking animals that we then have to find someone to buy from us. What do you think?"

"Anything would be better than what we are doing now," said Vivian. "I like this idea. If we are going to be thieves, we should steal things of real value, things we can use ourselves. Yes, I think this is a good plan."

We rode out from San Rafael through the country we had traveled for many years. We skirted all the settlements we came to, especially Santa Fe, and ended up on the well-defined Santa Fe Trail a few miles south of the town. We found a good place to hide and watch where the road southeast to Galisteo forked off. After we waited for less than an hour, a single wagon made its way toward us from Santa Fe and turned onto the Galisteo road. The wagon was piled high with cargo covered with a canvas tarp. The two mules pulling it were straining with the heavy wagon and its load.

"Isn't that the gringo teamster who is always in the cantinas of Abiquiu?" I asked.

"Yes, I think it is. Do you suppose he's drunk now?"

"I think he probably is, but we cannot take a chance that he will recognize us."

I took the bandanna from around my neck and pulled it over my nose. Vivian did the same. We had talked about doing this to prevent being recognized. I felt like a real bandit.

"Do you see anyone else on the road?" I asked Vivian.

He stood up and looked in all directions. "There is nothing, nobody in sight, and no dust rising for miles."

"Good, we go. Check your pistol. Ready?"

We mounted our horses and quickly caught up with the wagon. Altering my voice, I ordered the man down from the wagon. The teamster obeyed, staggering slightly when his feet hit the ground.

"He is drunk," Vivian murmured. "Sit down in the dirt, you drunken fool."

"What? What you want? I don't talk Mesican."

"Sit. Sit." Vivian waved his pistol and pointed to the ground. The teamster finally sat in the dust of the road, his legs extended in front of him. Vivian went around to his back and roughly jerked the man's arms up and placed his hands on top of his head. "Stay like that, you drunken fool. Hands on top of your head or I will shoot you."

The teamster looked around, then twisted his body to look at Vivian. "What? I told you I don't talk Mesican."

Vivian patted the top of his own head with his left hand and pretended to shoot the pistol in his right hand by shouting 'bam' and jerking the pistol upwards.

The teamster got the message. "All right, I understand. I'll keep my hands on my head."

I got into the bed of the wagon and threw off the tarp. We couldn't take the wagon with everything in it because we would have to stay on the roads. "Let's sort through all this and throw what we can use into the road. We'll take one of the mules and make a pack it can carry."

We sorted through the goods on the wagon, finding clothing, ribbon, thread and needles, cloth, some iron pots, and a box with four new revolvers and ammunition for them. There were also bags of corn flour, beans, and even some canned fruits.

"Look, here are bags of coffee and sugar. Let's take them also." As he spoke, Vivian continued to glance at the road in both directions, looking for dust rising from anyone coming toward us.

I quickly rigged a large pack for the mule, using the canvas that had covered the goods in the bed of the wagon and new rope that was part of the cargo. I balanced the pack over the back of the mule and tied it in place. "Now let's tie this drunken fool to the tongue of the wagon. He can help the mule pull it down the road while we ride away."

After we tied the teamster next to the remaining mule, we slapped the mule on the rear and got him moving, struggling to pull the wagon and the man down the road. Laughing, we mounted our horses, our saddlebags also burdened by loot, and led the loaded mule toward San Rafael.

We reached home with our bounty and celebrated our good fortune. Our wives and the children sorted through what we brought but asked no questions about where it came from. Jose Vincentes had returned home with the sheep— there was very little for them to eat because of the draught. The sheep were crowded into our largest corral and fed from our fast-dwindling supply of hay from last fall. We slaughtered a lamb, and our wives prepared a feast with some of what we took from the wagon. Vivian and I basked in the happiness of our family.

Two days later, I heard the approach of many horses. I peeked out of a window to see a squad of soldiers led by an officer and a man with a badge on his coat.

"This is not good, Vivian. You go out to find out what they want, and I will stay hidden inside with our guns loaded and ready."

They rode up to the house, and Vivian stepped outside.

The officer spoke in halting Spanish. "Are you Jose Espinosa?"

"I am known as Vivian, but yes, I am he."

The officer sat more upright in his saddle. "We are on a recruiting mission and want to know if you and your brother, Felipe, would like to join the army. We have heard that things are difficult for your family, and the army pays well. You would be able to purchase food and other goods from the army store at Fort Garland at reduced prices."

I moved closer to the window to hear what was being said, wondering how the officer knew our names.

Vivian answered the officer. "I might be willing to join, but only if my brother wants to as well. He is not here at this moment, but I will talk to him about it when he comes home. If you come back tomorrow morning, we will let you know what we decide."

The officer hesitated. I presumed he was considering his answer. "Well, it is a good opportunity for both you and your brother. We will return in the morning to talk to you."

Inside, Jose Vincente came up behind me and whispered, "Are you and Vivian going to join the gringo army?"

"Shush, they will hear you. Join us when Vivian and I discuss this after the soldiers leave. Be quiet and listen. You could learn something."

After the soldiers left, Vivian and I sat down and discussed the situation. "Why do you think they came looking for us, and why did the officer need all those men if they just want to recruit us into their army?" I asked.

"I think they know about what happened with the wagon," Vivian said. "The whole time that officer was talking, I watched the gringo sergeant. He was nervously looking all around as if he expected trouble. However, did you notice that all the other soldiers were Mexican? Maybe they are actually trying to recruit Mexicans."

"I don't think so, Vivian. Why would that man with the badge be with soldiers on a recruiting mission? I think they were here to arrest us both. That drunk might have recognized us and told them who robbed him."

"Then we should leave here now," said Vivian.

"No, then they would know we did something wrong. Maybe they are really trying to recruit Mexicans as soldiers. Let's prepare as though they did come to arrest us, though."

We cut an opening through the wall of the jacal into one of the rooms of the house. I told the family members what Vivian and I had decided. "If they are trying to trick us and arrest us, Jose, I want you and Secundina to pass us loaded guns through this opening. We will pass back guns for you to reload. Do you understand what you need to do?"

"I am very worried about this, Felipe," Secundina said. "Perhaps everyone except the four of us should be gone, visiting a neighbor."

"Yes, that is a good idea. We don't want anyone in the house hurt. Jose Vincente, do you understand what Vivian and I need from you and Secundina?"

"Yes, we will do as you say," Jose replied.

"Good, now we are going to hide our horses and everything else we might need out by the river in case we have to escape in a hurry. Jose, you get the roan horse and load him up with all our camping gear, then tie him up in the same place where we hide our horses."

The next morning, the detachment of soldiers and the marshal returned. Vivian again met them outside. I watched and listened, this time from the jacal.

The officer spoke. "Well, Vivian, what have you and Felipe decided? Will you join us? The army will pay twenty-five dollars to each of you when you sign the papers, and you will receive twenty dollars a month and food, uniforms, and a warm place to sleep. It is a good life, and you will be able to support your families."

I thought he had rehearsed the speech. He delivered it while looking around, perhaps hoping to spot me.

Vivian spoke up, looking past the officer at the marshal. "Why is the marshal with you if all you want to do is recruit my brother and me into your army?"

"Oh, he's just along because he knows most of you folks and where you live." The officer dismounted and walked slowly toward Vivian. "He's just showing us around. What have you decided?"

I suspected he was going to try and grab Vivian.

Vivian took a long step backward. "My brother and I have decided we do not want to be in your army."

The officer lunged at Vivian. "You are my prisoner."

"No, I am not." Vivian tore loose and ran into the jacal, where I was waiting with a revolver in each hand and two more tucked into my belt. I handed one of the revolvers to Vivian, and we both ran out the door and into the midst of the soldiers, firing. A Mexican corporal was hit, fell off his horse, and lay still. The rest of the soldiers, still mounted, scattered in all directions. The officer started to mount, but his horse shied and ran after the others, dragging him along, one hand on the pommel, the other on the cantle of the saddle, while he tried desperately to get his left foot into the stirrup and mount. Vivian and I ran into the thick underbrush of willows and cottonwoods along the banks of the Conejos River.

The marshal had his pistol out and was in close pursuit when his horse stepped on a fallen log. The log rolled, the horse stumbled, and the marshal pitched forward over the horse's head. He rolled over, and his right leg slammed into a tree trunk. I heard the long bone of his thigh break; it sounded almost like a gunshot.

Vivian and I were hiding in thick underbrush close enough to watch and listen to everything that happened next. The officer finally got his horse stopped, mounted, and gathered his troops, cursing loudly at their total ineptitude. The sergeant flinched but did not respond to the tongue-lashing he received for not keeping his troopers under control. They found the marshal and splinted his broken leg.

The officer spoke rapidly to the marshal, but not loud enough for me to hear or understand what he said. But the marshal grunted in a loud voice. "Take me to the fort, no doctor in Conejos." I smiled, able to translate what he said into Spanish.

The officer shouted something to the sergeant, who repeated the order to the Mexican soldiers in Spanish. "The lieutenant says to tether your horses, form into ranks, and follow me into the house. We are going to search for the stolen goods."

I shook my head. The drunken teamster must have recognized us. Maybe he was just acting drunk.

The sergeant stomped to the house, peered through the door and, in a loud voice, ordered Jose and my wife out into the yard while his soldiers searched for the stolen merchandise.

"Sergeant!" the officer shouted. "Do you have the list of what was stolen from the teamster?"

The sergeant reached into a coat pocket, pulled out a piece of paper, and waved it at the officer. Soon all that we had stolen was piled in the yard. All we had left for our efforts were the four revolvers we had in our hands, the ammunition, and what we had eaten the night before. Following the officer's commands, the sergeant told the men to take one of our two wagons and load the stolen goods into it. Then they took two mattresses from the house and made a bed in our other wagon for the marshal. They wrapped the dead corporal with a threadbare blanket, also taken from the house, and put him in the first wagon with our loot. While all this was happening Vivian, and I did our best to stay quiet. Jose and my wife stood leaning against the house, stricken looks on their faces.

I whispered to Vivian, "If they make a move to take or injure Jose or Secundina, we will charge them, firing our pistols." He nodded.

The officer was on his horse, muttering to himself. The horse pranced a bit, and he got the animal under control, pressing his knees inward and pulling back on the reins. He sat quietly, then raised his voice and shouted, "This is just not right! Those thieving bastards can't get away with this." He then gave the sergeant more orders. The sergeant ordered the troopers to strip the house of everything. They put everything we had in the wagon with the corporal—every bit of bedding, food, pots, pans, clothing, all were taken from us.

Vivian grabbed my arm and whispered into my ear, "We need to stop them. They are going to leave our family completely destitute."

"No. That's what that officer wants. He doesn't know we are hiding and watching but suspects that we are. We won't be able to surprise them as we did before."

Vivian and I watched from our hiding place in horror as the soldiers brought our crude furniture out to the yard and smashed it. Everything else of any value was finally loaded into the wagon with the dead man.

"What's that damn noise over there?" The officer shouted.

"The corral is full of sheep, sir."

The officer thought for just a minute or two and gave another order.

"Now he wants us to kill all the sheep," the sergeant explained in a loud voice. "He wants the Espinosas to regret killing the corporal and stealing from the Americans. He doesn't like sheep—says they smell bad."

The sergeant marched his squad over to the corral and ordered them to fire into the flock. Estrella and Hermana ran to protect their charges, snarling and barking at the soldiers.

"Shoot those damn dogs," the officer ordered, pulling his own pistol.

The sergeant shot Estrella, then Hermana. I started to push out through the brush with the revolver in my right hand.

Vivian grabbed my arm and held me back. "There are too many of them, Felipe. You are right—they will not scatter and run as they did when we surprised them earlier. We might kill some of them, but they will kill us. Then what will our family do?"

I responded through clenched teeth. "You are right, but the gringos will pay for this."

As the dogs bled out, they looked back at Jose, wondering what they had done wrong. Jose stood barefoot in two inches of dust, horrified, his mouth open in a silent scream, tears trailing through the dust on his face.

Vivian and I wiped away our own tears but remained silently hidden. My heart was pounding in my ears. I dug my fingernails hard into my palms to stop me from rushing out with both pistols spitting lead.

The troops were finally ordered to mount up, and the officer led them away slowly. As soon as they were out of sight, Vivian and I came out of hiding. Both Secundina and Jose were weeping. I picked up Estrella. Her head and shoulders hung down on one side of my arms, her rear legs over the other side. She wasn't dead long enough to stiffen.

"You both stop crying! Crying won't solve anything. We are going to bury the dogs. They did nothing to deserve this fate," I told them, my teeth clenched.

Secundina stopped crying and ran to face me. She grabbed my arm, and I almost dropped Estrella. She was angrier than I had ever seen her. "What will we do to live?" She shouted. "We have no food, no clothing, no furniture. What am I supposed to feed the children? How can we cook without pots and pans? You and Vivian have brought disaster on us."

"Be quiet, calm yourself. Vivian and I will fix this. We will provide for the family, but all of you must be patient and give us time. There is plenty of meat in the corral. Go to the neighbors and tell them to come quickly to gut and skin the dead sheep. They can take the meat and fleece. Tell them the soldiers killed the sheep and took everything. They don't have to know why the soldiers came. Tell them that Vivian and I will return and have gifts for them if they take care of all of you until then. We will leave you our camping pot to cook in and the neighbors will have more things to let you use until we return."

As I spoke, I allowed the rage within to take over. I could feel my face flush, and I clenched my hands as I squeezed the dead dog in my arms. Vivian picked up Hermana and followed me to the back of the corral. "Jose," I called out, "please bring some flat pieces of wood from the furniture. We will use them to dig graves for the dogs." As the three of us dug, I kept thinking, *I hate them. I hate all the gringos. I will have revenge on them. They will not escape me.* Then I took Vivian's arm to stop his digging. "We will go out, find solitary gringos, kill them, and take everything of value. If you don't go with me, I will go alone."

"I am with you, Felipe," answered Vivian. "We will get even with these gringos who treat us as if we are dirt. They cannot continue to take from us."

Jose stopped digging and said, "I want to go with you. I will help you kill gringos."

"No, Jose, you must be the man here and do your best to take care of the women and children. It is a great responsibility. Vivian and I must be able to depend on you to do this, or we cannot go. Do you understand?"

Jose hung his head and dragged the big toe of his right foot through the dust. "Yes, I understand. I will take care of them, but I would rather be with you."

"Thank you. You are a good man. More brother than nephew."

After we finished burying our dogs and started butchering the dead sheep, we sent Jose and Secundina to tell the neighbors about the dead sheep. Soon they started arriving to help with the butchering and to take their share. It was cold enough for the meat to keep when hung outside. The neighbors responded with what they could, but they were as poor as we were. They supplied one cooking pot, an old iron skillet, six blankets, thin from long use, and small quantities of corn, wheat, and beans. One neighbor told Secundina she was welcome to come to her house and use her grinding rock to grind corn for tortillas.

Early the next morning, Vivian and I decided that the family, with the neighbors' help, could survive until we returned. We told the family what we planned to do and promised to return as soon as possible. Then we mounted our horses and headed north, leading the packhorse. We took a wide berth around Fort Garland. We talked about the possibility of lying in wait to kill soldiers but decided they would rarely ride out alone and even if they did, other than their arms, they would have little of value to us. We crossed over Sangre de Cristo Pass and turned north again, riding nearly forty miles, and we found an old Indian trail that took us into the mountains, where we made camp.

On the morning of 16 March, we rode downstream. After a few miles, we spotted a small sawmill in a gulch. We dismounted and hid our horses in a thick grove of trees. Hiding behind trees and brush, we slowly made our way closer, then hid behind some rocks to watch. The sawmill was not operating, but a man made his way from the mill to a nearby log cabin and disappeared inside. We watched as he left the cabin and climbed to a small meadow where his horse was grazing. We mounted and rode into the meadow, where the man waited to greet us. Vivian pulled out one of his revolvers and shot him through the heart.

"We must make it look as though the Indians did this," I said. I dismounted, took my knife, scalped him, and then carved a large cross on his chest while I spoke in a loud voice. "This is the sign that we do this for the Mother Mary, to whom we pray for forgiveness. This gringo was an enemy of the church. We are justified in killing all enemies of the church. It is also vengeance for our papa who the gringos caused to die of a broken heart, and our dogs who were innocent of any wrongdoing." Then I went through his pockets and took all his coins.

We ransacked the small log cabin, taking blankets and cooking utensils, but the sawmill produced nothing else of value to us. We took the man's horse and rode to the Arkansas River where we broke through ice at both edges to cross. Shivering from the near-freezing water that soaked our feet and legs up to our knees, we rode north, hugging the base of the mountains, until we reached Red Creek. In a nearby meadow, we found a small herd of unattended cattle grazing. We roped one of the steers, cut its throat, and butchered it, but only took away about fifty pounds of meat, leaving the rest to rot. Following Red Creek upstream, we rode until dark, then camped and roasted some of the meat.

With the extra blankets we took from the cabin at the sawmill, we each had enough blankets under our folded buffalo robes to keep us warm. The next morning, I took Vivian's shoulder as he was starting to gather things. "Brother, I think we should rest here today and let the horses graze and rest. We may need them to be fresh soon. Perhaps the gringo has been found and they are tracking us."

"I have been watching," Vivian replied. "I saw no sign of anyone following us, but you are right, Felipe. The horses should be ready to run if we must."

The following morning, we ate the last of the roasted beef, then traveled north for ten miles to a canyon about thirty-five miles northeast of Canyon City. As we rode slowly along the top of the canyon, we spotted another sawmill. We hid our horses in a stand of trees and worked our way to the edge of the canyon, finding a vantage point that allowed us to spy on what was happening below.

While we watched, two men worked on the mill, chinking with mud, while a third man shingled the roof of the cabin. Late in the afternoon the man came down from the roof and hung a blanket over the door opening of the cabin. Smoke from the metal chimney of a wood stove curled up into the cloudless sky. The other two lay down their tools, washed up in the creek, dried their hands on their shirttails, and walked to the cabin.

Vivian and I crept closer to hear what was being said. One of the men picked up a rifle, handed a pistol to the other man, and shouted something into the cabin. The man inside answered them. They turned and walked down a trail next to the running water. Shortly after they were out of sight, the man in the cabin came out with an axe and started splitting firewood logs. We approached the cabin. The man, seeing we were not Indians, waited in front of the cabin, the axe in his hand, no doubt wondering who we were and what we wanted.

When we were only a few feet away, he greeted us. "Howdy."

I was holding my pistol down at my side where the man couldn't see it. Enough time had passed, and the two other men had been walking fast, so I thought a gunshot would probably go unnoticed. Without saying a word, I raised the revolver and shot him in the head. He fell over backward, stiff as a felled tree, dead before his head touched the ground.

"We must make it look like Indians again," said Vivian. He picked up the axe, raised it high above his head, and brought it down with sufficient force to split the dead man's head from the top of his skull all the way to his mouth.

I stabbed the corpse on the left side of the chest with my hunting knife, wiped the knife off on my right thigh, and replaced it in its sheath. "Let's move fast and see if these gringos have anything of value. The other two may have heard the gunshot and started back."

I searched the dead man's pockets and found some coins and paper money. We ransacked the cabin, emptying every suitcase, every box, and every bag we found. I found a small leather pouch which contained more money. I stuffed it under my belt. We took everything that seemed to be of value, but again the pickings were small. We found some canned food, bags of wheat and corn flour, a crock containing sourdough starter, a pair of gold-rimmed spectacles, a gold watch and chain, a satin vest with embroidered flowers on the front, and a daybook with 'McPherson' stamped in gold leaf on the leather binding.

With our pack horse carrying the additional stolen items, we made our way into the foothills and made camp next to a small stream well hidden in a grove of trees. We ate our fill of some of the food we took from the cabin and rolled up in our bedrolls to sleep.

Vivian raised up onto his left elbow to face me. "Did you feel any remorse when you killed that gringo today?"

"Remorse? No more than I did when you killed the first one. I only think about Papa and all they have taken from us. We are doing our duty for the glory of the church and Mother Mary. Why should I have remorse? Do you feel remorse?"

"A little today. What I did was brutal, but maybe they will blame it on the natives. No, you are right. We are doing the Lord's work. These gringos stole from us, and we are making the score even. I have no remorse, my brother. Goodnight."

Three days later, we rode into Denver, where we were not known. We split up and each took some of the plunder to sell for whatever we could get for it. I went into a store where the owner was Mexican. He was interested in the gold watch and chain and traded it for a supply of beans and cans of meat and fruit. I spotted a copy of a newspaper with the name *Verdad*. It had articles in both English and Spanish. A headline grabbed my attention: "Owners of two sawmills murdered." I picked up the paper and saw another small stack of newspapers titled *El Mercurio de Nueve York*. All the articles in this one were in Spanish, including another article about the sawmill murders, with the name of the author, Daniel Cosa. I took a copy of that paper as well.

"How does this man from New York know about sawmill murders way out here?" I asked the owner.

"Ah, he is a correspondent who lives here in Denver and writes articles for the paper in New York. He sends the articles to them by telegraph. Amazing, no?"

"Yes, remarkable. I would like to buy and take these with me to read about these murders. Do they know who did it? Was it the same for both?"

"You can read about it. They think maybe Indians did it."

Vivian and I left Denver and camped not far away. We each took a newspaper and took turns describing the articles about the murders.

"Listen to this, Vivian. It says the first man we killed was fifty-eight-year-old Franklin Bruce. He was a farmer and millwright who lived with his wife and four children on a farm only a few miles downstream of the mill." I couldn't help but feel some sadness for the wife and children but then thought about our family and transferred the sadness to them. "The first paragraph is a graphic description of what had been done to the man." I didn't need to read that to Vivian. "Then it says he married a childless widow in 1839 in Vermont. Shortly after their marriage, they moved to Indiana, then to Michigan, then to Illinois, and from there to Wisconsin. Each move was a new attempt to scrape a living from the land. Two years after moving to Wisconsin, the couple's second daughter was born, giving the family two boys and two girls. Shortly after settling in Wisconsin, he built a sawmill, and the family prospered. In 1860, a flood demolished his sawmill, but Bruce was able to salvage most of his machinery. He learned of a wagon train forming to go to the gold fields in Colorado, loaded his family, and with what remained of his sawmill, headed west."

I looked at Vivian. "Does reading about these men and their families change anything for you?"

"Some, but not much. My article makes it clear he had almost as much grief as we do, but nothing was stolen from him by the government as they did to us. This article from *Verdad* is long enough to be a short story. 'Bruce joined a wagon train of eleven wagons. His family made friends with two other families, and they all decided to stop for winter in Canyon City.' They make these gringos sound like heroes! Then it goes on to talk about how the families went to different places. Bruce went to California Gulch but decided being a miner wasn't for him. He took his family and started looking for farmland, found a place on Hardscrabble Creek, and with the help of his sons, built a house, cleared the fields, built a diversion dam, and dug an irrigation ditch for the fields. When that was done, he found a location upstream where the water flowed strong enough, even in the dry months, to turn a water wheel."

"There was also that pine forest nearby," I added.

"Yes, I remember that. Well, the article says he built his mill that fall and winter and waited for the spring thaw to power the mill. He was a hard worker. I'll give him that. The paper says that Murdock McPherson and Henry Harkens, Bruce's companions on the trip west, also tried their hands at gold mining, but found it 'hard work for little reward.' They decided mining camps were not decent places for their families. McPherson and Harkens recruited two other men to join them as partners to build and operate a sawmill. The two that we saw walking away, McPherson and Bassett, returned just before dark and discovered Harkens where we left him. They thought he had been killed by Indians and ran back to where they had just visited the Priests' farm."

I considered saying something to Vivian but noticed he was concentrating on the article. I had seen that look on his face many times when we were studying; he wanted to commit every word to his memory. I said nothing, wanting him to continue.

"All of them spent a sleepless night with guns loaded expecting to be attacked by Indians. Listen to this, it's almost poetic: 'The three men, and sixteen-year-old Henry, watched as the sun gradually rose east of the Priests' cabin. Shadows from the tall pines gradually shortened as daylight illuminated the recently plowed fields, pastures, and nearby groves of trees. There was no sign of Indians."

"This article is also very dramatic," I said. "Listen to this. 'Mr. Priest jogged to the corral, where three horses looked up as he approached. He was furtively twisting to see in all directions. He grabbed the halter of the nearest horse and put on the bridle and saddle he had snatched from the shed attached to the corral. Then he led the horse out of the corral, mounted the horse, and galloped off to the southwest to the Smith ranch. Within an hour, he returned with Smith and four of his ranch hands'."

Both of us were pleased with the reactions to the trouble we had caused. We were getting even with the gringos. I continued reading from my article. "It says that Smith sent men to other places to bring help, and by noon there were twenty-five men gathered at the sawmill. They looked for tracks of Indians but couldn't find anything. They dug a grave and buried Harkens. I looked up to see that Vivian was listening carefully. Uh, oh. Listen to this, Vivian. 'The sheriff of Canyon City and his deputy rode up to find out what happened. The men told them what they had found, and the sheriff explained they were tracking two men who had killed Franklin Bruce at his sawmill. The tracks had led them to this spot. They didn't think the perpetrators were Indians'." I scratched an itch behind my left ear.

"It goes on to say that McPherson asked if they knew who the murderers were, but the sheriff said they did not. Then they asked the sheriff if he wanted a posse, but he told them he and his deputy had enough supplies for the two of them for a week. If they formed a posse, they would have to go back for supplies, and the trail would get cold. He told them he and his deputy could cover more ground and be quieter than a big posse. He said the two of them could deal with the two killers when they caught up with them."

"The sheriff and his deputy are after us. This next part is important for us, we need to know everything about them. The article says, 'During this exchange, the sheriff's deputy, named Alfredo, the half-breed son of a mountain man father and Apache mother who inherited his mother's looks and temperament, remained silent. Alfredo's father abandoned them when he was four. He and his mother lived with her tribe until he was thirteen when his mother took Alfredo to Canon City. The sheriff hired the boy's mother as a housekeeper and nurse for his wife, who was slowly dying from tuberculosis. He treated the boy like a family member. Alfredo is now in his early twenties. He is taciturn but an extremely competent hunter and tracker, skills learned while with his mother's tribe. The sheriff relies on him and trusts him. They found the tracks of the perpetrators and followed them north toward Colorado City, but before reaching that settlement, the tracks turned west toward Ute Pass. At the beginning of the pass, Alfredo lost the trail where the tracks mixed with those of a hundred or more animals. The sheriff and his deputy returned to Canyon City'."

"I'm certainly glad those two didn't catch up with us," Vivian said. "We don't need a sheriff and his half-breed adopted son chasing us."

I nodded my agreement. That night we slept peacefully, not really worried about being found.

The following morning, after entering Ute Pass, we doubled back to the entrance and left the trail, obliterating our tracks for several hundred yards. Then we rode west until we found an old Indian trail that took us to Four Mile Creek. After reaching the creek, we followed it downstream until we reached a small gulch protected by rock bluffs on the north and west sides. The southern end was open, allowing the sun to warm the area. The bluffs protected our campsite from the prevailing winds. In the bottom of the gulch, a bubbling spring watered several thickets of willows and cattails that provided seclusion. There were also several clumps of wild grapevines growing close to the spring, hence its name, Grape Springs. Away from the spring, spread out along the bottom of the gulch, were several small meadows with good grass for the horses.

After making camp, I told Vivian, "I think we should hide here for a week or longer until anyone looking for us gets tired. It will allow the horses to rest. It looks like many deer come to this spring to drink, and we can kill one or more for meat. We have plenty of corn and flour. Do you agree?"

"Yes, I am of accord. I do not know if anyone will be looking for us, but that sheriff and his deputy worry me. Maybe they are after us again. If so, it is a good idea to hide for a while."

A week later, Vivian and I hid our stolen goods among the trees in a willow thicket. We followed a trail heading northwest for forty miles without encountering any other travelers and eventually reached Snyder Creek. We followed the creek north, pushing through thick stands of trees and brush until we spotted a trail going through the mountains. On one of our hunting trips, many years previously, we had been to the top of Kenosha Pass but from the other side. We rode over the pass, then two miles down Kenosha Gulch and set up camp for the night.

A cold mist that was starting to form snow forced us to build a lean-to shelter. We built up a fire in front of the shelter and rested comfortably that night after eating a rabbit Vivian shot that afternoon. Our camp was a short distance northeast of the road going from Denver to Fairplay and only a mile or so away from a roadhouse known as Kenosha House.

We left our camp each morning and watched the road from various vantage points for several days. Late in the afternoon of 8 April, we spotted what appeared to be a heavily loaded wagon, its contents covered with a tarp. We decided the two men on the wagon were probably on their way to Denver.

"If they come from Fairplay," I observed, "and they are heavily armed, perhaps the wagon is full of gold."

"It's possible. Let's follow them."

A short time later, the men pulled off the road and set up camp in a gulch. They were only about two and a half miles northeast of Kenosha House. We watched as the two unhitched their horses, groomed them, led them to a small meadow, and hobbled them so they could graze but not wander off. We waited until they built a fire, cooked a pot of stew, rolled up in their bedrolls, and went to sleep. We crept up carefully until we were only a few feet from the sleeping men. I shot one of them in the chest while Vivian jumped on the other one and stabbed him in the chest three times. The man shook Vivian off, jumped to his feet, and ran four hundred yards down the gulch with us close behind. He finally collapsed and died. We left him where he fell and returned to the camp. The wagon contained only some broken parts from a mowing machine. We gathered up the dead men's rifles and pistols, took their camping gear and food, and returned to our own camp for the night.

"That was a lot of work for not much reward," said Vivian.

I agreed. "Well, we didn't get lucky—the wagon could have been loaded with gold, but it wasn't. It was worth a try."

The next day, we rode back over Kenosha Pass and turned south, and after thirty miles at a rapid pace, we crossed over Wilkerson Pass from west to east. Seven miles southeast of Wilkerson Pass, we found our next victim. It was dusk, and the place we found was isolated, no neighbors for many miles in any direction. We waited until it was dark, then rode up to the house, tied our horses to the front porch pillars, and crept inside, revolvers drawn. We found a man alone in the house, sound asleep. I prodded him awake with the muzzle of my revolver. "Get up, you gringo fool," I said in Spanish.

"What? What are you saying? What are you two doing in my house? What do you want?"

I used one of my few English words. "Outside." We marched him outside the house in his long johns and bare feet. Once off the porch, he tried to run, but we quickly caught him.

"Don't waste a bullet on him," I told Vivian. "We will slit his throat to make it look like Indians killed him."

We left the mutilated corpse in the dirt near the corral and ransacked the house, again taking everything useful or sellable. Some documents with a name on them we left on the floor. We rode off to the south that same night and arrived back at Grape Springs the following morning.

We remained hidden in our camp at Grape Springs for two weeks and decided to head back north to the same area where we had killed the two men with the wagon. We reached the road and turned our horses toward Fairplay. About three miles northwest of Fairplay was a place the gringos called Cottage Grove. On the evening of 2 May, a Saturday, we shot a man through the head and performed our usual butchery on his corpse. A couple of days later, we came across two men at Red Hills, northeast of Fairplay. The men were squatting on the ground, resting their horses. Vivian shot one of the men through the heart. I shot the other man in the wrist. The wounded man ran off, but Vivian and I quickly caught up to him on our horses. Vivian jumped off his horse and knocked the man to the ground. He held him down while I crushed his head with a rock.

We were both splattered with blood and brains. I felt powerful but possessed by some sort of demon, no longer able to control my rage at all gringos. I was becoming obsessed with killing every one of them we could find. Vivian was grinning, his pupils dilated, his eyes wandering aimlessly. "We are paying back the gringos. Getting vengeance, Verdad?"

I wiped off my face with the back of my left hand and stared at the transferred blood. Suddenly, I had to sit down.

Vivian asked, "Why are you sitting? Are you hurt?"

I blinked several times, then looked at Vivian's worried face. "Uh, no…Suddenly I feel very tired."

"Well, get up. We need to take everything these two had and get away from this place."

A week later, we struck again. We saw a man driving a wagon loaded with lumber on the road from Alma to Fairplay. Vivian and I were hiding alongside the road in a stand of trees and brush. As the wagon approached, I shot the driver in the chest with my rifle. The bullet knocked the man backward against the lumber. He fell sideways onto the seat and rolled down into the footwell. The driver got back up onto the seat and slapped the horses with the reins to go faster. Vivian was taking aim as I reloaded my rifle, but a load of lumber shielded the driver. We watched as he regained the seat and urged the horses forward.

As we rode back to our camp, Vivian complained. "That gringo has told everyone about us by now. We should have gone after him and killed him. I don't understand what happened. I know you shot him in the chest, and he was knocked down. How could he get back up and drive those horses away from us?"

"Who knows? Perhaps he turned to the side at the last moment, and I just grazed him. We were too close to the town—we wouldn't have caught him before he got there. All they know is that we are not gringos murdering their own. They can't know for certain if we are Mexican or Indian. Besides, we are a long way from that place now. We will go back to Grape Springs and wait for a couple of weeks until they get tired of hunting for us. Then we can go to a different place and kill some more of these gringos. You have not lost your taste for this, have you, Vivian? We are just making the score even."

"Yes, I know. I agree with what you say. We will be safe in our camp. They will forget about us in two or three weeks, and then we can kill more of them. However, maybe we should go home first. We have taken many things that will be useful for our family."

"Yes, it is true we have many things the family can use, especially the money. Perhaps we should think about going home."

I wanted to continue the killing. Robbing the men was no longer a priority, but what Vivian said about going home made sense. However, if the people from Fairplay made a posse and came after us, they might have found our trail and caught us. We could not risk leading them to our home.

"Vivian, I think you are right, but let's go back to Grape Springs, wait a week or more, and then start home. Most certainly the family can use what we have, and we did tell them we would return soon. We have been away too long."

One of the items we took from the cabin after killing Harkins was a journal of blank pages, the cover stamped with the name McPherson. While camped at Grape Springs previously, I started writing in the journal, just random thoughts at first, then to justify the murders of the gringo men. I wanted to leave a record of our accomplishments and the reason for the killings for our children.

On our eighth day at Grape Springs, I woke up when Vivian got out of his bedroll and built up the fire.

"Ah, Felipe, you are up. I'm going to go retrieve our animals. I think maybe we should leave here today and go home. I miss my wife and maybe my child has been born."

"Yes, of course. I will get up." I did so and followed the path he had taken. I paused as Vivian emerged from the thicket of willows, put a bridle on one of the horses, and bent to remove its hobbles. I saw black smoke and fire erupt from a rifle from another group of trees at least two hundred yards away. A large lead ball smashed into Vivian, knocking him flat on his back, the reins of his horse still in his hand. I rushed back to our camp, grabbed my rifle, pistols, and ammunition, and left via the escape route we had chosen in case the camp was discovered. I emerged from the willows and sprinted toward the closest hill, where I knew I could find cover. I glanced to my right and saw two men walking toward Vivian, their revolvers drawn. I jumped into a ravine, running hard with a revolver in my right hand and my rifle in my left. We had made a crude path from the ravine up a slope leading to a red rock bluff that looked down at the camp.

Then someone shouted, "There goes the other one, up that bluff! After him, men. Don't let him get away!"

I heard the sound of many men chasing me, but I knew all the places where I could hide and catch my breath before getting to the cave where we had stashed extra ammunition and a container of water. I reached the cave, breathing hard, and crawled into it. There was a large boulder hiding the entrance, and part of the mountain extended over the boulder, hiding it from view from the top. Once the men stopped looking for me, I would be able to watch what they were doing from the top of the boulder. After the men chasing me reached the top of the bluff, one of them shouted down.

"There's no sign of him, Mr. McCannon. He's got away from us. No telling where he got to. We're coming down."

I listened as they scrambled back to the camp, kicking rocks loose and making a lot of noise, especially when they slid down steep slopes on their buttocks. When I was certain they were off the mountain, I climbed to the top of the boulder and peeked down.

I saw a large man, probably McCannon, take off his hat and rub his hand over his head. "Don't worry," he shouted at the men approaching him. "He can't get far. He's on foot. I'm going to make certain the other one is finished."

I could see Vivian, still on his back. I had seen the rifle ball hit him high on the right side of his chest. But he must have been still breathing, still alive. He still held on to the reins of his horse. Before the big man and the others reached Vivian, he rolled over on his side, pulling his pistol. As they approached, Vivian fired. He must have been weak from the loss of blood. I could see his arm shaking. He missed. One of the men was carrying a shotgun. He fired, hitting Vivian's horse in the neck. It dropped to the ground next to Vivian, who fired at the man holding the shotgun but missed him as well. The man they called McCannon returned fire. The ball from his rifle hit Vivian in the face, and his head exploded. Two men bent over Vivian. One of them took his spurs as a souvenir. I saw McCannon remove the leather thong covered with red beads from around Vivian's neck. Attached to the thong was a gold medallion with a likeness of the Virgin Mary and the words 'N.S.D. Guadalupe, De Mexico, A. 1805' etched into the metal. The medallion had belonged to our papa, the only memento Vivian had of him.

While McCannon was inspecting the medallion, rage overcame me. I stood up on my boulder, raised my rifle, and fired. The bullet hit the brim of the big man's hat, nicked his ear, and tore his shirt. I fired my revolver, but he was much too far away. I ducked and ran just as one of the men squeezed off a shot from his rifle. The posse spent another hour looking for me, but I was well hidden. They finally returned to our camp and packed up what they found there.

They took everything—coats, clothing, boots, blankets, buffalo robes, cooking and camping equipment, combs, knives, and a large cache of rifles, pistols, and ammunition. They found Harkins' gold-rimmed spectacles and McPherson's embroidered satin vest. I knew they had found a leather pouch with over a hundred dollars' worth of gold dust in a pocket of Vivian's pants. Two of the horses we had could be identified by their brands as belonging to murder victims. I expected there would be someone in the posse who would recognize Vivian. They would know exactly who they were after.

I was in trouble. I was at least a hundred and fifty miles from home, and I was without a horse, food, or blankets. I had only the clothes I was wearing, my rifle, a revolver, a sheath knife, and the journal in the pocket of my coat. I also had my powder horn, bullet bag, and percussion caps along with a pouch with some silver dollars and paper money. I didn't know if the paper money was worth anything, but I was hopeful. I was capable of finding a piece of flint with which to strike sparks using my knife so I could start a fire. I could kill animals for food, once I was out of earshot of the posse. I knew people were hunting me, but I could make certain nobody followed or caught me unawares. I did not know if the posse had left some men behind to watch in case I showed myself. I couldn't risk going to Vivian to bury him. I was very careful to keep myself hidden from anyone who might be near the camp, and I made a wide circle before heading south, traveling at night and hiding during the day.

After three days, I came upon a remote ranch in the middle of the night. I stole a horse, saddle, and bridle. Four days later, after riding a circuitous route, I was back in San Rafael, but without much succor for my destitute family. I told them what had happened to Vivian and about all the plunder we had intended to bring them. I put all the money I had in my wife's hand.

Disbelief on her face, she left her hand extended. "This is all you have to show for killing so many gringos?" She turned her back to me, still holding the pouch of money.

I had no answer for her or any other members of the family. I was angry with myself when I thought of all the valuable goods we had in our hands and lost. I was unable to forgive myself for not leaving Grape Springs a day earlier so we could have brought home all that plunder. I was despondent when I thought about the loss of my brother, and I started making plans to avenge him as well as Papa, our sheep, the two dogs, and all our belongings. However, I could not leave until I provided more for my family.

I built a small hut in a dense thicket of willows and cottonwoods next to the Conejos River, away from the family's house and fields. During the day, I hid in the hut, occasionally making short trips into the mountains to hunt for deer, elk, and small game to supply the family with meat. When the ground warmed enough that spring, I helped Jose Vincente with the planting while keeping my features hidden under a large sombrero. I always had an escape route planned and my guns and supplies were cached so I could grab them on the run. I kept my eyes and ears tuned constantly, hoping to spot any lawmen or soldiers before they could spot me.

On Easter morning, I participated in the annual ceremonies conducted by the Penitente Brotherhood of the three villages along the Conejos River. The picador of the Brotherhood pricked the flesh of the small of my back with a sharp piece of flint. He then handed me the disciplina, and I scourged the bleeding wounds on my back. After an hour of praying on my knees, the coadjutor washed my back using cold rosemary tea. After two hours of rest, we repeated the process, and this time I asked others in the Brotherhood to apply the disciplina to my back, urging them to use more and more force. Finally, I lifted a timber eight feet long, with a crossbar of four feet, to my shoulder. While encouraging my compadres to scourge my back, I dragged the heavy cross to a small hill where a hole was waiting. My arms were bound to the crossbar with heavy rope. The brothers tied my feet together and attached them to the post. They positioned the post at the mouth of the hole and raised it. Within minutes, the ropes on my arms rubbed the skin raw, stinging, and then a dull ache. I ignored it. I lost all feeling in my arms, but pain pounded at my head.

Searing pain brought tears to my eyes. It wasn't physical pain; it was the pain of loss. Loss of my papa, loss of our home in El Rito, loss of my brother Vivian, loss of those two wonderful sheepdogs, loss of the love and respect of my family. I hung on the cross until sunset, crying to Jesus, Mary, and God for forgiveness for my many sins, but I made a silent promise to continue to avenge my father and my brother, and most importantly, to protect my church.

Not long after I suffered on the cross, I saddled the same horse I had stolen during my escape and started back to Grape Springs. Again, I traveled only at night, hiding during the day, and taking wide detours around any kind of civilization. I found the remains of Vivian, left where he had fallen. The bastards hadn't even bothered to bury him. There were only a few shredded pieces of cloth and a sun-dried carcass stripped of flesh. Some bones had been scattered away from the corpse by winged and four-legged scavengers. I reverently gathered all the remains I could find and put one of his feet in my pocket. Then I dug a grave and buried my brother, covering the grave with rocks.

I fell to my knees and prayed steadily for most of an hour, palms together in front of my face. I got up, went to the horse, and removed a braided rawhide scourge from a saddlebag. I went back to the grave, knelt again, and removed my shirt. For the next two hours, I was on my knees, silently praying to the Virgin, whipping the scourge over one shoulder and then the other until my back was stripped of flayed, bleeding flesh.

Finally, I sighed and said aloud, "Lord Jesus and Mother Mary, I am truly sorry and repent of my sins, especially the sin of not yet killing enough gringos to avenge Papa, and now I have to avenge Vivian as well. I am penitent but unworthy of your notice. If you grant me your blessings, I will avenge both my brother and my father. Perhaps I can no longer cope with what has happened to me, God, but the gringos invaded, took our lands, and by their actions threaten the Holy Church. I am your soldier. I will give my life to protect your church. Please help me do this."

Chapter 20
Felipe

I left my brother's grave and returned home. That same summer of 1863, my nephew returned from Conejos where he traded some fresh produce for supplies. He had also acquired a Spanish-language newspaper. He handed the newspaper to me and said, "Look at that article on the second page."

The article told about how the McCannon posse killed Vivian and that a reward had been offered for my capture.

"I don't think any of our neighbors will turn you in for the reward, Felipe, but perhaps you need to think about moving on. Are you going to avenge Papa and Vivian or not?"

Jose Vincente was now a full-grown man of twenty-three years. He was correct—I needed to return to my pursuit of vengeance; however, I had decided I could not be as effective working alone as with a partner. I needed someone who would understand why the gringos had to pay for all they had done to us and for their ongoing efforts to denigrate our people and the Catholic Church.

"The gringos have stolen everything from us, Jose. You know how your mother and grandmother and the rest of our family must live. Once we were a family of some substance, but the gringos took everything from us. You know I have always thought of you more as a brother than a nephew. You are of my blood, and I love you. I hope you have the same love for me. I am going to show you something now, and I am asking that you make an oath while you hold this in your hand."

"Of course, Felipe. I will do whatever you ask of me."

I slowly unfolded the sheepskin I was holding. It contained Vivian's shriveled brown foot, skeletal in appearance. "This is the left foot of your brother and mine, Vivian Espinosa," I said, my voice choked with emotion. "It is all we have of him; most of the rest was in the bellies and the shit of the buzzards and coyotes that devoured his body. Take it in your hands. Swear to me that you will be my compadre and help me avenge Vivian, and your grandfather, and the two sheepdogs I know you loved."

Jose swallowed hard and pulled back. Then he steeled himself and took the relic from me, dubiously holding it in his hands. "I swear to you, and our Lord Jesus, that I will avenge our brother Vivian and our grandfather Pedro. I will follow you and obey you and kill the gringos as they killed our blameless dogs."

A week later, I took Jose with me on a raid. We robbed and killed two men. A week later, we distributed all the plunder among the family. After spending a week with the family, Jose and I again saddled up and rode northeast out of San Rafael, leading a stolen pack mule carrying supplies. The sun was bright in the cloudless sky, but there was a brisk breeze, and we both shivered under our old, thin wool serapes. I diverted around Fort Garland and all towns, villages, isolated farms, and ranches where someone might spot us. We went to the Sangre de Cristo Creek trail and followed it over the pass. Just over the pass, we left the trail and rode to the headwaters of South Abeyta Creek, and then we went downstream a short distance into a heavily wooded gulch.

I swiveled in my saddle to look at Jose. "This will be our camp. It is hidden, and there is sufficient grass for the animals. Each morning we will ride to the Sangre de Cristo Pass. There we will find a place to hide and watch. We will rob and kill any gringos that try to use that road. Is this agreeable to you?"

"Of course."

"After we kill some gringos, they will send men to try and kill us. Before that happens, we will go east. On the plains, we will find isolated ranches. We will kill all the gringos we find."

"I will do whatever you say, Uncle."

For almost two weeks, the only traffic over the pass was convoys of two to five wagons with at least two men in each wagon, too many for us to attack. Mid-morning of 10 October, Jose and I were in our usual spot, only twelve miles from Fort Garland. We were hidden behind a large boulder overlooking the trail with our horses tethered out of sight a short distance away. I watched the trail while Jose stretched out on the ground, resting his head against a boulder, basking in the warm sun, protected from the cold breeze. I touched Jose on the head, then put a finger to my lips.

"Now comes a buggy pulled by two mules, only one man and a woman in it. Get ready," I whispered.

As the buggy approached, Jose and I jumped up and fired our pistols in the air. The driver whipped the mules into a run. They ran past us as we fired at the mules. A few hundred yards down the road, one mule fell dead, stopping the buggy. Jose and I ran up to the buggy, firing until our revolvers were empty. The second mule fell. The driver jumped out of the buggy and ran up one side of the canyon, abandoning his passenger. Jose and I followed him, doing our best to reload our revolvers as we ran. I looked over my shoulder to see the woman passenger climb down from the buggy and scramble up the opposite side of the canyon into some boulders.

While we were trying to find the driver, a wagon entered the canyon. I motioned to Jose to duck down behind a large rock with me. The two men in the wagon stopped because the buggy and two dead mules blocked the road. We saw the woman run to them, sliding down the side of the canyon, dislodging rocks and boulders in her haste. The two astonished men gaped at her.

The woman seemed to know the older of two men and was talking animatedly, waving her arms about as she spoke. The man took her arm and looked around in all directions. I was sure he didn't see me because he lifted the corner of the tarp concealing the contents of his wagon and helped her climb in under it.

"Keep looking for the gringo, Jose," I whispered. "I will find out who the two with the wagon are. Perhaps they have something of value to us."

I came out from where I was hiding and trotted toward the road, jumping over brush and rocks. "What people are you?" I hollered, brandishing my revolver. "If you have weapons, throw them on the ground."

"As you can see, we are Mexican," answered the older man, with considerable calm. "We have no weapons, Señor. We are poor farmers, nothing more. We cannot and will not fight with you."

"Did a gringo run past you on the road?"

"No, Señor, but we did see a man running down that mountain." The old man pointed in the opposite direction of Fort Garland.

"That is the gringo we are after. We will catch him and kill him," I told him.

"What did he do to deserve this fate, Señor?" The other man asked.

"That's none of your business. Did you see a woman?"

The younger of the two men responded. "What woman? We saw no woman."

At that most inopportune moment, the woman sneezed. "Put that prostitute of the gringo out of your wagon. I should kill you for lying to me and hiding her. I saw you help her into the wagon and hide. Get out, woman, or I will shoot you dead where you are." I had no intention of shooting her. She was a woman and bore no responsibility for what had happened to our family.

As the woman came down from the wagon, I saw she was Mexican, her face somehow familiar.

"This is Señorita Dolores Sanchez," said the old man. "She is known to me and is not a prostitute, but a respectable lady. I cannot allow you to kill her. She asked for my protection, and to honor our Lord Jesus, I must protect her. You will have to kill me to take her."

She held in her hand a large silver cross attached to a silver chain around her neck. "Don Pedro, you must not die because of me. Think of your wife and family. Who will take care of them? I know of these men, they are Penitentes, good Catholics. They won't hurt me."

She knew me. I tried desperately to think of why she looked so familiar. Dolores Sanchez? I couldn't remember ever meeting a Señorita Sanchez.

"What are you carrying in this wagon?" I demanded, still waving my pistol.

"We have only flour and bread," said the old man. "If you want, we will leave you some bread, eh, amigo?"

I was still concentrating, trying to remember why I should know Dolores Sanchez. "Yes, yes, we can use some bread," I replied, still searching for a memory.

The younger man climbed into the bed of the wagon, flipped the tarp forward, took out a basket filled with loaves of bread, and placed it near the tailgate.

"Here is bread enough to last you for a time, amigo. I will put it down here, next to the road. Is that good?" The old man asked.

I had a vague recollection of meeting the señorita at a fiesta and smiled to myself. "Fine, get back in the wagon and drive off, slowly," I murmured.

"That's good, amigo. May the señorita come with us? She has done nothing to warrant your hatred."

He had used up all my patience. I shouted at him, "Go! Do not look back. I will decide what happens to this woman, but if she dies, you tell your pueblo that the Espinosas from the Rio Conejos valley killed her for being with a gringo."

I watched as the two men got back on the wagon and slowly continued on their way. They went around a curve and out of sight. I walked over to the dead mules and cut lengths of harness straps.

"Señorita, lie down on the side of the road," I ordered.

She was not unattractive. I guessed she couldn't be more than thirty years old. The skin on her face was smooth, unmarked by wrinkles, and her hair was hidden by a scarf, but I could see it was a light brown color. She had on boots, and gloves covered her hands. I had no intention of harming her. I tied her hands and feet with the straps of leather, but not tight. "How do you know me?" I asked her.

"I have relatives in San Rafael, and we were introduced at a fiesta."

"I have a vague recollection of that but didn't remember your name. Why were you with the gringo?"

"I hired him, his name is Philbrook, to drive me from Trinidad to Fort Garland where I planned to spend the night. The next day, he was to take me to Costilla to visit relatives."

She was calm and showed no fear of me. A brave woman.

I left her tied up and joined Jose in the hunt for Philbrook. With amusement, I walked away and went behind a large boulder to watch what she did. It took only a few minutes for her to free herself. I watched as she climbed up the side of the canyon opposite the direction I had taken. She scrambled all the way to the top and found an outcropping of rocks with a small cave hidden behind some brush. She crawled into the cave. I wanted to let her escape. Even though, if rescued, she would no doubt tell who we were, I could not bring myself to kill an innocent Mexican woman, nor did I want to take her cross or whatever money she had.

As the sun set, we gave up looking for the driver. We returned to the buggy, taking everything we could find of value to us, and left for our camp.

Later, Jose looked up from the can of beans he was stirring with his knife while it warmed in some coals from our campfire. "I don't understand, Felipe. Why did you not shoot the woman? She knows you and probably me, although I didn't recognize her. She will tell the authorities who we are, no?"

"Probably. But do you really want to kill women? How can they be responsible for all the bad things that have been done to our family? I think that woman is quite brave. I respect her. Our fight is with the gringos, not a Mexican woman."

Jose thought for a long time and said, "I understand. I also have no desire to kill women, especially not Mexican women."

I smiled and said, "Bueno." Jose understood that what we did was vengeance for what the gringos did to us. I hoped he also understood that we were defending the church as well.

Chapter 21
Tom

I spent two years dividing my time between the Costilla farm with my family and the Trinchera ranch. I kept my growing herds of cattle at Costilla and during the winter fed them hay harvested from the Costilla pastures. This spring I moved a large number of horses and mules to the Trinchera ranch, taking several men with me to help herd the animals and drive two wagons full of supplies.

After we reached the Trinchera property, I put four men to work making adobe bricks. I intended to build additional rooms for my house, a new barn, and some outbuildings for storage. I put three men to plowing and planting. There was plenty of work to do, and I kept my workers busy from dawn to dusk, but I still needed additional help. Maria Pascuala was again pregnant and suffering more than usual, and with her and the rest of my family in Costilla, there was nobody to cook, wash and mend clothing, clean the houses, and attend to all that needed to be done to keep me and my workers comfortable at Trinchera. We were eating tortillas and beans and not much else, and I was sick of it. My house was a mess, the workers' houses even worse. My clothes, what there was of them, were torn and dirty.

Early one morning in May, three Mexicans rode into my yard. With them was a Navajo girl sitting uncomfortably on top of the pack on their pack animal. She was small but clearly had reached adulthood. Judging by her expression, she was unhappy with her situation but resigned. I wondered what her story was.

One of the Mexicans hailed me. "Hola, Señor Tomas."

I watched them from the doorway of my house, squinting into the sun. Shading my eyes with my left hand, I stared at the face of the man who had called out. I kept my right hand at my side, close enough to draw the pistol holstered in front of my left thigh. I didn't know the speaker or either of the other men and wondered how they knew me.

"Who are you?" I said.

"You don't know us, Señor Tomas, but we came here from Taos. Your friend, Señor St. Vrain, told us where we could find you. He told us you might have use for a girl to cook and clean for you. This Navajo girl is a good worker, and she is for sale."

"How do you know St. Vrain?" I asked, still suspicious, although I had complained to him the last time, I was in Taos about being tired of cooking my own food.

The same man answered, sitting comfortably on his horse, careful to keep both of his hands where I could see them. "Oh, we did some work for him. He is a fair man and paid us well."

"So, you say that she can cook. What can she cook?" I glanced at the two silent ones, who were sitting with both of their hands on their saddle horns. Well, I thought, they are all being careful to keep their hands where I can see them.

"We have been on the trail for three days, and she cooks for us venison and beans, and she makes very thin tortillas from wheat flour. She does something with rabbit that is delicious, and if you have the ingredients, she can bake bread and sweets. She does laundry and also mends torn clothing."

"How much do you want for her?"

"We will accept seventy dollars. She is very good at cooking, and she is clean, for a Navajo."

"Climb down, girl. Let's have a look at you," I ordered.

The girl slid off the pack and landed solidly on her feet. She stood still as I walked around her. I took one of her hands in mine, then the other. They were clean enough but rough from work. She let each hand drop to her side when I released them.

"Open your mouth, girl. Let's have a look at your teeth."

The girl opened her mouth, and I peered in. She had all her teeth, and her mouth smelled of some herb she had chewed, although I couldn't place it. She seemed calm, not scared of me. Then she gave me a faint smile.

"Do you speak Spanish, girl?"

"Si, Patron."

"I'll give sixty for her."

"We paid almost that much for her, Señor. We must make a small profit, no? She is a very good cook."

"Sixty-five. My last offer. Take it or move on." I started to move to the house.

"You are a very tough negotiator, Señor. All right, sixty-five. By the way, you should take care. The Espinosas are robbing and killing again."

"I know they are thought to be the ones that robbed and killed several men. But Vivian was killed by that posse. Why do you think the Espinosas are the ones doing the killing?"

"Well, people say so. There seem to be two of them, and they kill men who are on their own and then rob them."

"That so? Not my concern. Stay on your horses. I'll get your money from the house."

As the three men rode away, I put my arm over the girl's shoulders, a sign that she was mine and, I hoped, a sign that I would protect her. She flinched but did not try to move away. I wondered what the poor girl had been through. Without trying to escape my arm, she turned to me and ventured another half-smile.

"Don't worry, girl. You are safe here with me. How old were you when you were taken from your people?"

She pinched her eyebrows together, concentrating. "I was fourteen, I think. I don't remember. It was long ago."

"How long ago? Years, months, weeks?"

"I was with the people those men bought me from for four winters. Those men who bought me weren't nice."

"Who took you from your tribe?"

"The Tabaquache Utes. I was away from our hogan, with the sheep. Three of them found me and carried me to Abiquiu and sold me to a family."

"What family?"

"Bernal. Manuel de Jesus Bernal."

"Big family. My wife is also of the Bernal family. Were they good to you?"

"Yes, they were kind. But last winter, the Señor died, and there were too many to feed. The Señora sold me to those men two weeks ago. They only paid forty dollars."

I grinned. "I knew they made more profit than they would admit to. Anyhow, you are safe with me. I wanted to take you away from them. What is your name?"

"I was called Dominga by the Bernal family."

"That's good enough for me. Come inside, Dominga. I will show you where you can sleep, and then you can get busy. There are eight men here. We all work hard and need a lot of good food to keep going."

Two weeks later, I moved the large bed I had been building for myself into the bedroom of my four-room house, which also contained a parlor, dining room, and kitchen. The following morning, before dawn, Dominga vacated her straw mattress on the floor of the kitchen and crawled into my bed. I made room for her under my two wool blankets.

"I am cold," she said.

"I will keep you warm," I whispered, slipping my hand under her loose blouse, and gently fingering the nipple of her left breast until it was hard. She pressed closer, moaning softly into my neck. I had not visited the Costilla farm for some time and was missing Maria Pascuala. However, whenever I was with her of late, she was pregnant and not interested in sex or had just given birth. I was thirty-nine years old and had needs. I understood now why Charley took in Siccamo.

It was another good year. All but two of my mares gave birth, either to horse or mule foals. One of my men, an experienced horse trainer, broke the yearlings and finished them before they were two, so they were accustomed to both the saddle and a pack. The army bought all the horses and mules I could supply, at top prices. The fields, planted with corn, wheat, and beans, all produced abundant crops. Most of the harvest was sold to the army, and the surplus was kept in my new storage buildings for later sale.

The late October sun had set, and Dominga and I were in bed. I gently rubbed her abdomen, just beginning to swell from the growing child within.

"Soon it will be time to bring hay for the animals from Costilla for the winter."

Dominga was silent for some time. I was making a list in my mind of all that had to be done before the move. I thought she had fallen asleep, but she brought me back by suddenly saying, "What will become of me and the child?"

I was puzzled. "What do you mean? You will come with us, of course. There is no need to speak of the father of this child. I will have a little house built for you, away from the main house. You will help Maria Pascuala and our daughters take care of the house, cook, mend, and do the other chores. I will let everyone know that your primary job is to be the housekeeper for the Trinchera ranch. There is no problem."

"Your wife will know."

"Nonsense. She might suspect, but she will not know. She is a good woman. She understands the needs of a man. She will say nothing, do nothing. Do not occupy yourself with these concerns. Just do as I tell you. Everything will work out."

"As you say, Señor Tomas. You paid for me, and I will do as I am told."

"Good. Now stop talking. You know what I like."

"Yes, Señor." She smiled.

Late the next afternoon, while I was giving instructions to my men about what and how to pack for the trip back to Costilla, an army courier rode up.

"Mr. Tobin?"

"That be me."

"Compliments of Colonel Tappan, sir, he requests that you come to Fort Garland prepared for a trip into the mountains. There's two men out robbing an' killing folks. The colonel wants you to track them down."

"Does he know who the men are?" I asked.

"If he does, he didn't share that information with me, sir."

I was afraid that it was the Espinosas, as the man who sold Dominga to me had said. But robbing and killing innocent people wasn't right. No matter who they were, they needed to be stopped. "All right, you ride back and tell your colonel I'll be there as soon as I can get my men and my housekeeper on the road to my Costilla place."

The next afternoon I was ushered into Tappan's office. The colonel stood to welcome me, offering me his hand.

"Mr. Tobin, I'm glad you could answer the call. Do you know about the terrible murders throughout this region that have been taking place? They have all been one or two men living alone or traveling who were killed and then robbed. Men who were innocent of any wrongdoing. I have been ordered to catch the perpetrators and bring them to justice."

"Yes, most everyone in these parts knows about the murders. But they've been mostly north and east of here, haven't they?"

The colonel rubbed his forehead and sat down behind his desk. "Yes. Well, I've got a Miss Dolores Sanchez here who says two Espinosas attacked her on the Sangre de Cristo Pass road. She and her driver were on their way here and then on to Costilla where she planned to visit relatives. She tells me she has known you for some time." The colonel turned toward the door and shouted, "Orderly, please bring Miss Sanchez here."

"Dolores Sanchez. Yes, sir. I know her. She's kin to my brother's wife. Most everyone living in these parts for any amount of time is related somehow. How does she know they were Espinosas?"

"Please take a seat, Mr. Tobin. I know many people here are related, but be that as it may, I would like you to talk to Miss Sanchez. There is no doubt that someone shot and killed the two mules that were pulling the buggy she was riding in. That person also threatened to kill the driver. All her possessions from the buggy were stolen, but her driver escaped. He arrived here the night before we found her. He reported that the two men were Mexicans. I sent a sergeant out with a squad to try to catch them and to look for the woman this Mr. Philbrook said he was bringing here. They found Miss Sanchez but didn't find any trace of the two men who stopped them."

The orderly led Dolores into the office, and the colonel and I stood. She ran to me and gave me an abrazo. I smiled and returned the hug.

She spoke to me in Spanish. "Don Tomas, I am so happy to see you! I told the colonel you are the one who can track these men down and stop them from killing more people."

I continued in Spanish. "Please, Dolores, sit here. You know who these men are, for certain?"

Dolores sat in the chair but kept hold of my arm. "Yes, I recognized Felipe, and I'm certain the one with him was his nephew, Jose Vincente. Pedro Garcia—you know Pedro, verdad? He came along with his wagon and stopped to help me. Felipe even told Don Pedro that they were the Espinosas. They wanted to kill me. I do not know why. I did nothing to them."

I was very upset and troubled that it was true that the Espinosas were committing these crimes. I paced the room.

"Will one of you please tell me what's going on? I don't speak Spanish," said the colonel. "I gather Miss Sanchez told you there were two of them, one middle-aged, the other a youngster."

I switched to English. "Yes, sorry, Colonel. She told me who the two men were."

Dolores also switched to English. "I recognized Felipe from a fiesta a couple of years ago, but he acted like he didn't know who I was."

"She recognized both Felipe Espinosa and his nephew Jose Vincente," I added. "Since his brother was killed, Felipe has apparently recruited the young man to help him continue his crimes."

The colonel got up from his chair. "Thank you, Miss Sanchez. I can see you are still very tired. Do you want to go back to your room and rest?"

"Yes, gracias, Colonel. Don Tomas, you need to stop the two of them from doing more evil."

"I will, Dolores. Rest easy."

She left the office, and the colonel looked at me from behind his table. "Do you know Leon Constantine?"

"Yes, sir. He used to work for Bill Bent, and then he and Antoine Lebrie partnered up with Leandro Beral and Louis Clouthier. They all worked for Bent together. Three years back, they started farming near Hardscrabble and built a general store in Canyon City. I know them all. I heard Constantine got his self another place on the Huerfano River, him, and Beaubois. They all be Frenchies from Canada."

"Yes, well, that's all very interesting, I'm sure. Mr. Constantine was recently found murdered in the Sangre de Christos along with another man who wasn't identified, maybe this man Beaubois. The Espinosas are suspects in those murders. My orders are to rid the country of these murderers, Mr. Tobin. I want you to track them down and bring me their heads."

The news that Felipe and Jose had killed Leon Constantine and maybe Beaubois made me angry at the Espinosas, who had, for reasons I couldn't understand, killed so many men, all Americans. I spoke up to the colonel. "Since they're murdering men like Leon, and now this business with Dolores, I reckon it be time for me to stop 'em. You said you sent a sergeant out to try and catch them. Can I hear from him what happened?"

The colonel called out for the orderly to fetch the sergeant. We waited in uncomfortable silence while I tried to imagine where Felipe and Jose had got to and why they were out killing and robbing. The sergeant knocked at the door, entered, and saluted the colonel.

"All right, Sergeant, please give Mr. Tobin here your report on the mission I sent you on."

"Yes, sir. We found the buggy and two dead mules. Everything was taken from the buggy. Didn't find no suitcases or anything else of value."

"What happened then?" I asked.

"I had the squad fan out and look for any sign of them murderers, but we didn't find nothing."

"No tracks? Did they have horses?"

"Dunno, I ain't much of a tracker. We saw lots of tracks on the road—horses, mules, and ox—but they went off both ways. The ground's rocky, and not one of the soldiers could find any sign of where them two got off the road."

"Anything else?" I asked.

"Well, I had the boys shove them mules off the road. They were blocking it and we pushed the buggy off to the side of the road. I reckon Mr. Philbrook will be wanting to get him some new mules and fetch it. He'll need a harness, too. The Espinosas cut up his harness."

"All right, Sergeant. You're excused, but please find the quartermaster and send him to me." After the sergeant left the room, the colonel turned to me. "I sent for the quartermaster to have him get everything a patrol will need to go with you to track these murderers down. How long do you think it might take?"

"Can't say. Depends on how good they are at hiding their tracks. I wouldn't think more than a couple of weeks, maybe less if we get lucky."

Chapter 22
Felipe

Two days after I allowed Dolores Sanchez to escape, we were feeling safe in our camp. Our fire flickered red, blue, and orange against the trees and underbrush surrounding us. We were satiated with roasted meat from the steer we had butchered.

Jose added another piece of firewood to the fire. "Tell me again, Uncle, how we came to be here doing the work of the Holy Mother Mary and avenging Papa and Vivian. I need to understand how we are getting vengeance and protecting the church at the same time."

I looked up from the leather-bound daybook in which I was writing. "I am certain you remember when the gringos robbed us while we still lived in El Rito. We were not hidalgos, but everyone in the pueblo owned some irrigated lands, and all had a share of the many cattle, sheep, and horses that we grazed on the common lands. We were also able to harvest lumber and firewood from those lands that were ours, legally granted to our people by the Mexican government. Then the gringos came, started a war with Mexico, and conquered us. They denied our heritage and used their gringo laws to steal all our common lands. They left us destitute, peons, and serfs where we had been lords. Even more egregious, they denigrated the Catholic Church. The Blessed Virgin talks to me and insists that we take retribution." I held up my hand, the palm arresting any movement or speech from Jose. "Wait, she speaks to me now." I nodded, pretending to be listening to a voice Jose couldn't possibly hear. "Si …Si…I understand."

I needed Jose to believe that we were doing what the Virgin Mary ordered and that she spoke directly to me. I continued. "Do not forget that your uncle Vivian was murdered by the gringos at Grape Springs. I need you to remember the dense thicket of willows and cattails watered by a small spring. I showed you where I had buried the sun-bleached bones of your uncle. We dug down a small distance and placed Vivian's foot with the rest of his remains."

Jose's face showed wrinkles above his nose, and his mouth was turned down at the corners. I was afraid he had begun to doubt me. I thought again about the morning when Vivian was killed, and I summoned tears. I wiped my hand across my face, brushing them away impatiently. "Vivian came out of the trees early in the morning to get the horses. They shot, without warning, from ambush, the gringo cowards! Vivian pulled his pistol and fired at the gringos, but another bullet hit him just above the nose. I got away with my rifle, my pistol, and the clothes I was wearing. I had to leave everything else we took from those gringos we killed, except for this." I waved the leather daybook at Jose. "In this book, I record our vendetta. Listen, I want you to know my thoughts and my reasoning. Do you want to know what I am writing?"

"Yes, Uncle. I need to know and understand all your thoughts."

I read aloud from the journal: "They ruined our family and the other families of El Rito, taking away our common lands. When Vivian and I retaliated, they came to where we had moved and took everything from our house, first our beds and blankets, then our provisions, they removed what little furniture we had and smashed it, and finally, they killed all our sheep and executed Estrella and Hermana. Seeing this, Vivian and I declared, 'We would rather be dead than see such infamies committed on our families'!" I closed the book. "These are the reasons we had to go out and kill Americans, Jose— retribution for the infamies committed on our families."

"You know of some that Vivian and I killed, Jose, but of some you don't know. It is a sufficient number, however. Ask in New Mexico if any other two men have ever been known to kill as many as the Espinosas! In total, the three of us have killed thirty-two. I have kept track in this book."

I continued. "This next part is my defense for all the murders. I want my family to understand. I am a poor poet, but this is what is in my heart." I read from the book again. "I, Felipe, on this the forty-third night of my company with the angels, offer this testimony and prayer:

I am blessed with the milk from the breast of Holy Mother Mary!
I am covered with the cloak of Holy St. Salvador!
I am defended by the sword of Holy St. Paul!
I am looking after animals and my enemies.

They have hands and cannot touch me,

They have feet and cannot catch me,

They have eyes and cannot see me,

They have ears and cannot hear me.

I am as free as our Lord was originally. Amen—Jesus!

Flying along a narrow path, I met Jesus Christ.

Jesus Christ be my father. Mother Mary be my mother.

Holy St. Clement be my sponsor, so that the devil may not meet me by day or night.

I will be sitting on the lap of the Virgin Mary until I die in her arms. Amen—Jesus."

As I read the words out loud, I wondered at the sound of them. Was I losing all semblance of sanity? Was I acting as a madman, unable to control what I did? How could this end?

Chapter 23
Tom

I rode Jen, still my favorite mount, the six miles from my ranch on Trinchera Creek to the fort. Over my strong objections about the number of men who were to go with me, Colonel Tappan insisted that Lieutenant Horace W. Baldwin and fifteen soldiers accompany me on the hunt for the Espinosas. A private citizen, Loring Jinks, happened to be at the fort conducting some business, and he was eager to be in on the capture of the desperados. I don't know why the colonel agreed to it, but Jinks was allowed to come along. So, I insisted that the colonel should also allow twelve-year-old Juan Montoya to come along. I knew the boy and his family well. Juan worked for the quartermaster at the fort, and this temporary assignment with me would mean extra income for the Montoya family, a large one with many mouths to feed.

"I'll be needing someone to take care of my mule while I be tracking on foot," I told the colonel. "Juan can do that for me. I assume he will be paid extra for his service by the army. Otherwise, I don't see how I can do this."

The colonel sighed. "All right, Mr. Tobin. I'll make certain both you and he are on the payroll for the time it takes to get the Espinosas."

"But he'll continue to be paid by the quartermaster," I said.

"Yes, yes. Just get this done. Bring me their heads."

I wondered, since that was the second time said that if he really wanted me to bring him Felipe's and Jose's heads. It was late before Lieutenant Baldwin managed to get all the necessary supplies and equipment, choose the troopers, and issue their instructions. Riding Jen, I came through the gate out into the cold darkness followed by Baldwin, sixteen soldiers, one civilian, and one boy. Heavy cloud cover hid the moon, but I could see my breath in the reflected light from the fort. I was wearing homespun wool pants and shirt, and my bearskin coat, the fur side in. I was happy to be warm. I had jammed my hat securely on my head to keep it in place should the wind come up. My Hawken rifle rested on Jen's neck, in front of the pommel of the saddle. In its oxtail holster was the new 0.36 caliber Colt model 1851 Navy revolver I had recently bought. It was an unusual time for a patrol to leave Fort Garland, well after midnight, October 12, 1863, but I told the lieutenant it was important to get to the last place the Espinosas were seen. I held the rifle steady with my right hand, my left hand holding the reins. As the last horse left the opening, I looked back at the interior parade grounds of the fort. The colonel was standing with his hands on his hips watching us leave as the gate closed.

We rode through the night until the sun peaked over the mountains as I led the troops into the western access to Sangre de Cristo Pass. At the highest point of the pass, I stopped to speak with Lt. Baldwin.

"I believe you should rest your men here for a while," I said. "I'll see if I can cut some track of those hombres. I'm pretty certain they came this way."

"Probably a good idea, Mr. Tobin. The men are getting tired, and the horses could use a rest as well. I'm not comfortable with you going off alone, though. I'll assign some men to go with you."

"All right, but they need to take off all that jangles and move quiet like. Do you think you have someone that can do that? They need to follow me, keep up, and not spook them varmints we're after."

Baldwin called four of his men over. "You four accompany Mr. Tobin and follow his instructions to the letter. Understood?"

It was mid-afternoon when I told the four men to dismount, hold their horses, and wait for me as I followed tracks, I thought were most likely those of the Espinosas. They led to the top of the ridge in front of us. I hunkered down before crossing the ridge, peered over a rock, and spotted a wisp of smoke from the far end of the valley below. I pulled my revolver from its oxtail holster. The signal I arranged with Baldwin to join me required that I fire two quick rounds, followed by a pause and a third. I doubted that the Espinosas would recognize it for what it was.

I turned to the soldiers standing behind me. "You all stay here and wait for the lieutenant. I'm going to flush those two varmints. When the rest of the soldiers get here, you can all follow. I'm going to move that way and circle around to that meadow." I pointed to my destination.

I proceeded on foot, my rifle in my right hand, loaded and ready. I moved carefully in a broad, mile-wide half-circle through a forest of pine and then a thick grove of aspen. Brilliant gold aspen leaves fell like spring rain onto my bent back. I put my toes down first, then my heels to muffle the crunch of the leaves. I moved through the dense woods to the edge of a clearing. They were waiting for me, and I realized they must have known what my signal was. They both fired at me with their rifles, but they were more than four hundred yards away and their rifles couldn't cover the distance with any accuracy. I fired my Hawken and the ball almost hit the one I thought was Felipe in the head. He yelled something to Jose, and they scurried to their horses tethered another hundred yards away. They jumped onto the horses and, pulling an already loaded packhorse, whipped their horses with their reins as they galloped toward a thick grove of pines on the opposite me. I finished reloading the Hawken and brought it up to fire but lowered it just before the two disappeared into the trees. With me standing it was a long and too difficult shot. I sat down to wait.

Lieutenant Baldwin and the soldiers found me about a half hour later.

"That was them, but I missed a long shot. I believe we should go back toward the pass and camp in the canyon," I said.

"Why on earth should we do that?" The lieutenant asked.

"Because they were ready and waiting for me. If we go after them now, they'll know we're not just some routine patrol. They'll keep pushing hard and get away. Felipe was taught to hunt by a man with Injun blood, he'll know how to cover his tracks. If we hunker down and rest, maybe they'll think they're safe and hole up. Now I know what their horse tracks look like for certain. If Felipe doesn't bother to cover their tracks for too long a distance I'll get them, Lieutenant. Don't you worry."

"How far back do you want to go?" Baldwin asked.

"You remember that creek we crossed some miles back? There's a flat meadow there just off the road, good water, plenty firewood, plenty grass for the horses. Any noise your men make won't matter."

"Ok then, let's move out."

When we arrived at the campsite I had in mind, we found it occupied by Tom Burns, a freighter who was returning from Denver to his home in Canon City. His heavy freight wagon, pulled by four strong draft horses, was half-full of goods.

I had known Burns for several years and trusted him. We talked awhile and then called Lieutenant Baldwin over to where we were squatting, warming our hands at a small fire.

"Got us an idea, Lieutenant," I said. "I think they might circle around and come back this away to throw us off. How about we put some of your soldier boys in Tom's wagon in the morning, cover them up with his tarp, and send him on his way? If the Espinosas circle around and spot a wagon with only one man, it'll be appetizing for them. If they attack, your boys can rise up shooting. The rest of us can trail along behind far enough to not be seen, and when we hear the shooting, we come up fast."

The lieutenant turned to face me. "That sounds like a good plan if you really think there's a chance they'll circle around, Mr. Tobin. But it will be dangerous for you, Mr. Burns. If they shoot from ambush, you could be in real danger."

"Don't you worry about me, Lieutenant," Burns answered. "I don't think the Espinosas are good enough shots to get me from far off, and I know this road. I know all the good places for an ambush. I'll keep a close eye out and keep moving around on the seat like I'm getting bounced. Count me in. I'd like to be in on the kill of those murdering bastards. They killed two of my friends."

"All right then, as long as you can accept the danger you're going to be in, we'll do as you suggest," replied the lieutenant.

That evening the camp was a noisy scene, filled with laughter and loud talk. That suited me just fine. If the Espinosas had circled around, they would be watching, and I wanted them to think the soldiers were easy to surprise. In the morning, I would take the troops in the opposite direction that Burns took, before turning around to follow the wagon. The lieutenant had split his troops into small groups huddled around several separate cooking fires. Most sat on their bedrolls to eat. Baldwin broke out a bottle of whiskey and gave each man a small portion to ward off the cold. I ignored the offer but Burns took his share and mine. The night was clear, and the mountain sky burned bright with stars. A large harvest moon cast an orange glow. Eventually, the men spread their bedrolls out around the fires.

The next morning, we maneuvered the wagon so the tailgate faced a steep slope. While Tom hitched up his horses, four soldiers slipped quickly under the canvas tarp into the bed of the wagon. Burns started slowly down the

Sangre de Cristo Canyon toward Canon City while I led the company of soldiers, making more noise than was necessary, back up toward the pass.

Burns drove slowly down, keeping the brakes of the wagon engaged, as if carrying a heavy cargo. Either the Espinosas were not in the canyon, or they suspected a trap. Burns stopped at the exit from the canyon, and the four soldiers were happy to climb out from under the hot tarp. They were all standing in the road when I arrived with Jen at a lope.

"Well, it was a good idea, but I guess the Espinosas decided not to take the bait if they were watching," I told the lieutenant. "It could be they're up on that peak over yonder." I motioned with a slight indication of my head. "From up there, you can see most of this part of the road, so if they're there, they know we planned an ambush. I'm gonna take you and your boys over toward the north side of the canyon. There's a branch of the creek that runs down from the pass that can't be seen from that peak." I waved my arm in the general direction of the same peak where I thought they might be watching us. "We'll follow that creek up and maybe get a jump on them tomorrow."

"Well, the idea was good—too bad it didn't pan out," said Burns. "I expect the Espinosas are a might wary, but I'll bet on you getting them before too long."

"Thanks, Tom, I appreciate that. Oh, we'll get them all right, if not today, soon."

Burns climbed back onto the seat of his wagon, clucked at his horses, and continued on his way. I didn't tell Lieutenant Baldwin that I had just caught a glint of sunlight reflecting from some metal near the peak of the mountain I had indicated. Maybe it was the Espinosas watching us, maybe not. If it was, I wanted them to lose sight of us so I could circle around and track them.

I led the troops into the thick undergrowth. Jen and the horses forced their way through until we reached the place where two branches of the same creek fell from the summit of the pass. Between the two branches, the forest was less dense, but the way to the pass was filled with rocks and large boulders. The troops followed me, carefully picking their way through. Jen did not stumble, but several of the horses struggled to get up the rocky, boulder-clogged route. Three of them almost went down, but all managed to right themselves as we made our way slowly up. It was almost evening when we reached a flat area less than two hundred yards from where the road topped the pass. That night, we camped without fires.

Before bedding down for the night, I went to check on Jen. "Well, old girl, I expect we'll cut their trail sometime tomorrow. They'll come off the back of that mountain to avoid us, and I'll find 'em."

Chapter 24
Tom

At dawn the following morning, I suggested the lieutenant deploy his soldiers over as wide an area as possible and look for signs on either side of the road going down off the pass. After an hour, one of the troopers found many horse tracks crossing the road. I dismounted to examine them.

"Appears to be Injuns. Utes more than likely. This be their traditional haunts. At least twenty ponies, all carrying, but they split up here. They're hunting, be my guess. Only two or three in each group. The Espinosas might have joined up with them or be following one of the groups. We need to check them all, look for the prints of three shod horses."

Lieutenant Baldwin split his men up and they scattered, each small group following a set of tracks. Baldwin and I took six of the soldiers with us, Juan Montoya following. We started a wide sweep with me carefully scanning for signs. It wasn't long until the civilian, Loring Jenks, and the other groups of soldiers were out of contact with us.

About half an hour before sundown, I took Baldwin, his six soldiers, and Juan down to Pass Creek, and we set up camp on Veta Mountain. The rest of the troopers were scattered, left to fend for themselves overnight. I was happy not to have the lot of them making my job harder.

At dawn the following day, I led the lieutenant and the men with him off the mountain to La Veta Creek. We followed the creek east, downstream. Mid-morning, I spotted the tracks of two steers following behind the tracks of three shod horses. It was them. I got down from Jen, handed her reins to Juan and told him to stay put. I followed the trail on foot, bent over, almost sniffing the tracks. The rest of the men followed on horseback at a distance, keeping me in sight.

An hour later, I scampered off the trail I was following and scared up a steer from the undergrowth. I recognized the brand of two of my old friends, John Francisco and Henry Daigre, whose ranch was only about ten miles from where we now stood. I motioned for Lieutenant Baldwin to join me.

"See here, Lieutenant?" I showed him the tracks I had been following. "They're headed into those thick groves of aspens down there, then I expect they'll circle that peak to the south." I pointed with the Hawken. "They kept one of the steers they stole. I reckon they'll butcher the one they kept for meat. The bush is thick down there, so you won't get through with the horses, and your soldiers make too much noise. Won't wash. It'll spook them. You all hang back. You can circle around to the south along that ridge," I pointed again with the rifle, "and wait. When I jump them, you'll hear old Hawk speak, and then you all come on up fast."

Baldwin frowned. "I want to be with you when you find them."

"Only if you can stay behind and not make any noise," I said.

One of the soldiers spoke up. "I'll go with you."

"So will I," said Juan Montoya, who did not want to be separated from me.

The Hawken would have to be reloaded after firing, and I might need more firepower. "All right, but the three of you keep behind me, and mind where you put your feet. Stay quiet. The rest of you stay here."

I took off in a ground-eating jog in the general direction I had indicated. The three following me did a fair job of being quiet and keeping up. The forest was thick, the undergrowth dense. Sometimes we had to crawl under or over fallen trees. The sun was starting its descent when I saw the tracks leading into another thick stand of aspens, pines, and undergrowth that I knew surrounded the spring where Cuchera Creek began. Crows and magpies circled above.

One of the soldiers who had been separated from us the previous day rode up and joined the group I was leading. They all followed me another hundred yards through the thick trees. The crows and magpies were still circling overhead, focused on a potential meal. They didn't warn the Espinosas by flying off. The group following me did everything they could not to make noise, but they were unable to move quietly. I squatted down, raised my hand to stop them, and then motioned them forward slowly, one at a time. Putting my finger to my lips, I huddled with each and whispered instructions. "You all wait here. Stay squatted down and damn quiet. When I lift my hand, cock your gun, but don't fire until I do." I looked each of them in the face and waited until I was sure he understood.

I carefully adjusted the percussion caps in the leather holder around my neck, making sure they were secure. I put two lead balls from my shooting pouch into my mouth and stalked forward, my Hawken held out in front, ready.

I sensed movement about two hundred and fifty yards away and stopped. It was the back of Felipe's head moving as he tore the meat from a rib with his teeth. I lay flat on the ground, my rifle propped on a fallen log. Felipe must have sensed me. He turned, spotted me, and jumped up, dropping the rib, grabbing at his pistol butt as he ran, shouting for Jose to escape. I sighted, leading him, and shouted, "Stop, Felipe!" He didn't. I squeezed the trigger. Through a cloud of black powder smoke, belching fire, and a thunderous explosion, the lead ball flew, passed through Felipe's chest, and knocked him to the ground.

I tipped my powder horn into the muzzle, spat a bullet into the barrel, and rammed it down without a patch. As I fit a new percussion cap in place, young Jose Espinosa, sprinting hard, bounded out of a ravine, headed for a thick grove of quaking aspen.

I shouted to the men. "Shoot, boys! Shoot! Don't let him get to those trees."

Two shots rang out from behind me, but they both missed with their short-range carbines.

Jose was only two steps from the safety of the trees when I was finally able to fire. He collapsed, twitched twice, while reaching his outstretched arms to the safety of the trees. Then he lay still. I approached Felipe with my revolver in my hand, but he was dead, as was Jose when I reached him.

I was troubled. I had made the decision to not let them get away again, but now I was upset for shooting them both in the back. However, if they had got away, I knew it would be harder to find them. I told myself I had to stop them—they were responsible for so many murders and could not be allowed to continue. While waiting for the lieutenant and his troops to get to me, I remembered the colonel telling me to bring him their heads. He didn't want them to go on trial—he wanted them dead.

When the lieutenant arrived with the rest of his soldiers, I said, "Do you think the colonel really wanted me to kill them?"

"I'm certain he did," the lieutenant answered. "If we had captured and arrested them, it would have meant a trial and all the expenses associated with it. They would have had the opportunity to tell why they were doing this and would certainly have gained sympathy from the Mexicans."

"Well, he told me to bring him their heads, and that's what I'll do. Maybe that will make him consider what he orders folks to do the next time."

The next day, unannounced, I walked into the colonel's office at Fort Garland carrying a flour sack. There were two shiny new notches on the barrel of my Hawken.

"Got 'em," I announced.

"That so?" The colonel replied, looking up from his desk.

I reached into the sack and pulled Felipe's head out by the hair, dropping it on the floor. It rolled almost two feet toward the colonel. I reached into the sack again and removed Jose's head, holding it up, then dropped it on the floor.

The colonel showed no emotion, not even a hint of disgust. "The Rocky Mountain News offered a $2,500 reward for them," he said.

"I didn't hunt them down for money, and you said to bring you their heads. I shoot them both in the back to keep 'em from getting away." I was still upset about that. "It was my duty as an American citizen, same as serving in your army." I placed a leather-bound book on the table. "Felipe," I pointed at the head on the floor, "had this in his pocket."

The colonel glanced at the gold-lettered name on the journal, picked it up, and leafed through it. "It's all in Spanish. I'll get it translated." He took a blank sheet of paper from a pile on his desk, wrote something on it, and signed his name at the bottom. "This paper says you brought me the heads of the murdering Espinosas on this day. Put your mark on it."

Biting my lower lip, I carefully printed my name. TOBIN. I gave him back the paper and left the office without saying anything else.

I learned later that he did have the book translated, and the entire translation was published in several newspapers.

The day after I rolled the heads of Felipe and Jose Espinosa across his office floor, Colonel Tappan wrote an official order of congratulations to all the troopers who had gone out to rescue Dolores Sanchez and to those who accompanied me when I killed the Espinosas. He neglected to mention either Loring Jenks or Juan Montoya. The only credit he gave me was as a guide to the expedition.

Still troubled by what I had done, I returned to retrieve the headless remains of Felipe and Jose Vincente Espinosa and buried them near San

Rafael. I was also troubled by the abject poverty of Secundina Espinosa and her children. For many years, I provided them with food and money when I could afford it. As a result, the family respected me enough to ask me to serve as an official witness at the wedding of Felipe's daughter, Maria Vincente Espinosa.

Author's Note

On April 3, 1893, after numerous formal appeals by an old and destitute Tom Tobin and his family, Colorado Senate Bill No. 165 was approved. The state allocated $1,000 to him for killing the Espinosas.

Bibliography

Carter, Harvey L. (1966) *Tom Tobin. The Mountain Men and Fur Trade of the Far West.* Edited by Roy R. Hafen. Glendale, CA: The Arthur H. Clark Co.

Chapman, Arthur (1924) *The Story of Colorado, Out Where the West Begins.* Chicago and New York: Rand McNally.

Chittenden, Hiram Martin (1986) *The American Fur Trade of the Far West,* Vol. 1 and 2. Lincoln, NE: University of Nebraska Press.

Darley, Alex M. (1968) *The Passionists of the Southwest: Or The Holy Brotherhood, A Revelation of the Penitentes*, 2nd ed. Glorieta, NM: Rio Grande Press.

Davis, W.W.H. (1982) *El Gringo: New Mexico and Her People.* Lincoln, NE: University of Nebraska Press.

Ebright, Malcolm (1994) *Land Grants and Lawsuits in Northern New Mexico.* Albuquerque: University of New Mexico Press.

Goetzman, William H. (1963) 'The Mountain Man as Jacksonian Man,' *American Quarterly* 15, **3**, 402-415.

Hayward, Walt, and Brad McDade (1997) 'A Glossary of American Mountain Men Terms, Words & Expressions,' *The American Mountain Man* (website), http://www.xmission.com/~drudy/amm/gloss.html

Laycock, George (1996) *The Mountain Men: The Dramatic History and Lore of the First Frontiersmen*, Lyons & Buford.

Maguire, James H., Peter Wild, and Donald A. Barclay, eds. (1997) *A Rendezvous Reader: Tall, Tangled, and True Tales of the Mountain Men 1805–1850*. Salt Lake City: University of Utah Press.

Perkins, James E. (1999) *Tom Tobin: Frontiersman*. Pueblo West, CO: Herodotus Press.

Secrest, Clark (Autumn 2000) 'The Bloody Espinosas: Avenging Angels of the Conejos,' *Colorado Heritage*.

Wheelan, Joseph (2007) *Invading Mexico: America's Continental Dream and the Mexican War, 1846–1848*. New York: Carroll & Graf Publishers.

Works Progress Administration Federal Writers' Project (1941) *Colorado: A Guide to the Highest State*, The American Guide series. New York: Hastings House Publishers.